SING IT TO HER BONES

"Talley . . . demonstrates both a penchant for storytelling
and a flair for character development."
—*The Baltimore Sun*

"A powerful, moving story . . . Marcia Talley's Hannah Ives
is a great new character and voice for mystery lovers."
—Steven Womack, Edgar Award–winning author of
Dirty Money

"[An] assured and accomplished first novel . . . More
Hannah Ives, please! This is one to watch."
—Kate Charles, author of *Unruly Passions*

"[SING IT TO HER BONES] is rich in local color as
well as plotting and writing. It is a promising
introduction to a new writer and a new character
we want to see again—and soon."
—*The Washington Times*

"A dazzling debut mystery . . . this is a series with
the right stuff. Don't miss this one."
—*MLB News*

"No one can match Marcia Talley's unsentimental view
of the tangled, complex relationships among adult family
members: people who must be, at one and the same
time, parents, children, sisters, wives. That she can
tell a good story while she's at it—and is even funny—
is Talley's special gift."
—SJ Rozan, Anthony and Shamus
award-winning author of *Stone Quarry*

OCCASION OF REVENGE

A Hannah Ives Mystery

Marcia Talley

A Dell Book

Published by
Dell Publishing
a division of
Random House, Inc.
1540 Broadway
New York, New York 10036

Dell® is a registered trademark of Random House, Inc., and
the colophon is a trademark of Random House, Inc.

ISBN: 0-440-23520-0

Printed in the United States of America

Published simultaneously in Canada

August 2001

OPM

10 9 8 7 6 5 4 3 2 1

Acknowledgments

So many wonderful people helped me while I was writing this book that I hardly know where to begin with my thank-yous.

To my family—my husband, Barry, and my daughters, Laura Geyer and Sarah Glass—you were always there when I needed you. Really, I couldn't have done it without you.

To my sisters—Susan Woythaler, Alison Jacobs, Deborah Kelchner, and Katherine Carstens—who will know why.

To friends and family who gave me a warm bed, hot meals, and a quiet place to write while I toured—Alison and Joe Jacobs, Susan and Saul Woythaler, Betty Lou and David Walsman, Terri Ryburn-LaMonte, and Elizabeth Talley—I can come out and play now.

To Chief Wayne M. Bradley and Captain Robert A. Edler, Jr., of the Chestertown Police Department, Chestertown, Maryland; and to Corporal Arthur Griffies of Maryland State Police Barracks "J" in Annapolis, Maryland, for cheerfully answering my questions. If I got it wrong, it's entirely my fault, not theirs.

To Suzanne Fischer of Chestertown, Maryland, for so generously inviting me into her home and for allowing me to put a body in her bathtub.

To Janice Gary, Executive Director, and the staff of First Night Annapolis—especially Jan "Red" Adkins—for their courtesy and for letting me paw through their archives.

To Luci Zahray, "The Poison Lady," who proves every day how dangerous a home can be!

To S. Brent Morris, Charles Mylander, and Chuck Hanna, because I've never been very good at math: Thanks 10^6.

To Jackie Cantor—editor, advocate, and friend, above and beyond—and to Abby Zidle, a rare gem.

To my agent, Jimmy Vines, for believing in me.

To my writers' groups—Sujata Massey, John Mann, Janice McLane, and Karen Diegmueller in Baltimore, and Janet Benrey, Trish Marshall, Mary Ellen Hughes, Ray Flynt, Bonnie Settle, Caroline Buppert, Christiane Carlson-Thies, and Sherriel Mattingly in Annapolis—for tough love. Sherriel, if you should ever tire of librarianship, I am sure there's a job waiting for you at Hallmark Cards.

To Linda Sprenkle, fellow adventurer, location scout, and dear friend.

To Barbara Parker, friend, feng shui consultant, and Web maven, extraordinaire.

(*http://hometown.aol.com/mardtal/homepage.htm*).

And to Kate Charles and Deborah Crombie—dearest of friends, confidantes, and advisers—the reason why ten-cents-a-minute long-distance services had to be invented.

Talk not to me: I will go sit and weep,
Till I can find occasion of revenge.

—William Shakespeare
The Taming of the Shrew
Act 2, Scene 1

OCCASION
OF REVENGE

chapter

1

TWO YEARS AGO I DIDN'T THINK I'D LIVE LONG
enough to make it to my next chemotherapy session,
let alone see my widowed sister-in-law happily remarried. But God had been gracious, sending good health
my way and Dennis Rutherford to Connie.

Nothing less could have persuaded me to appear
at St. Philip's that bright Saturday afternoon, to stand
in the brides' room in front of a full-length mirror
wearing an idiotic grin and the matron-of-honor dress
from hell. Connie cheerfully assured me I would be
able to wear it later on, but I secretly doubted that outfit would ever make it out of the plastic dry-cleaning
bag I planned to hide it in once her wedding reception
was over.

While Connie hovered nearby, fussing with the veil
on her Jackie Kennedy–esque hat and looking radiant
in a white linen sheath topped with an elaborately em-
broidered bolero jacket, I zipped myself into a dress
with defensive shoulder pads that made me look like a
wedge of lemon meringue pie. Frankly, with her artist's

eye, I'd expected better from Connie, but for some reason she'd set her mind on this particular number, a cocktail dress in a bilious shade of yellow that turned my olive skin a sallow green. I leaned toward the mirror. I smiled. At least the low-cut bodice showed off the swell of my newly reconstructed breast to advantage. The short, narrow skirt made the most of my ankles, too, slim above dyed-to-match T-strap pumps. But my daughter Emily was right: Even with camouflaging pearl-tone panty hose, my knees were not ready for prime time.

Veil adjusted to her satisfaction, Connie picked up the bouquet of stephanotis and gardenias she would carry down the aisle. I had a single gardenia clamped to the side of my head with four hundred bobby pins, and my brownish hair had been tortured into a twist with so much hair spray that if a hurricane had swept through the church just then, leaving nothing of St. Philip's standing but its eighteenth-century pulpit, I'd have been found miles away in a tree, stone cold dead but with nary a hair out of place.

A trumpet fanfare blared from the organ in the sanctuary. I shivered. I'm a sucker for trumpets. Even the Hallelujah chorus from *The Messiah* makes me swoon.

I pulled a tissue out of my sleeve and handed it to Connie so she could blot her lipstick. "Ready?"

She gave me a hug. "Hannah, darling, I've been ready for this day for over a year!"

My sister-in-law's parents had passed away years ago, so she had dispensed with the usual giving-the-bride-away bit. It was just me, marching down the aisle to Jeremiah Clarke with Connie trailing stunningly behind.

I was so nervous—Did I have the ring? Was every-thing set with the caterers? It wouldn't *dare* rain, would it?—that the ceremony itself remains pretty much of a blur. I remember how yummy the best man looked in his tuxedo—of course, I was married to him—and holding my breath when Reverend Lattimore got to the speak-now-or-forever-hold-your-peace part. But the pregnant pause was filled only with the intrepid hum of the heat pump trying to warm up the church on that crisp November day, until Connie, hearing no objections, curled her free hand into a fist and pumped it toward herself: *Yes!* I couldn't suppress a nervous giggle.

During the homily, while Reverend Lattimore droned on about Perfect Love, paraphrasing heavily from Hosea, Ruth, and Song of Solomon, I noticed Dennis's daughter, Maggie, looking like a daffodil perched on the edge of her pew in the first row on the groom's side. With her black hair and pale Irish skin, the color so complemented her that I began to suspect a conspiracy in the nuptial color scheme department. Connie'd do anything to keep Maggie—who had a long way to go before completely accepting her father's choice of bride—happy. The two rows behind Maggie were occupied by men with commendable posture whom I took to be police officers, colleagues of the groom.

On the bride's side of the aisle sat my sister Ruth, her rapidly silvering hair intricately braided. Next to her, eleven-month-old Chloe squirmed happily on her mother's—my daughter, Emily's—lap. Emily's husband, Dante, whose given name is Daniel Shemansky, had moved his family back east from Colorado to accept a job at New Life, a health spa in the Blue Ridge Mountains of Virginia so exclusive that if you didn't Know Some-body, you had to have reservations years in advance. I was delighted he'd be massaging bodies closer to home. And until they found a place of their own, they were staying with Paul and me in Annapolis, an equally de-lightful arrangement.

In the row behind Emily sat my sister Georgina and her husband, Scott, distracted. No doubt they were re-considering the advisability of bringing children under the age of ten to a wedding. Both were trying to retain control of their twin sons, Sean and Dylan, now eight, who were being encouraged to draw pictures on their wedding programs, while five-year-old Julie perched primly, cradling her toy rabbit. Abby's poor, fur-free ears had been coaxed into a white lace doll bonnet, its strings tied under the rabbit's chin in an enormous, untidy bow.

And behind them, Daddy. By the prismatic light streaming in through a stained-glass window, Daddy looked flushed and happier than I had seen him since the death of our mother. He wore that sappy half-happy, half-solemn look you get at weddings, where your mouth smiles but you have to keep hauling out the tissues to dab at your eyes.

I gazed around the sanctuary, imprinting these joy-ous faces on my brain, praying they'd erase the painful memory of my previous visit to St. Philip's on the occa-sion of young Katie Dunbar's funeral. That sad day would never fade altogether, of course, but my heart soared when the organist swooped into Charpentier's trumpet tune, her feet in black lace-up oxfords pump-ing up and down like well-oiled pistons along the pedal board.

As Paul and I recessed behind the bride and groom

past the row where my father sat, he whispered an aside to a frizzy-headed blonde sitting in the pew next to him, then smiled broadly in my direction. He winked. I sent a thousand-watt beam back. Not hard for someone wearing a sunshine suit.

Although I had worried about it, too, during the exchange of vows, the stretch limo Paul had arranged was dutifully waiting at the curb. After posing on the church steps for an untold number of photographs, Dennis extracted his daughter, Maggie, from a private conversation with Reverend Lattimore, I waved a see-ya-later to my daughter and her little family, and the wedding party settled in behind tinted windows for the three-block drive to historic Dulaney House, picking grass seed out of our hair and clothes. "If it rains," I commented cheerfully, "I'm going to sprout like a Chia Pet."

"Do you believe that nonsense about the rice?" Paul asked as he adjusted my hairdo and poked a few more bobby pins into my sagging gardenia. At the rehearsal, Reverend Lattimore had forbidden rice, citing a wedding where the out-of-town guests had thrown Minute Rice. The seagulls, he said, had swooped down, eaten it, puffed up, and died in the courtyard of the Hillcrest Nursing Home across the street.

"Urban legend." The limo eased to a halt. "Or at least a village one."

Connie leaned across the seat, her hand resting lightly on Dennis's knee. The new half-carat diamond-and-platinum ring she wore caught the sun, sending a dot of light ricocheting across the upholstery. "Speaking of legends, Washington actually slept here, you know." She indicated a second-story window on the far left of Dulaney House. "He was coming from Virginia to resign his commission at the Annapolis State House and he waited here for the weather to improve before crossing the Truxton by ferry."

I ducked my head and stared at the spot where Connie was pointing. An ordinary window. "You sure?" I chuckled. "George Washington didn't live enough nights in his whole life to sleep everywhere attributed to him. When would he have time for Martha at Mount Vernon?" We unfolded ourselves from the vehicle, Connie and Dennis first, and entered the house.

If old George had actually stayed at Dulaney House on that cold December day in 1783, I doubt he'd ever seen it looking so beautiful. Constructed solidly of brick with generous windows and bright white trim, the central three-story house was flanked by identical one-story wings, connected to the main house by passageways called hyphens. An ornately carved doorway led into an entrance hall where a central stairway curved up and away to our right. We passed straight through into the ballroom, where a string quartet had arranged itself on a fine Oriental rug near a wall of French doors leading out into the garden. They were playing one of Vivaldi's seasons—"Winter," I think, appropriate to that fine November day two days after Thanksgiving. In contrast, baskets of flowers screamed spring. Arrangements of tulips, daffodils, and lilies decorated tall pedestals flanking the doors. Smaller arrangements had been placed on circular tables covered with white damask tablecloths. Servers in black pants, white shirts, and festive bow ties snaked smoothly through the crowd bearing platters of crab balls, egg rolls, and shrimps, while two bartenders near a walk-in fireplace at the far end of the ballroom efficiently mixed drinks.

Daddy was already there, standing at the bar, holding a glass of wine in one hand while the bartender handed him what looked like a super-dry martini on the rocks. While Paul disappeared into the cloakroom with our coats I hurried over to greet my father.

"Two-fisted drinker?" I forced a smile.

"No." He kissed my cheek. "It's for Darlene." He gestured with the martini. "Over there."

I sighted along his arm until I saw, at the end of it, the blond woman who had been sitting next to him in church. I pasted a smile on my face—what Paul calls my perma-grin: stretched lips, full teeth, like rigor mortis had set in. "She doesn't look like the martini type."

"She isn't." He waved the glass under my nose and I caught the unexpected odor of mouthwash.

"Yuck. What's that?"

"Peppermint schnapps." He raised a bushy eyebrow. "Want one?"

"Daddy, I'd rather drink battery acid." I tipped my wineglass to my lips and took a sip of cool, crisp chardonnay, studying his lined but still handsome face over the rim.

"I'd have to agree, but Darlene says it's not a special occasion if she can't have her schnapps." Daddy planted a light kiss on my forehead. "Save a dance for me, sweetheart?"

"Of course, silly." But I was speaking to his back as Daddy turned and glided off to the lady-in-waiting, leaving me stranded by the bar, feeling like a wallflower.

"Penny for your thoughts."

"Paul!"

Confirming my suspicions about the lemon meringue pie, Paul said, "You look good enough to eat," and nibbled on my neck in lieu of an appetizer.

"So do you. I wish we were sailing off to the Caribbean along with the happy couple over there." I gestured with my glass in the direction of the hallway where Paul's sister, Connie, was standing with her new husband in the curve of the staircase, manning an informal receiving line.

"Maybe on my sabbatical next year."

"Hah! That'll be the day! What's a math professor going to do on a sailboat that will count as research?"

"Think."

"About what?"

"Patterns."

"Like what?"

"The parabolic arcs of flying fish trajectories."

I laughed out loud. "I can't believe that anybody would pay you to do research like that."

Paul led me over to the bar where we joined a short line. "Ah, that's where you're wrong, my dear. It's rumored that someone's about to offer a million-dollar prize to the first person who can prove Goldbach's Conjecture."

"What's that?"

We wandered over to our table and sat down. "Goldbach stated that every even number greater than two is the sum of two primes." Paul patted the breast pocket of his tux jacket and I worried that he'd pull out a pen and start illustrating this for me on the tablecloth, but fortunately the only thing in his pocket was a decorative handkerchief.

"That seems fairly obvious," I said, "even for a French major."

"Ah, yes," Paul replied. "But nobody's ever been able to *prove* it."

"I see." I sipped my wine. "It's like extracting the square root of pi. It could go on and on and on."

He nodded.

"Well, I'm sure you'll figure out something, and when you do—sweetheart, honey lamb, sugar pie"—I grinned at him, toothily—"I'll be sure to sign on as first mate."

"How about chief cook and communications officer?"

"That, too." The way he was looking at me, I thought he might have a second honeymoon on his mind—starting that night.

"Look, there's old Mr. Schneider!" Paul kissed the air next to my cheek. "Let me say hello to the old boy." He loped off in the direction of a tuxedoed gentleman in a wheelchair being pushed by an attendant up a ramp from the garden and into the ballroom. Mr. Schneider was the father of Dennis's deceased first wife.

"Oh, my poor ears and whiskers!" The bride, looking flushed, materialized on my right so suddenly that I nearly spilled my wine.

"Dennis deserted you already? The cad!"

Connie flopped into a chair, removed a punishing high-heeled shoe, and began massaging her toes. "We gave up on the receiving line. Dennis is off in the library, back-slapping with his buddies. Get me a drink, would you?"

"Wine?"

"That would be lovely."

"White or red?"

Connie indicated the pristine white landscape of her wedding outfit and made a face. "Duh!"

I returned from the bar with a glass of white wine

for Connie just as Daddy's new friend cut loose with a high-pitched cackle that carried over the sawing of the strings launching into "Spring."

"Who's that?" I asked Connie, pointing toward the cackle.

She shrugged. "And Guest."

"Huh?"

"That's all I know. When your father RSVPed, it was for two: Captain George Alexander and Guest. I forgot to tell you." She cast a fashion-critical eye over Darlene's cocktail dress, a lacy froth of Pepto-Bismol pink with a flouncy skirt that hovered three inches north of her knees and a bodice that plunged a couple of inches too far south of her generous bosom.

"I hope she doesn't sneeze," I said. Darlene held the stem of her glass between her thumb and forefinger, laughed again, then pirouetted away toward the meats table on dainty toes stuffed into size five sling-back, open-toed stiletto heels. "That's Daddy's *date*?"

" 'Fraid so."

"But it's only eight months since Mother died," I managed to croak around the lump in my throat.

Connie started to say something but ended up grinning me an apology over her shoulder as she was whisked aside by a sophisticated couple in their late seventies, immaculately dressed and carrying a large, beautifully wrapped wedding package.

I looked around for Paul and found him at the antipasto table, stacking his plate with marinated mushrooms and asparagus spears while talking to my sister Ruth. Ruth wore an ankle-length, multilayered caftany thing in a sheer natural linen. I snitched an asparagus spear from Paul's plate, bit off the bud end, then pointed the stem at Darlene. "Daddy has a date."

Ruth turned to look where Daddy was holding forth with Darlene and another woman whom I recognized as Ellie from the nearby Country Store. Ruth's eyes brightened. "The lady in blue?"

"I wish. No, the lady in pink. Darlene somebody-or-other."

Ruth sputtered into her wine. "Oh, gawd! Where'd she buy that dress? Togs for Tarts?"

"Well, at least your father's not sitting at home feeling sorry for himself." Paul slipped an arm around my shoulders. "Nothing is going to bring your mother back," Paul continued reasonably with a sympathetic one-armed hug that squished air audibly out of my shoulder pads. "Let the old guy have a little fun."

It was hard to think of my father as old. A 1950 graduate of the Naval Academy, he'd given the Navy thirty years, then worked another nineteen years building airplanes in Seattle before retiring to Annapolis last year. The month Mother died, he had turned seventy.

"That doesn't look like fun," Ruth said. "It looks like trouble with a capital T and that rhymes with D and that stands for *fool*."

Paul nibbled on a carrot stick and stared in Darlene's direction. "You can't judge a book by its cover, girls."

I groaned. "May I write that down, Mr. Shakespeare?"

"Maybe she's a great conversationalist. A Harvard grad running a multinational corporation. A scholar with an advanced degree in comparative literature from Yale." He turned to Ruth. "How come you don't know this woman, Ruth? You see your father every day."

After Mom died, my divorced sister had given up her poky, overpriced apartment on Conduit Street in downtown Annapolis and moved into our parents' home in the Providence community. Daddy, she discovered, barely knew how to balance a checkbook or file his income taxes. Mother had always taken care of the bookkeeping. And cooking? Forget about it.

Ruth shook her head. "He's never mentioned her. Probably too embarrassed." She sipped her wine. "But he has been spending more evenings out lately." She snorted. "He told me he was bowling."

Daddy must have said something funny because Darlene threw her head back, open-mouthed. He would have had time to count her fillings. I was beginning to recognize her laugh, full and deep-throated, ending in a giggle.

"I think I have a very good idea where *her* talents lie," offered Ruth, sourly.

"Take a pill, Ruth."

Ruth smiled at Paul, sickly sweet. "I do believe I will, Mr. Ives." She reached around him, selected a fringed toothpick from a silver cup and speared a crab ball, then dredged it through the cocktail sauce.

"Why don't you go introduce yourselves, girls?"

I displayed my empty wineglass. "First, I'll need another one of these."

Ruth, still chewing, speared another crab ball and sailed off in the opposite direction. "I think it's *his* job to introduce his girlfriend to *us*," she called over her shoulder. "I'm going to find Georgina."

"Last time I saw Georgina, she was in the tent in the garden fixing fruit-and-cheese plates for the kids," Paul said.

Ruth, her mouth full of crab, nodded, waved, and disappeared outside. I watched as she weaved among the boxwood hedges, then strolled down the well-manicured lawn which sloped gently away from the historic mansion toward the Chesapeake Bay.

Paul took my elbow and steered me toward the bar. We had just refilled our glasses when the music died.

"Ladies and gentlemen!" The first chair violin, a painfully thin bleached blonde clad entirely in black, had trouble being heard over the celebration. Paul tapped a fork against his plate and after several seconds the room grew quiet and guests began drifting into the ballroom from the adjoining rooms and from the garden. The waif lifted her bow high, like a baton. "Ladies and gentlemen, I give you . . . Mr. and Mrs. Dennis Rutherford!"

Connie and Dennis appeared from the hallway, holding hands and beaming at one another like star-struck teens. The skinny violinist, who could have put a heaping plate of crab balls to good use, set her bow to the violin and played a few introductory chords before turning to her musicians and segueing into "Mexicali Rose." Paul leaned toward me. " 'Mexicali Rose'?"

With my lips close to my husband's ear I whispered, "Maybe there's a Mexican holiday we don't know anything about."

At the end of the second bar of music, Dennis swung Connie wide, twirled her into his arms, then waltzed her around the dance floor in graceful, sweeping circles. They could have been on wheels.

I turned to Paul. "Holy Toledo! It's international ballroom on PBS."

"Dennis told me they've been taking lessons."

I watched, admiring and amazed. Tears formed in the corners of my eyes. "It's so beautiful!" I jabbed Paul with my elbow. "I've been trying to get you to take lessons for years, you bum!"

"Maybe someday."

Before I could extract a promise to that effect, our daughter, Emily, appeared. She looked beautiful, too, in a slinky, floor-length slip the color of caramel that she proudly claimed she'd bought for fifty cents at Goodwill. Since leaving home for Colorado Springs, she had let her ragged, badly dyed hair grow out. Now it hung, sleek and smooth, the color of dark molasses, just touching her shoulders. She'd applied light touches of makeup to her eyes and cheeks and exchanged the black lipstick of her rebellious years for a burgundy gloss. Dante loomed tall behind her, dressed in black slacks and a white shirt. I doubted my son-in-law owned a suit. If it hadn't been for his colorful tie, I might have mistaken him for one of the waiters.

"I'm trying to get your father to dance," I explained to Emily, who was balancing Chloe on her hip. The strings swung into "I Only Have Eyes for You" and the floor began to fill with other dancers. Suddenly, twenty-two pounds, all of it Chloe, was in my arms.

"C'mon, Dad," Emily said. "Let's dance." Without waiting for a reply, she seized Paul's hand and dragged him onto the floor. Smiling crookedly, he held her, stiffly at first, then with more confidence as his elbows unlocked and his arms relaxed. He began rocking from one foot to the other, leading his daughter around the ballroom with a skip, half shuffle, skip, slide.

Leaving me with Dante.

I always managed to put my foot in it where conversations with Dante were concerned. Chloe saved me the trouble of having to think of something to say by grabbing my earring, a string of dangling pearls, and yanking—hard.

"Ouch!" My hand shot to my ear. "You little imp!"

Dante, who had been watching Emily dance with

her father with a grin on his face, turned to see what all the commotion was about. "You OK, Mrs. Ives?"

I laughed, pried Chloe's fingers from the earring, and slipped it into my pocket for safekeeping. I attempted to distract my granddaughter by making faces and talking to her like an idiot. "Widdle Chloe want something to eat, huh?"

Dante held out his arms to his daughter. As his cuffs crept higher on his wrists, I could see portions of the elaborate tattoos that decorated his arms—the business end of a rattlesnake; the talons of an eagle. Until I had had a nipple tattooed on my reconstructed breast, the artwork on Dante was the closest I'd ever come to a tattoo. "Here, Mrs. Ives. Let me take her," Dante volunteered. "She's going to make a mess of your dress."

"That's OK," I said, thinking there wasn't much Chloe could do that would break my heart over this dress. But in a few minutes, my granddaughter metamorphosed into a writhing sack of eels. I handed her back to her father gratefully. "Thanks."

Dante settled his daughter on his hip and plugged a pacifier into her mouth. When a vigorous sucking motion signaled that Chloe had a firm grip on the nipple, he turned to me. "I'd ask you to dance, but one of us . . ." He jiggled Chloe up and down.

I was relieved. I was still working on my relationship with Dante. It had not started out on the best of terms when he'd dropped out of Haverford College just a semester before graduation to move out west, taking my besotted daughter, who had graduated from Bryn Mawr with honors a year earlier, with him.

"Just look at your grandfather-in-law," I said at last. "Who?" Looking puzzled, Dante's gaze drifted from

Chloe's plump face to the dance floor. After a moment, he chuckled. "Oh, I see."

Daddy was squiring Darlene around the floor like a pro. Darlene's skirt swirled away from her body, revealing shapely thighs encased in hot pink panty hose. I willed their label to say Queen Size, Super Support, but there wasn't a chance of that. Although she must have been well over fifty, Darlene had the legs of a twenty-year-old.

I scowled in my father's direction. "Acting like a teenager."

Dante nodded sagely, his ponytail wagging. "Whatever."

"I think it's disgusting." Dante's head swiveled in my direction and I immediately regretted my candor. "Sorry." I smiled apologetically. "It seems like just yesterday that Mom . . ." I took a deep breath and held it, then turned my eyes back to the dance floor where Daddy and Darlene were sharing a sprightly fox-trot. "She's certainly peppy, I'll give her that."

"She's not so bad." Dante shifted Chloe to the other hip and repositioned the pacifier, which had fallen into the folds of the hand-smocking on her white piqué dress.

Someone snapped a picture and I flinched at the flash. I squinted up at my son-in-law. "You've met her, then?"

"Briefly. Emily and I talked with her for all of two seconds back at the church. She's a widow living over in Chestertown."

Chestertown was a community over the Bay Bridge on Maryland's Eastern Shore, about an hour's drive from Annapolis. "Chestertown? How'd Daddy hook up with someone way over there?"

Dante shrugged. "Don't know. You'll have to ask him."

I was thinking about this when the music stopped. Paul and Emily reappeared, looking flushed from their efforts at contemporary ballroom. "The musicians are taking a break," Emily said, sounding disappointed. Too bad. Now that Emily had broken the ice, I was hoping Paul would trip the light fantastic with *me* while the force was still with him.

Behind Paul's back I watched Daddy as he led Darlene from the dance floor over to the bar. They picked up refills, then wandered out to the garden. I saw them again briefly, participating with enthusiasm when we toasted the bride and groom with chilled champagne. My backbone stiffened by wine, I was headed in their direction with a million questions on my mind when Paul asked me to dance and everything else flew out of my head.

When I thought about Daddy and Darlene again, it was cake cutting time, but they were nowhere to be seen. I waited until the last notes of "Good Night, Sweetheart" had died away, until the caterers began wrapping up the leftovers in heavy-duty aluminum foil, until the flowers had been loaded into a van headed for the nursing home, but I never got that dance Daddy had promised me.

I emerged from the bathroom with my hair still damp from the shower to find Paul waiting, propped up on two pillows. He whipped the sheet away from my side of the bed and patted the mattress. I smiled, slid in next to him, and snuggled close, my cheek resting comfortably on his chest.

"Sorry it's so goopy."

He nuzzled my neck. "What's goopy?"

"My hair. All that hair spray. I brushed it hard, but . . ."

"You can wash it in the morning." His kiss began near my right ear, meandered down my cheek, and finally found my mouth. I wrapped my legs around his and melted into him.

The end of a perfect day.

In the past two years, I'd learned the fine art of appreciating perfect days whenever they came my way. And it was a good thing Connie's wedding was an eleven on a scale of one to ten, because it was the last perfect day I would see for a good, long time.

THE TELEPHONE RANG, JOLTING ME OUT OF A THOR-
oughly satisfying dream, an action/adventure film, as
I recall, featuring Pierce Brosnan and Sean Connery
dueling with spear guns for my attentions. I observed,
aloof and amused, from the deck of a luxury yacht, sipping a dry martini—shaken, not stirred—fetchingly
clad in a form-fitting black-and-pink skin-diving suit.
Me, not the martini.

"Hullo?" I managed, resurfacing so fast I was in
danger of getting the bends.

"Hannah, Daddy didn't come home last night."

"What?" I groped around on the bedside table until
I found the alarm clock. Six-thirty. I groaned.

"His bed hasn't been slept in."

Paul turned away from me, burrowing under the
covers. "Who the hell is that?" he mumbled.

I covered the receiver with my hand. "Ruth. She's
worried that Daddy isn't home."

Paul flipped down the comforter and sat up. "Well,

it doesn't take Sherlock Holmes to figure that one out, Watson."

I laid a hand on his leg and returned my attention to my sister. "Are you sure? Maybe he's asleep on the sofa. Or in the family room."

"Nuh-uh. I checked."

"In the bathroom?"

"Nope."

"Is there a message on the answering machine?"

"No."

I rubbed my eyes. "Look, he probably took Darlene home and one thing led to another . . ."

"Probably, but he could have called me, Hannah."

"He could have, but that probably wasn't the first thing on his mind."

"The stomach turns."

I flopped back on my pillow, the receiver clamped to my ear. "My feelings, exactly."

"All I ask is a little common courtesy, Hannah. I cook, I clean, I iron his shirts. The least he could do is let me know when he isn't coming home so I don't worry." She heaved an exasperated sigh. "If it had been *me* not coming home, he'd've had a fit."

By now, I was wide awake. Paul, listening to my half of the conversation, propped himself up on an elbow and used his free hand to trace little circles on my arm. I crossed my eyes, stuck out my tongue, and playfully swatted at his hand.

Ruth had a point. Although Daddy was doing her a favor by letting her live at home rent free, Ruth more than made up for it by what she contributed to the running of the household. If Daddy had to pay someone—several someones—to cook, clean, wash, iron, pay the bills, and keep up the yard, he'd have to take out a second mortgage. Ruth considered her stay transitional and mutually beneficial. She'd agreed to help get Daddy back on his feet while she saved enough money from Mother Earth, her shop on Main Street, to make a down payment on a home of her own. Lord knows Eric Gannon wasn't in a position to help her out. Ruth's ex was throwing all his money at a sweet Gen-Xer named Candee these days.

"Daddy probably thinks that by letting me live here for free and giving me the car he doesn't owe me anything," Ruth complained.

When Ruth's aging VW Golf had died the previous summer in a shuddering heap of cracked windshield, bald tires, and rusting quarter panels, Daddy had signed over the title of Mom's Corolla to her. With his passion for fairness, I'd received Mother's emerald engagement ring and he'd given Georgina her beaver coat, but the rest of Mom's things he'd kept, as if by parting with them he'd be admitting to himself that she was really gone. One day we'd have to go through Mom's closet and dresser drawers, but not now. The pain was still too fresh and too deep.

"He's a grown-up, Ruth," I reminded my sister. "To him, you're still a kid. He probably doesn't think he needs to account for his actions to you."

"Still, it's rude. What if he's been in an accident?"

"Unlikely. He left the reception with Darlene surgically attached to his arm." I wrapped my fingers around Paul's incurably roving hand. "Look, if he hasn't returned home by noon, let me know and we'll send out a search party."

"Where?"

"Darlene's, to begin with. The local bars."

"That's not funny, Hannah. Besides, do you know where Darlene lives?"

"Somewhere in Chestertown."

"What's her last name?"

"I haven't a clue."

"Great. So we just drive over to Chestertown and ask around for somebody, anybody named Darlene?"

I hadn't been to Chestertown for several years, but I remembered it as a small, friendly place, home to Washington College and featuring a waterfront lined with stately colonial and Georgian-style homes. Chestertown had all the charm but none of the size of Annapolis; folks were likely to know one another there. Recalling Darlene's startling hair and revealing wardrobe, I imagined that if we approached enough people and described her, eventually someone would be able to tell us who she was.

"What if Daddy's lying in a ditch somewhere?" Ruth worried.

"In that case, somebody would have called."

"Should I check the hospitals?"

"Don't be silly." I thought for a minute. "He did have his wallet with him, didn't he?"

"I assume so, but I don't know for sure. It isn't on his dresser, anyway. I checked."

I felt the mattress heave as Paul slid out of bed. "Coffee?" he pantomimed. I nodded and watched with affection as he padded toward the hallway in his bare feet.

"When he gets home, I'm going to kill him," Ruth grumped.

"Killing would be too quick. Why don't you tie him

to a chair until he promises to keep you posted on his whereabouts?"

Ruth snorted. "He has no consideration. No consideration at all." The rant continued. "I have to open up the store in a couple of hours."

"Today's Sunday, Ruth. You don't open up until noon on Sunday. And if you're a little late, people will just have to wait for their aromatherapy kits. Nobody ever died from running out of patchouli."

"Maybe I'll feel better after I have my coffee." I heard the sound of running water. Ruth must have been calling from the kitchen. "Wait a minute!"

"What? What?"

"Why, the old devil!" Ruth whispered. "He's tiptoeing up the driveway now! I can see him out the kitchen window. Must have parked his car out front. Ha! Old tomcat probably thinks he can sneak in and climb into bed without me being any the wiser. Well, do I have a surprise for *him*!"

I took a deep breath. "Don't do anything stupid now, Ruth."

"Nothing he doesn't deserve for making me worry like this. I don't need any more gray hairs, thank you very much."

With a half-smile on my lips, I imagined the scene. "Call me later."

"And he'll probably be wanting breakfast, too."

Just before the telephone clicked into silence, I heard Ruth drawl, "Well, good morning, Casanova."

I waited a good ten minutes for Ruth to cool her jets, staring straight up, watching slivers of early morning sunlight creep across the ceiling. Then I called back.

Ruth answered on the first ring. "Plato's Ethical Culture Parlor."

"Oh, har de har har. What if I'd been somebody important?"

"I knew it was you."

"Oh?"

"Who else would be calling at this hour?"

I directed a raspberry into the receiver. "Don't forget who woke up who, Ruth. Or is it whom?"

"Well, I wasn't sleeping, so I figured I'd share the joy."

"Thoughtful of you." In the background I could hear the high-pitched squeal of the coffee grinder. I could almost smell the aroma of fresh-brewed Starbucks breakfast blend wafting down the telephone lines. Then I had to laugh. Paul was coming through the bedroom door holding a mug of steaming coffee in each hand.

I blew him a kiss, reached for my mug, and sipped at it gratefully. "So, what's his story, Ruth?"

"He spent the night in Chestertown with You Know Who, just like you said."

"Sometimes I hate to be right."

Ruth sighed heavily. "I don't know what he sees in her."

"She makes me laugh." It was Daddy's military voice, crisp and clean-cut. I imagined him leaning over Ruth's shoulder, addressing the receiver as if it were a raw recruit.

"Keep that up, and I'll go deaf." Ruth's voice gradually faded. "Excuse me, Hannah, while I go repair my eardrum."

"You should have called home, Daddy," I said when my father took control of the telephone.

"Sorry, dear. I didn't think."

"Ruth was worried sick."

"I said I'm sorry."

"So, Darlene makes you laugh, huh? So do Laurel and Hardy movies, but you don't have to buy them dinner."

"You know what I mean, Hannah. Since your mother died . . ." He paused. "Well, I have *needs*, dear."

In the uncomfortable silence that followed, I realized that this was the closest my father had ever come to discussing sex with me. He quickly changed the subject. "Look, why don't you and Paul come over for dinner tonight? Bring everybody."

"Dante's gone back to Virginia," I said. "He has to be at work this morning."

"Tonight?" That was from Ruth. Daddy must have covered the receiver with his hand because there was a muffled discussion before Ruth came back on the line, sounding exasperated. "Well, don't expect Julia Child," she snapped.

"When did I ever?" Ruth could arrange your kitchen according to the principles of feng shui, but ask her to put seven basic ingredients into a harmonious casserole and you'd be out of luck. "I'll bring bread and a salad," I reassured her.

"Great! If Georgina brings dessert, I think I can manage."

"Georgina, Scott . . ." I did a quick mental head count. "With you, Dad, us, and all the kids, that makes eleven."

"Twelve," she corrected.

"Twelve?"

"Don't forget Darlene."

Indeed, from that day forward, there'd be very little danger that I'd ever forget Darlene.

chapter

3

SHE ARRIVED LATE. FASHIONABLY LATE. CLAUDIA Schiffer on a Versace runway couldn't have done it with more style. From the moment she glided over the threshold of my father's house and into the entrance hall, Darlene was in control, keenly aware that all eyes were on her. A cold front had moved across Maryland overnight, and against the unseasonably chilly weather she wore a red wool cloak, which she unbuttoned and swirled off her shoulders like a matador, launching it in my general direction. Perversely, I just missed catching it.

"Here, allow me." Emily bent to retrieve the cloak, knocking heads with Darlene in the process.

"Ouch!" Vigorously rubbing her head, Darlene straightened to her full five foot two plus at least three inches of trendy stacked heels. Above them, she wore sleek black capri pants and a sweater the color of bubblegum. I had read that capri pants were back in style, but I couldn't help thinking that she looked like a refugee from the old *Dick Van Dyke Show*.

"I'm so sorry!" Emily's face wore a look of genuine concern. "Are you all right?"

Darlene handed my daughter the cloak. "I guess I'll live." She looked over Emily's shoulder, one pale eyebrow raised. "Where's your grandfather?"

"In the kitchen."

"This way?" she asked, taking a tentative step down the hall. When Emily pointed, she sailed off in that direction, the neck of a paper-bag-encased wine bottle clutched in her hand. "Georgie!"

I glanced at Emily, who had covered her mouth with her hand to keep from laughing. "Georgie?" I mouthed. For a weird moment I thought Darlene was calling for Georgina.

Emily waggled her index finger. "Pink is *definitely* her color." She scooped up Chloe, who had been sitting on the carpet experimenting with her shoelaces, trying to determine if they were edible, and we followed our guest, arriving in time to observe Darlene plant a wet kiss squarely on Daddy's mouth. My stomach lurched.

Fortunately, Ruth's back was turned. A storm cloud still hovered over her, and I didn't think she'd be in the mood to watch the opening round of the Nookie Olympics, Senior Division. Ruth stood at the stove tending a pot of steaming water. On the counter next to it were two one-pound boxes of pasta. "This is for you." Darlene thrust the wine in Ruth's direction.

Ruth turned. A strand of silver hair had escaped from her leather headband to dangle in a corkscrew over her forehead. She swiped at it with the back of a hand which held a large wooden spoon. "Uh, thanks," she mumbled. "Red or white?"

"Georgie said we were having spaghetti. So red."

"Just put it on the counter, OK?"

Daddy reached over, took the bag from Darlene's hand, slipped the bottle out, and stared at it as if committing every word printed on the label to memory. "Turning Leaf," he said. "A fine, fine wine." He kissed Darlene's cheek. "Thank you."

Ruth rolled her eyes ceilingward, turned back to the stove, and began punishing the sauce.

Darlene inhaled deeply. "Ah! Homemade spaghetti sauce!" She stepped toward the stove, until Ruth stopped her with a look that would have turned Mother Teresa to stone. Homemade? I had seen four empty jars of Prego in the kitchen trash can, but I'd never tell.

"Thank you." Ruth managed a smile, but I hoped none of the saccharine in her voice would drip into the spaghetti.

"Here," I said, taking the wine from my father. "Let's open it and let it breathe."

While I coaxed a stubborn cork out of the bottle, Ruth bent over, turned the heat down under the sauce, then wiped her hands on a towel which had been tucked into the waistband of her slacks. "May I fix you a drink, Darlene? Peppermint schnapps?" I'd seen more convincing smiles on guests of honor at funeral homes.

Darlene had been standing next to my father, gazing up at him as if he were the learned professor and she were an infatuated student. "Hmmm?"

"A drink. Schnapps?"

"No, thanks." She wandered toward the refrigerator, her hand running along the countertop as if checking it for dust. "That's only for *special* occasions."

So what is this? I wanted to yell. *A tax audit?*

Ruth recoiled as if she had been slapped. In a just world she would have upended the pot of sauce over Darlene's head.

I set the wine on the counter and stepped between the stove and the fridge, effectively blocking Darlene's view of my older sister who was coming to a boil almost as quickly as the pasta. "Would you like to see the house, Darlene?" I gave my father a straight-mouthed look. "Daddy, why don't you show Darlene the house."

But before anybody could move, the doorbell rang. Daddy turned his head, whether in response to the doorbell or to my question it was impossible to tell.

"I'll get it!" Emily leapt at the opportunity to get out of Dodge. She breezed down the narrow hallway, her skirt a bright patchwork quilt floating a few inches above her Birkenstocks. When she opened the door, Sean, Dylan, and Julie tumbled in, red-cheeked, followed by a blast of cold air, my sister, and her husband. Sean and Dylan made a beeline for the pool table in the basement, passing me with a perfunctory "Hi, Aunt Hannah!" before disappearing down the stairs. Julie remained in the hallway where she patiently peeled off her jacket, one sleeve at a time, and handed it to Emily.

His hand cupping her elbow, Daddy and Darlene passed by, headed toward the living room.

"Who are you?" asked Julie, who stood blocking the doorway, a bedraggled Abigail rabbit clutched under one arm.

Darlene stooped to Julie's eye level. "My name is Darlene," she cooed. "And isn't that a lovely teddy!"

Julie twisted her body sideways until Abby was safely out of the stranger's reach. "Abby is a *rabbit*!"

"So she is." Darlene reached out to pat Julie's copper curls but missed as Julie turned and darted away, leaving our guest squatting unsteadily next to Mother's Oriental umbrella stand. Figuring Daddy would sort it out, I threw an arm around Georgina and kissed the air next to Scott's cheek. "So glad you could come," I whispered as I relieved Georgina of a double-stacked pie carrier. I jerked my head toward the living room door through which Darlene had just disappeared. "Ruth's already in a snit. This could get ugly."

Emily had been hanging up coats, but she turned on me then. "Honestly, Mother. Give Granddaddy a break. Darlene's not so bad."

"How do you know?" Scott asked as he helped Georgina remove her coat and hat.

"Well, I don't, really, but at least Gramps isn't mooning around the house all day."

Georgina combed her long, copper-colored hair with her fingers. "Hat hair," she said. "I hate it." Then she turned to Emily. "That's one point in Darlene's favor, then. Keeping Daddy occupied."

Scott laughed. "Well, I for one am looking forward to seeing more of this paragon of virtue."

Thinking about the low-cut sweater Darlene had chosen for the evening, I said, "Then you won't have long to wait. The paragon has taken Daddy and her ample bosom into the living room."

"What's a pair of gones?" piped up Julie who had appeared, unaccountably, on the other side of the accordion gate that kept Chloe from crawling upstairs.

"Paragon," corrected Emily. "It means super-special, like Abby."

"Can Chloe play?" Julie asked.

Emily gave her cousin's ponytail a playful tug. "Sure, squirt. Let's take the baby and go down and see what the boys are up to."

Thank God for Emily! While the grown-ups spent the cocktail hour do-si-do-ing about the kitchen and living room, she kept the children occupied downstairs with popcorn and Coca-Cola, watching, from the periodic roar wafting up from the family room and from Julie's delighted squeal—"Ooooh! Flying cows!"—the *Twister* video. I thought *Twister* was a bit intense for little kids—it had scared *me* spitless—but they'd seen it seven or eight times already so it was probably a little late for me to object.

Meanwhile, Darlene and Daddy had migrated to the kitchen. Spreading a cracker with brie, she extended it toward my father, who was noisily lobbing ice cubes into a shaker. "Now, George, you've already had one martini!"

Was she some sort of fool? Everybody knew that the drink he was fixing had to be his third or fourth, at least.

Daddy added a splash of vermouth to the vodka already in the shaker and shook the nasty mixture vigorously. He took the cracker from Darlene's fingers and popped it into his mouth whole. "Just cleansing my palate." He poured his drink, sipped it experimentally, then turned to Ruth. "When's dinner?"

Ruth scowled over her shoulder. Some of the water from the pasta pot she was emptying into a colander in the sink slopped over onto the counter. "Five-minute warning. Tell everybody to wash their hands and come to the table."

After the rocky start, I was determined that the dinner would proceed pleasantly. Sitting on my father's left, I told Darlene about the St. John's College library where I was cataloging the collection of L.K. Bromley, the famous American mystery writer. I brought everyone up to date on my volunteer work for the Susan G. Komen Breast Cancer Foundation. Somewhere in the middle of asking Scott a question about the big account he had just landed, I noticed Darlene was shoving her spaghetti around on her plate, turning it over with her fork as if she were hoeing a garden. A tidy pile of mushroom bits grew to one side of her plate.

Ruth noticed it, too. "Something wrong with your spaghetti, Darlene?"

Darlene glanced up at Ruth. "I'm allergic to mushrooms."

"Oh?" By the grim set of her jaw, I could tell Ruth didn't believe that for one minute.

Daddy laid down his fork and patted Darlene's hand. "Ruth will fix you something else, won't you, Ruth?"

Without saying a word, Ruth stood, shoved back her chair, walked around the table, and snatched Darlene's plate. I hurriedly excused myself to see if I could help. By the time I got to the kitchen, Ruth had tipped Darlene's dinner into the garbage disposal and flipped up the switch so violently I thought it would fall off the wall. Over the grinding she snarled, "What the hell does he think I am? A short-order cook?"

Even though Daddy had been a bit over the line, I found myself coming to his defense. "She is his guest, Ruth. He just wants to make her happy."

"Well, next time he can make her happy at the Maryland Inn or Cantler's." She sluiced the remaining sauce off Darlene's plate, then mounded it high with fresh pasta. "Get the butter out of the fridge for me, will you?"

I handed Ruth the Land-o'-Lakes and said, "Look, Ruth. I don't like Darlene much, either, but what can we do? Daddy's a grown-up, and he's clearly smitten. I keep thinking, what would I do if Daddy didn't like Paul?"

Ruth stared at me thoughtfully, a carving knife in her hand.

"I'd want him to give Paul a *chance*. At least try to get to know him better. Wouldn't you?"

Ruth used the knife like a machete to hack off a chunk of butter, then she dropped the butter on top of the pasta and sprinkled it with chopped parsley, ground pepper, and a generous portion of grated cheese. "I guess so." She passed the plate under my nose for inspection. *"Voilà!"*

The aroma of freshly grated parmesan teased my nostrils. "Yum."

"She can like it or lump it," Ruth shot over her shoulder on the way back to the dining room.

I picked up the tall wooden pepper grinder and followed my obstinate sister. By the time I breezed through the door, Darlene had her new dinner and Daddy was fussing over her like a nanny. "There. Is that better?"

"It's fine, Georgie." The smile she gave Ruth reminded me of the car salesman in Glen Burnie from whom I bought my used Le Baron.

"Ah, good." He nodded.

"Tell me, Darlene," Ruth asked just as Darlene had raised a full fork of spaghetti to her lips. "Where did you and Daddy meet?"

Darlene lowered her fork and smiled. "We met at McGarvey's. My son, Darryl, works there."

"Oh? Doing what?" Ruth leaned forward, her hands neatly folded on the tablecloth in front of her.

"He's a waiter."

I thought about all the times I'd eaten at McGarvey's Saloon and tried to match my recollections of the wait staff there with the face of the woman sitting directly across from me. I couldn't do it. I closed my eyes. If Daddy's romance stayed on course, one of those waiters might soon be my stepbrother.

I killed some time helping Sean grate parmesan on his pasta while I thought about it. So, Darlene had a son. Yet she wore no wedding band, just an ornate turquoise-and-silver ring on the pinky of her right hand and a plain, gold school ring of some kind on the other. Paul must have been wondering the same thing. "What happened to Darryl's father?" he asked gently.

Darlene lowered her eyes. "I'm a widow."

Daddy had been nodding at his place, his head hanging so low it was in danger of crashing into his plate. Suddenly, he perked up. "Darlene has two children. Deirdre is twenty-eight, three years older than Darryl."

Darlene speared a cucumber with her fork. "My first husband died when Deirdre was eleven."

Georgina touched her arm. "I'm sorry."

"It was a long time ago."

Opposite Daddy at the head of the table, Ruth sat glowering like a malevolent Buddha, her eyes like slits. I glared back at her, willing her to keep her mouth clamped shut before something rude tumbled out. So, the glamorous Darlene had been married at least twice. But, as much as I wanted details about Darlene's background, for the sake of family harmony I swallowed my questions, even though I was in danger of getting an ulcer from all the nervous acid and tomato sauce churning around in my stomach.

Thankfully, Emily changed the subject, telling us all about New Life Spa in Virginia where Dante had already begun work. "It's so la-de-dah," she spoke directly to Darlene, "that you need to make an appointment *years* ahead of time."

"Like Greenbrier?"

"You've been to Greenbrier?"

"Once," Darlene said. "In another life."

Emily studied Darlene curiously, as if waiting for her to elaborate, but when the seconds lengthened and there was nothing more, she said, "It's sort of like Greenbrier, but way up in the Blue Ridge near Front Royal."

"Does the spa provide housing?" Scott wanted to know. Typical. He's an accountant.

Emily shook her head. "I wish! No, we've been house-hunting. Fortunately, New Life pays well enough that we'll actually be able to afford a small house, if we stay outside the Washington metropolitan area."

Darlene twirled her fork idly in Ruth's impromptu culinary masterpiece. Apparently she didn't like the pasta parmesan, either, because there was a mound of it still on her plate. "Are you going to work?" She smiled at Emily. "Outside the home, I mean."

Emily grinned fondly at Chloe who perched next to her in a high chair, calmly squeezing warm French bread between her fingers, making sure it was thoroughly dead before licking what was left of it off her knuckles. "No. Dante and I plan to homeschool our children."

This was news to me, but clearly not to Paul, who smiled benignly at his daughter across the table. Or perhaps he had retreated from the battlefield and was mentally far, far away, working on some theorem. Either way, we would discuss this homeschooling nonsense later.

"I sent Darryl and Deirdre to Catholic schools," Darlene said. "It was all I could afford."

I had decided that the conversation was going nowhere and had shanghaied Georgina to help me clear the table when Daddy gazed at Darlene, his eyelids at half mast. "Poor Darlene. She's lost three husbands."

I nearly dropped the dirty dishes I had been balancing, plate upon plate.

"It's still hard to talk about." Darlene bowed her head. Emily skillfully steered the conversation back to the more happy topic of Darlene's children. Between trips to the kitchen I learned that Deirdre was a graduate student in biology at the University of Maryland and lived in a condo in Bowie.

After a few moments, Ruth joined us at the kitchen sink. "She's lost three husbands? How careless of her!"

Georgina arranged a row of salad bowls on the top rack of the dishwasher. "Well, it's not exactly her fault, is it?"

"How do we know?"

"Ruth!" My sister had been watching too many reruns of *Murder, She Wrote*.

"I'd give my eyeteeth to know what happened to them."

"Why don't you just ask?"

Ruth gave me an Oh, Sure look. "She's after his money. I just know it."

"You don't know anything of the kind," I said. "Did you see the car she's driving?"

Ruth shook her head.

"A Porsche."

Georgina, who didn't have a car of her own, whistled. "They don't come in Cracker Jack boxes, do they?"

"No, ma'am." I tapped Ruth's cheek lightly. "She could have inherited tons of money from her former husbands, sweetie. Maybe she really *loves* Daddy."

If we had been taping a TV ad, Ruth's explosive *Ha!* would have shattered the wineglass she held. "You realize, don't you, my dears," she drawled, "that if Daddy marries That Person and he dies, she'll get everything. Grandmother's furniture. Mother's jewelry. This house. His car. Everything."

Georgina leaned against the kitchen table. "Don't be silly, Ruth. There'd be a will!"

I had to agree with Georgina. Daddy loved his family to distraction. He would never enter into a marriage without taking us, and his grandchildren, into consideration. "There'd be a prenup," I stated with confidence.

Ruth wasn't swayed. "Once he gets into the clutches of that hussy, absolutely nothing would surprise me."

"Don't you think you're being just a wee bit premature?" Georgina chided. "They've only just met and you already have them walking down the aisle."

"Georgina, dear, did you *look* at her?"

Georgina nodded.

Ruth upended her wineglass into the dishwasher. "I rest my case."

But during dessert—Georgina's homemade deep-dish

apple pie, warm from the oven, over which Darlene gushed her approval—Ruth melted a bit around the edges, like a scoop of ice cream à la mode, softening enough to ask Darlene where she had bought her sweater and making it sound as if she really cared.

Unfortunately, Darlene seemed preprogrammed to blow it. "You know, George," she said as we rose to leave the table, "if you put up a chair rail, you wouldn't have all those scuff marks on the wallpaper." She touched the paper, a beige silk floral that Mom and Dad had selected and hung themselves only weeks before Mother had been rushed to the hospital. Darlene leaned toward my father and said, sotto voce, but just loud enough for Ruth and me to hear, "If I ever move in, this ugly wallpaper will have to go."

Beside me, Ruth stiffened dangerously. I yanked her through the door into the kitchen just in the nick of time. Whether Ruth dropped or threw the dessert plate, I'll never know, but it hit the baseboard near the dishwasher, splashing melted ice cream all over my mother's hand-braided rug. "How *dare* she!" she raged. "That's it! I'm out of here! It's high time I found a place of my own." Her face was an alarming shade of red. "I've been nothing more than an unpaid servant ever since Mother died."

"Ruth . . ."

She shook off my restraining hand and took a step toward the back door. "Forget it, Hannah." I could tell Ruth was itching to pack her bags and get out of there. Right away. This minute. Slam the door and leave us all standing there, gaping, with dirty dishes piled sky high in the sink.

I folded Ruth into my arms. It was like hugging a marble column. "Cool it, Ruth," I whispered against her ear. "If you run out on him now, it'll leave the house wide open for Darlene to move right in."

Ruth began to tremble. "I'm going to kill her," she muttered.

I increased pressure on my sister's back, squeezing hard until the trembling stopped. "OK now?"

Ruth nodded.

"Ready to go back in there?" I pointed toward the dining room.

"Maybe."

With my hand against the small of her back, I urged Ruth into the dining room. Except for the dirty dishes, the room was now empty. We followed Daddy's deep baritone into the living room where we found him seated next to Darlene on the sofa. Georgina sat in Mother's chair, thank goodness; if Darlene had taken it, Ruth would surely have gone ballistic. I perched on the arm of the love seat next to Paul while Ruth chose to stand, lounging against the doorframe.

We had interrupted something.

Daddy looked at me. "Hannah, I've decided to move in with Darlene."

No wonder everyone was sitting there stiff as statues. "But . . ." Ruth began.

Darlene raised a hand. "He's not going to stay, girls. We've talked it over. He's just here to pick up his shaving gear."

"Daddy?" Ruth was blinking rapidly, close to tears.

"It's all settled." Darlene reached over and took my father's hand, drawing it into her lap. No one spoke for several moments. The clock on the mantel ticked as loudly as the telltale heart.

Ruth turned on our father. "Can't you talk? Does she talk for you now?"

Daddy sank back into the cushions. He looked like a scolded puppy—sad, confused, and a little frightened. "I have to live my own life."

"I don't believe this! After all I've—" Ruth's mouth snapped shut.

"Ruth, I love you. And I appreciate everything you've done, I really do. But it's time for me to do what *I* want for a change."

"But you're not even married!" Georgina protested. "It's not right!"

Darlene gazed serenely at our father. "I think somebody over seventy can live where and with whomever he wants."

"Georgina's right," Ruth said. "It's a sin, Daddy. Go ahead and ask her. Ask Darlene. What's her precious pope going to say?"

I stared in wonder. Since when did Ruth, our New Age flower child, care about religion? I was getting dizzy from the verbal Ping-Pong.

Darlene's head snapped around, taking in each one of us in turn. "You don't like me. None of you does." Her voice broke. "You're all against me."

Daddy wrapped a solicitous arm around his suffering girlfriend.

"To be real honest," Georgina commented, "we don't know very much about you."

"So, why are you treating me like . . . like dirt?"

"Don't be silly," Georgina soothed. "We've only seen you once before. How can you possibly say that?"

"I sense the coldness. What is it?" She looked directly at Ruth. "Do you think I'm a gold digger or something?"

"You said it, I didn't."

Darlene, her cheeks as pink as her sweater, sprang

to her feet and advanced toward my sister. "Ruth, I've tried so hard to be patient with you, to make allowances for how you must feel about this house and about your mother, but . . ."

"But what, Darlene?"

"Well, I hate to say it, but you're acting like a selfish brat!"

Ruth stepped aside deftly, turning to Daddy who was bent over, staring at his shoes. "Are you just going to sit there and let her talk to me like that?"

Daddy didn't answer.

Darlene grasped the back of a chair, the ring on her finger strangling the plump flesh, her knuckles white. Anger simmered in the dry green eyes that were directed at Ruth. "You know what your problem is?" Her voice dripped venom.

Ruth interrupted before Darlene could finish. "I think I'm looking at it." Ruth traded gaze for steady gaze.

Darlene sucked both thin red lips into her mouth.

Ruth, almost regal in her rage, faced our father in triumph. When Daddy looked away, she turned on Darlene. "Bitch!" And she spun on her toe and sailed out of the room.

No one spoke. In the deafening silence I could hear above the pounding of my own heart Daddy's labored breathing. I felt as if the world had slipped, violently and dangerously like tectonic plates in the San Andreas fault. Only a few seconds had passed, yet it seemed that a gap had opened in the living room floor; a wide gulf now separated us from our father. I might reach out across the yawning crevice but Daddy, now standing stiffly next to Darlene, was slipping farther and farther away.

After this unfortunate evening I hoped Daddy would see what a terrible person Darlene was, that he'd escort her down the drive to her car and we'd never see her again.

Wrong. Wrong. And wrong again.

ONE THING'S FOR SURE. RUTH IS HER FATHER'S
child. While she maintained an off-again-on-again
relationship with a local real estate agent and oc-
casionally dragged me along on halfhearted house-
hunting expeditions to look at South River Colony
condos or Eastport fixer-uppers, Daddy apparently
bought a spare can of shaving cream and a second
toothbrush and was blowing hot and cold about moving in permanently with Darlene.

As often as not, Daddy would be home for dinner
and Ruth, though exhausted from a day behind the
counter at Mother Earth would, more often than not,
be home to cook it for him.

We rarely saw Darlene.

Ruth counted every dinner served at home a major
victory in her silent tug of war with the widow Darlene
over our father. It wasn't that she didn't want to see
him happy, even remarried—someday. It was his choice
of a running mate that was giving her fits. If Daddy
had put an ad in the paper for someone the exact

opposite of our mother, she said, and if Darlene had applied, she'd have been the perfect candidate. We couldn't imagine what he saw in the woman.

"Isn't that obvious?" Paul said one evening two weeks before Christmas. He stood on a ladder, carefully positioning a crystal star on top of our Christmas tree, a plump, nine-foot spruce that graced the corner of the living room nearest the fireplace.

I hung a favorite blue glass horse on an upper branch where Chloe, who was playing at my feet with a strand of tinsel, couldn't reach it. "It's a guy thing, isn't it?"

"Uh-huh."

"Other than that, I mean." I retrieved the tinsel which appeared to be heading for Chloe's mouth and substituted her Tinky Winky doll.

Paul backed down the ladder, cocked his head to one side, and squinted up at the star. Satisfied, he turned to me and put his hands on my shoulders, his gray eyes unnaturally bright in the reflected candlelight. "Hannah, your father went straight from his mother—who cooked and cleaned and washed his clothes—to the Naval Academy—which told him when to go to bed and when to get up, even what to wear and what to think—to the Navy itself and marriage to your mother. Poor guy's never sown any wild oats. Maybe it's time."

"I just don't want him taken advantage of."

"You don't think he can look after himself?"

"No, I don't. He's not thinking with his head, Paul. Mr. Happy's in control here."

Paul laughed and pinched my cheek. "He usually is."

"You're impossible!" I thought he was going to hug

me, but I was holding a gilded angel with wings of delicate filigree and I was afraid he'd crush it. "Here," I said, handing him the angel. "See if you can't hang this out of harm's way."

Balancing on the ladder, Paul placed the angel on an upper branch, carefully facing her into the room. We'd bought her together for our first Christmas in Ohio more than twenty-five years ago. The only other decorations we could afford for that teeny, tiny tree had been a garland of popcorn, strung together with a needle and thread during an episode of *Star Trek,* and a box of colorful glass balls from the five-and-ten. We still had the glass balls, nestled in an egg carton, waiting to be hung.

I was reaching for a striped ball when Emily appeared in the doorway between the living and dining rooms, drying her hands on her jeans. "How's my girl?"

Chloe's face radiated joy at the appearance of her mother. She held out Tinky Winky, dripping with drool, for Emily's inspection. "Dah dah dah."

"Little ingrate," Emily said cheerfully. She swung Chloe into her arms and, using the tail of her linen shirt, wiped the baby's chin dry. "Bear her, feed her, change her diapers, and read her stories and the first word out of her mouth is *dah*." Emily boosted her daughter over her shoulder and with a firm grip on her ankles, slid Chloe down her back like Santa's sack. Emily jiggled her gently up and down until the little girl was convulsed with giggles. "Bath and beddie-bye and *Goodnight Moon* for you, sweetie pie!" She turned to smile at me. "I'll be back to help with the tree in a bit, OK?" Emily gazed wistfully at the boxes of decorations and sighed. "Speaking of *Dah* . . ." She swiveled her head around and spoke directly to Chloe's laughing pink face. "I wish your father could be here to help with the decorating."

Paul laid another log on the fire. "I realize the rich and famous need to be pummeled into shape for the holidays, but doesn't Dante get time off for Christmas?"

"Like, sure. Three whole days." Emily stiffened her back and thrust out her chin. "Zoh, ven I tell you ve haf mudge respect for zee family here at New Life, you vill zoh vant to verk vith us." She giggled. "But it will be great once we find a place of our own, won't it, Chloe? Then Daddy will come home to us at night."

Studying my daughter's face, roundly cherubic in the candlelight, I found myself softening toward my son-in-law. Clearly he cherished Emily and adored his daughter. He was also turning out to be a good provider. While he toiled on a Virginia mountaintop, working his fingers to blunted nubs, I worked to overcome my prejudices and get over the fact that Dante's degree came from the Rolf Institute in Boulder, Colorado, and not from Haverford.

Paul adjusted the damper in the fireplace. In the gentle draft the ornaments on the tree twinkled. With tears pricking the corners of my eyes I watched a sleigh I had made for my father out of Popsicle sticks revolve into view. I had been only eight when I painted it fire-engine red and stenciled *Daddy* on the slats in white. That treasure should have hung on the tree at my parents' house, but Daddy had declared that he didn't want a tree this year—it was too painful a reminder of Mother—so he'd hauled the decorations out of the attic and begged us to take the boxes away.

Ruth's box had ended up at my house. Any minute

she'd be showing up to help decorate. I prayed she wouldn't complain about where we'd put the tree. If I knew Ruth, she'd point out that there was better feng shui between the two front windows. Alas, the ancient Chinese hadn't been around in 1856 to advise our builders of that fact, or instruct them to install an electrical outlet on the wall there, so if I had anything to say about it, our tree was staying put.

I watched Emily skip upstairs with Chloe's head bobbing joyfully over her shoulder. Two minutes later I heard the bath water running. While Paul put the kettle on to boil for tea, I slipped a selection of Christmas CD's into the changer and happily unwrapped and hung our collection of ceramic angels while singing the alto part to "Silent Night" and "Angels We Have Heard on High." In the middle of a particularly fine *glo-o-o-ria*, Ruth materialized in a multilayered swirl of scarves, sweaters, and cold air. She froze when she saw the tree, her eyes glistening.

"You OK?" I asked. "You're not crying, are you?"

Ruth shook her head, then ran a mittened finger under each eye. "Just the cold."

I didn't believe her.

Ruth took off her mittens, stuffed them into the pocket of her sweater, and walked slowly around the tree, touching familiar ornaments. "Hannah, it's gorgeous." She knelt to inspect the Brio train that circled the tree stand on a lumpy green-and-white felt skirt. With a long index finger, she pushed the engine forward a foot. "I wish Daddy were here tonight."

"So do I, Ruth. I invited him, but he said he had other plans."

Ruth stood. "Right. Urgent business in Chestertown."

I looked at my sister and said what I knew she must be thinking. "I wonder if he's decorating Darlene's tree tonight."

Ruth shrugged.

"With—who is it?—Darwin and Deirdre?"

"Darryl," Ruth corrected. "Darryl and Deirdre."

"The Darling D's," Paul added. He set the tea tray down on top of the piano and drew Ruth to him in a one-armed hug.

"Darling?" Ruth ducked out from under Paul's arm and turned to face him. "Darling? Try dreadful, Paul. Or how about dangerous?"

I could tell by the look on his face that Paul didn't want to go there. "Tea?" He smiled, teeth gleaming, and gestured toward the tray.

"I need something stronger than tea tonight." She peeled off a Kaffe Fassett design I knew she had knit with her own two hands, laid it across the arm of the sofa, then fell onto the cushions, her legs sticking straight out in front of her. "How about a scotch on the rocks?"

While Paul went off to fix Ruth's drink, I moved empty boxes off the chair opposite my older sister and sat down in it. "What makes you think Darlene's dangerous?"

"Are you kidding, Hannah?" She sat up and leaned toward me, elbows resting on her knees. "Three men walked down the aisle with that hussy and none has lived to tell the tale."

Paul returned, carrying a tumbler full of crushed ice and a generous measure of scotch. "Your slushee, madame." It was ironic that none of us would have drunk like this around Daddy.

Ruth took a sip, smiled a thank-you to Paul, then

looked directly at me, her eyes like coal. "I don't want Daddy to be Number Four."

"Neither do I, at least not until we've had a chance to check Darlene out thoroughly."

Holding her glass in both hands, Ruth took another sip of her drink, then melted into the cushions. "So, what do you suggest?"

"I've already searched the Internet for Darlene Tinsley."

"And?"

"Nothing much, except her name appeared in the register of the Chestertown Garden Club. Then I tried just plain Tinsley and there were so many hits the blasted computer froze up on me."

Paul balanced himself on an arm of the sofa and raised his mug in a mock toast. "Thank you, Bill Gates." He took a sip of tea. "How about the son, Darryl? Didn't your father say he worked at McGarvey's?"

"Yes." I felt my face redden with embarrassment. "I even stopped by McGarvey's to talk to him. I told the guy at the bar I was Darryl's aunt, but he's taken a week off. He's on a ski trip out west somewhere. Won't be back until Monday."

"And darling Deirdre?"

I glared at my sister. "Ruth, get a grip. Deirdre could be a perfectly nice woman."

Ruth gave me an I-don't-care shrug and concentrated on her drink.

"But I couldn't find her, either. Directory assistance doesn't list her in Bowie and the university, as you might expect, is not in the home telephone number sharing business."

Paul set his mug down on the end table. "I have a radical idea! Why not just ask your father?"

"I did," I said, a bit miffed that he'd think I hadn't already thought of that.

"So did I," Ruth added.

"Paul, Daddy doesn't know any more about Darlene's past husbands than we do. He says that any time he mentions the subject, Darlene gets all choked up and teary-eyed. It's just too, too hard to talk about."

"Convenient."

"Maybe so, but he feels sorry for the woman and isn't about to push it."

Paul looked thoughtful. "Except for Tinsley, we don't even know their last names, do we? It's not common knowledge . . ." He drew an exaggerated breath. ". . . like Elizabeth Taylor Hilton Wilding Todd Fisher Burton Burton Warner Kotinsky."

I applauded appreciatively. "Very good! I doubt I could dredge that up out of *my* creaky database!"

"Before you go handing out any medals, I have to confess I saw it on A and E the other night."

"Nut!" I beamed at my husband, loving his crooked smile, his bright, intelligent eyes, and the unruly way his hair, slightly gray as if touched by frost, curled over the tips of his ears.

"Earth to Hannah." Ruth punched my arm.

"Uh, what I was going to say is that I asked my librarian friend, Penny, at Whitworth and Sullivan to run a search on the name Darlene Tinsley in the newspaper databases—"

"And?" Ruth interrupted.

"Nexis turned up nothing. And nothing for Darryl or Deirdre, either."

"You guys plotting again?" It was Emily, holding Chloe, pink from her bath and stuffed like a plump sausage into a blue-footed sleeper with Winnie-the-Pooh appliquéd on her chest.

I rose and gathered Chloe, slightly damp and smelling of Johnson's Baby Powder, into my arms.

"How old's this Darryl guy, anyway?" Emily asked.

"Twenty-five." I kissed the top of Chloe's head and felt a twinge. Emily had smelled just this way as a baby.

Emily, the grown-up, smiled. "Why don't you leave Darryl to me?"

Paul hugged his daughter, then took her chin in his hand and looked directly into her eyes. "Poor schnook will never know what hit him."

Emily shrugged. "Proud to do my bit for God and country." She held her arms out for Chloe. "Say good night to your grandma and grandpa and Auntie Ruth."

Anchored firmly in Emily's arms and swaying from side to side like the Leaning Tower of Pisa, Chloe planted sloppy kisses on cheeks all around before Emily took her upstairs to bed. Paul watched them disappear before turning to me. "Motherhood has certainly agreed with Emily, hasn't it?"

I couldn't argue with that. "It's like a miracle. Last Sunday in church I was saying to myself, Lord, I don't know who this young woman is, but I think we'll keep her."

Ruth balanced her glass on the arm of the sofa. "Maybe she left the evil twin back in Colorado?"

"Emily was never evil, Ruth. Just difficult."

"You call running away from home for months and months at a time 'difficult'?"

I sighed. "That's all in the past."

"Following that rock group?"

Thankfully Emily bounced back into the room just then, saving us from further Ruth-isms. We finished decorating, then sat back and relaxed, listening to the music, admiring the tree, and enjoying the cozy warmth of the fire as it burned ever lower in the grate. Ruth finished off a third scotch on the rocks and was so limp-limbed and mellow that when the time came, Paul had to drive her back to Providence in her own car, with me following.

Back at home, lying in the darkened bedroom next to my husband with a midnight showing of *Stalag 17* casting flickering shadows on the wallpaper, he asked, "Think Ruth's going to be OK?"

"Of course. I gave her a bottle of water and watched while she took two aspirins. Couldn't get her out of her clothes, though." I ran my hand slowly down Paul's arm. "She might be moving a little sluggishly in the morning."

"Come here, sweetheart," growled the Humphrey Bogart of Prince George Street.

Sometime later, we fell asleep with the TV on.

When the telephone rang, I struggled to open my eyes. On the screen, Lenny Briscoe sat opposite Mike Logan in *Law & Order*, pawing through some papers on his desk. *Why doesn't he answer his damn phone?* I patted around the covers, feeling for the remote, found it, and clicked off the TV.

But the phone kept ringing.

Three-oh-five. Shit! Nobody ever calls at that hour unless it's bad news. In the seconds before I picked up the receiver I remember thinking, *Thank goodness Emily is safe in her bed.* I prayed it would be a wrong number. A kid. A prank. "Hello?"

"Hannah! It's me, Ruth. The police called. There's been an accident!"

My head swam. "What?"

"A car accident! It's Daddy!"

"Is he OK?"

"They wouldn't say. It's a head injury. They've taken him to the emergency room. I'm going over there right now."

"Wait a minute!" I was already shaking Paul awake. "Don't you *dare* get behind the wheel, Ruth. Paul will be right over to pick you up!"

I turned on the bedside lamp. Paul looked at me with molelike eyes, rapidly blinking.

I covered the receiver with my hand. "Get dressed. Daddy's been in an accident, and you'll need to pick up Ruth. I'm going over to the hospital as fast as I can."

By the time I threw on the jeans I had abandoned on the carpet the night before, pulled a sweatshirt over my head, stuffed my bare feet into a pair of old jogging shoes, grabbed my parka from the front closet, and headed out the door, Paul was just pulling out of a precious parking spot directly across the street from our house. He powered the window halfway. "Get in. I'll give you a lift."

I leaned over, my breath a white cloud. "No. I'd rather walk."

"Hannah, it's nearly four in the morning! Get in this car!"

How could I explain? Eight months ago I was heading out this same door for the same emergency room, but that time I was in an ambulance with a pair of paramedics who were struggling to keep my mother's heart beating. How could this nightmare be happening again?

I kissed my fingers and pressed them against the window where they left misty white impressions on the glass. "Go get Ruth. I'll meet you at the hospital." And I turned and jogged away from him down Prince George Street.

IT WAS THE SAME RECEPTIONIST. THE SAME ONE, I swear, who was asking me the same damn questions in the same flat, emotionless voice. She'd probably taken a course—Pacification 101: Dealing with the Distraught Customer. My fingernails dug into my palms as I fought the urge to scream. I wanted to scream until I ran out of breath, until I fell, blue-faced and exhausted, to the cold, hard floor.

"I don't know his Social Security number."

The receptionist, Miss Prozac of 1999, managed a cool, dispassionate smile, but her fingers hadn't budged from the keyboard.

"I don't have a clue about his health insurance! Look in your computer! Look up my mother. My poor, dead mother." I slapped the counter with the flat of my hand. "Look up Lois Alexander. The information's the same."

In mid-rant, I felt a hand on my back and turned to see Paul, his face a misery of concern. "Sit down, Hannah. I'll take care of this."

Miss Prozac beamed at Paul, as if he'd just thrown her a life preserver. "Yes, please sit down, Mrs. Ivory. We can take care of this later."

"It's Ives," I corrected. The pressure of Paul's hand was firm but gentle on my back. "I-V-E-S."

Paul led me to a chair in the waiting room where I sat down heavily and tried to quiet the shaking of my hands by pressing them between my knees. "This is some sort of cosmic joke, Paul. Maybe we didn't handle it right the first time." He stood directly in front of me, blocking my view of the receptionist. I leaned my head against him and spoke into his belt buckle. "So now we have to do it all over again."

I sat back suddenly, remembering my sister. "Where's Ruth?"

"Her face was a mess. I sent her to the ladies' room." Paul reached down and smoothed a lock of hair back from my forehead. "So's your hair, sweetie."

I grasped his hand and held it against my cheek, like an anchor, fighting back fresh tears of anger and frustration. "Just keep me away from any mirrors."

Behind Paul a state trooper, large as a linebacker, loomed into view. Wearing a gray uniform with a Smoky the Bear hat tucked under his arm, he straight-armed his way through a swinging double door and crossed the room in our direction. "Are you Ruth Gannon?"

I looked up, surprised. "No, that's my sister. She'll be back in a minute." Suddenly I knew who this guy was. "Are you the officer who called about George Alexander?"

"Yes, ma'am. I'm Corporal Griffin." A patch on his left sleeve identified him as an officer with the Maryland Transportation Authority, the special police who patrol Maryland's bridges and tunnels.

"I'm his daughter. Is he OK?"

"Your father plowed his car into the back of a truck on the Bay Bridge."

"How badly is he hurt?"

"Aside from a pretty good gash on his forehead, not too bad. Fortunately, the air bags deployed and your father was wearing a seat belt."

"Thank God," Ruth said. She had returned from the bathroom and materialized at my elbow.

"Yes, ma'am. Some people think all they need is the air bag." He tapped an index finger next to his temple. "That kind of thinking gets you dead." Corporal Griffin shifted his considerable weight from one foot to the other. "Look, I gotta tell ya. They're doing a blood alcohol kit on him right now, but from your father's behavior at the scene and from what I learned from the paramedics, I'm afraid I had'ta issue a citation." Griffin reached into a slim portfolio that I hadn't noticed before. It had been tucked under his arm along with his hat. He pulled out a three-part form, tore off the pink sheet, and handed it to me. "Your father signed this form, agreeing to the test."

I looked at the bottom of the form where the YES box for an alcohol concentration test was checked and my father's familiar signature was scrawled over, around, and above the Driver Signature line. Another hand had filled in the date and time. I pointed at the line that said Signature of Officer. "Is that you?"

"Yes, ma'am. I'll be the investigating officer."

Ruth's eyes darted from Corporal Griffin, to me, to Paul, and back to Griffin again.

"You don't look surprised." Griffin fluttered the remaining copies of the DR-15 in front of Ruth and addressed her directly.

"Frankly, no," she admitted.

"Ruth!" I shot my sister a shut-up glare. "What's the next step?" I asked before Ruth could incriminate our father any further.

"We send the blood kit to our crime lab in Pikesville. The results will be back in two weeks."

"Then what?"

"If his blood alcohol level is higher than point one, we notify the MVA and his driver's license will be confiscated."

"Well," Ruth drawled, "that should cut down on his trips back and forth to see that witch in Chestertown."

"Be careful what you wish for, Ruth," I said. If Daddy's Little Problem got any more out of hand, she might be glad there was a Darlene in the picture.

Corporal Griffin sighed deeply, then laid his hat and portfolio on a chair. "Look, let's all sit down, OK? I got some questions and I'm sure you got some questions. Better now than later, huh?"

Griffin's chair creaked under his weight. His beefy body spilled over the seat on both sides, the nightmare seat mate in transatlantic flight hell. "As I said," he continued. "Your father was driving west in the westbound span when he ran into the back of a tractor trailer. A passing motorist called nine-one-one. I arrived about the same time the ambulance did."

Paul asked, "Was anybody else hurt?"

Officer Griffin shook his head. "Nope. The truck driver wasn't in his vehicle."

"Do you mean the truck was *stopped* on the bridge?" I was incredulous.

"Yes."

"Then how can it be Daddy's fault he ran into it?"

"Look, ma'am, that truck was lit up with blinking lights like Rocker Fellah Center. If your dad'a been sober, it never would'a happened."

"But . . ."

Paul silenced me by squeezing my hand, hard. "Does he need a lawyer?"

The officer shrugged. "If it was me, I'd get one."

"When can we see him?" I asked.

Griffin rose from his chair, tugged on the waistband of his uniform, and gathered up his belongings. "It's up to the doctor in charge, but someone should be out to talk to you soon." He reached into a breast pocket, pulled out a business card, and handed it to Ruth. "I'll be in touch."

"Thanks," Ruth said, although under the circumstances, I couldn't imagine what she was thanking the guy for.

After Corporal Griffin left I took the card from Ruth, read it, then handed it back to her. "Why you?" I asked, feeling unaccountably miffed.

She shrugged. "They called the house asking for Mom." Her voice broke. Huge tears slid down her cheeks.

"Oh, Ruth! I'm sorry!" I felt my cheeks grow wet. "Stop it! Now you're making *me* cry!" I hugged Ruth and began to blubber. My teardrops left gray splotches all over her white silk blouse.

"Girls, girls." Paul put his arms around both of us. "I find myself doing this a lot lately," he muttered into my hair. After a few seconds, he fumbled in his pants pocket and withdrew a couple of paper towels, an emergency supply that he must have yanked out of the dispenser in the men's room. "Here. You may need this."

I was blowing my nose noisily into the stiff brown paper when a doctor appeared. "Mrs. Ives?"

My head snapped around. "Yes?"

"I'm Dr. Wainwright." I shook the hand he extended. It was dry and very cold. "Your father's taken a good wallop to the head. It took twelve stitches to close the wound. He's got a concussion. I don't think it's particularly serious, but because of his age and the fact that it's a head injury, we're going to keep him a couple of days. Run a few tests."

"What kind of tests?"

"In addition to a head scan, we'll do a chest X ray and an electrocardiogram. Also a CBC, glucose, liver function, ABG—"

"Complete blood count I know, but what's an ABG?"

"Arterial blood gas."

"For a head injury?"

"Not exactly. The head injury may be just one of your father's problems, Mrs. Ives. I would be irresponsible if I released him from the hospital prematurely, before we've had a chance to determine the full extent of his injuries, and . . ." He looked at each of us in turn as if trying to predict our reactions to what he was about to say. ". . . And determine how much his recovery may be hampered by an alcohol dependency."

When none of us said anything, Dr. Wainwright continued. "I can see by the expression on your faces that I'm not telling you anything you don't already suspect." He waved his arm toward a bank of chairs and for the second time that morning, we sat down in them. "Look, the problem is this. If your father *is* an alcoholic, in anywhere from six to forty-eight hours he may begin to experience ethanol withdrawal. This can lead to seizures, hallucinations, delusions, vomiting . . ."

"D.t.'s?" I interrupted.

"Exactly. These tests I'm ordering will determine that risk, and then we will know how to treat him."

I studied Dr. Wainwright's earnest, caring face and remembered walking around for weeks with a lump in my breast and the wave of despair that washed over me when the very diagnosis I had feared turned out to be confirmed. *Cancer.* For months now, I'd worried about Daddy's drinking. Wondered if he'd crossed that fine line between drinking when he wanted to and drinking because he had to. *Alcoholism.* Before long, we'd know.

"Can we see him now?" Ruth asked.

"Of course. Follow me."

Dr. Wainwright led us to a large room that was separated into cubicles by curtains hung from ceiling tracks. Daddy lay on a gurney in the cube nearest the door. A large white bandage covered his scalp and forehead and an IV tube drained into his arm. Nearby, a cardiac monitor quietly bleeped.

"Daddy?"

I approached the gurney.

"Daddy?"

Daddy's eyes opened slowly. He shook his head and blinked several times as if trying to clear out the cobwebs and focus on my face. "Hannah?"

"Yes, it's me. And Ruth and Paul."

"Where's your mother?"

"Oh, Daddy!" I began to weep again.

Paul laid his hand on my father's. "Lois is dead, George, remember? She died last spring."

Daddy squeezed his eyes closed, as if to shut out this unwelcome news. He turned his head toward the wall.

"Daddy?" Ruth took a cautious step forward.

Daddy heaved a shuddering sigh, then reached up to touch the bandage on his forehead. "What happened?"

"You ran into a truck."

His eyes flew open. "I don't remember running into a truck."

"Take your time." Paul was reassuring. "It will come to you."

Daddy's fingers explored the perimeter of his bandage for a few long seconds, then suddenly he sat up, supporting himself unsteadily on one elbow. "Darlene!"

Paul put one hand on my father's chest and another on his back and helped him lie back down. "Don't worry, George. You were alone at the time. You must have been driving home from Chestertown."

Daddy scraped the back of his hand over the dark stubble that covered his chin. "I remember crossing Kent Narrows, but nothing after that."

"It's the concussion, Daddy," I said. "The doctor says they're going to keep you for a few days. Make sure you have no internal injuries."

"Does Darlene know?"

Ruth made a sour face. "I'll call her. Don't worry."

Daddy lowered his head and seemed to notice the disordered state of his clothing for the first time. Several buttons were missing from his blue oxford cloth shirt, which lay open, exposing a torn undershirt. He picked absentmindedly at some dried spots of blood that stained his shirt. "I'm a mess."

I had to agree. "You sure are, but I'll bring you some

clean clothes later this morning. In the meantime, I'm sure they'll have some cute little hospital gown you can put on."

"You betchum." The comment came from a nurse who suddenly appeared in the doorway with a green-shirted orderly in tow. "Yves Saint Laurent, Calvin Klein, you name it. We got 'em all." She positioned herself at the head of the gurney. "We're taking him to X ray now. Check back in a few hours for his room number."

I ran my hand over Daddy's short, wiry hair, and kissed his cheek. "Rest easy, Daddy."

The three of us stood there, watching, as the gurney with our father on it was trundled out of the room and down a long hallway. We watched, not speaking, until it disappeared through the door marked "Radiology."

"It's morning," said Ruth, "and I'm hungry."

But I was hardly paying attention. When I'd bent down to kiss my father, even the odor of the antiseptic they had used to treat his wound couldn't mask the sickly sweet chemical smell of alcohol metabolizing through his skin.

Daddy was in deep, deep trouble.

chapter

6

THE LIGHT OF A GRAY DAWN WAS SPREADING OVER
the city of Annapolis when we emerged from the hospital, walking stiffly and sluggishly, like bears crawling
from their dens after a long winter.

I stretched.

Paul yawned.

Ruth said, "Isn't anybody listening? I'm hungry."

I glanced at Paul and we said "Chick and Ruth's" almost at the same moment. No one needed to twist my
arm. I wasn't in any mood for cooking.

From the hospital, we walked east on Cathedral until it intersected with Conduit, then we veered left
toward town. Paul held my hand the whole way and I
felt light-headed, almost giddy, like back in the days
when we were dating. I recognized one contributing
factor, lack of sleep, and wondered when I'd get a
chance for a little shut-eye.

Chick & Ruth's Delly, an Annapolis institution since
1965, backs on Gorham Street near the municipal
parking garage and is just up Main Street from Mother

Earth. Paul pulled the back door open and we hustled through it into the upper dining room, then snaked our way through the closely packed tables and down the narrow stairway toward the front of the restaurant. Behind a long counter on our right, waitresses and countermen worked the drink machines, the sandwich lines, and the grill with practiced speed.

"This OK?" Paul indicated a booth near the front. "The Governor's Office," the booth that adjoined it, was roped off as usual, although I doubted that Parris N. Glendening would be bopping in for breakfast at seven-thirty on a Sunday morning.

Ruth slid a menu toward me across the black Formica tabletop, but I tucked it back on the elevated metal condiment shelf attached to the booth. "First things first," I said, squirming a bit to get comfortable on the lumpy vinyl chair. I extracted the cell phone from my bag. "I need to call Emily." I punched in our telephone number. "Order me a coffee, will you?"

Emily answered, breathless, on the first ring. "Where the hell *are* you?"

When I told her what had happened, she gasped, recovered, then sounded almost relieved. "I panicked, Mom, I swear to God, I panicked when I looked in your room and neither you nor Daddy was there."

It was a dig, but I couldn't resist. "Did you think we'd run away or something?"

"Not funny, Mother."

"I know. I'm sorry." The coffee had come, so I added some sugar and cream and gave it an absentminded stir. "Look, pumpkin, will you do me a favor?"

"What is it?"

I paused for a moment, not quite believing what I was about to say. Although I'd rather not see Darlene ever again, I had to be fair to Dad. He would want her to know.

"Mom? Are you there?"

"Sorry, I was just fixing my coffee. Look, honey. Would you call Darlene Tinsley and tell her about your grandfather's accident? I have her number written down in the flip-top phone book in the kitchen."

"OK, but you owe me." Emily paused. "You know I don't like her very much."

"Be nice, now. She's your grandfather's friend."

"For sure. And, Mom?"

"What?"

"I love you."

I pushed the End button and stared at the tiny display screen, nearly overcome with emotion. During Emily's troubled teenage years, I would gladly have paid a million dollars to hear her say those words. I laid down the phone and took a grateful sip of coffee, rich with cream and sugar, letting it roll over my tongue and down my throat like a soothing balm. I took time to survey the busy restaurant, but the cheerful orange booths and bright orange-and-yellow vinyl chairs and barstools did little to sunny up my disposition.

"Do you want to see the menu?" Paul asked, even though we both had it practically memorized. In any case, the main menu options were plastered all over the walls on colorful disks the size of dinner plates.

#311. The Parris N. Glendening. A baked potato with broccoli and cheese.

#14. The Bill Clinton. Turkey breast on whole wheat toast.

Al Gore was immortalized as a chicken sandwich, and when I got to Senator Barbara Mikulski, the open-face tuna on a bagel, I wondered, not for the first time, if there weren't just a bit of editorializing going on, with a decidedly Republican bent. Years ago, the Jimmy Carter sandwich had been peanut butter and bologna. I rest my case.

But it was too early for sandwiches.

Ruth ordered her usual bagel and Paul and I decided on the mushroom-and-cheese omelet which (Oh, joy!) comes with fries.

We gave our order to the waitress. Then, thinking about the copy of the citation in my purse, I said, "I wonder if Daddy knew what he was signing."

Paul shrugged. "It doesn't matter, honey. He'd have been in even bigger trouble if he didn't sign the darn thing. His driver's license would have been confiscated immediately."

"Does he have a lawyer, Ruth?"

"I don't think so; maybe in Seattle, but not in Annapolis."

"I'll call Murray Sullivan," Paul volunteered.

"Don't you know anybody else?" I hadn't laid eyes on Murray since the time Paul was accused of sexual harassment by a female midshipman and our marriage had nearly fallen apart. Thinking about it still hurt. I glanced at Paul sideways through my eyelashes. From the wistful look on his face, I could tell he knew what I was thinking.

He shrugged. "OK. I'll see what I can do."

I smiled at him gratefully.

Directly behind my husband's head there was a fourteen-year-old birth announcement, progressively yellowing, and every spare inch of wall was covered with photographs, drawings, and letters of appreciation to Chick and Ruth Levin who, framed newspaper articles reminded us, had passed away in 1995 and 1986 respectively.

Son Ted and his wife kept up the family business and its traditions now. It may have been dying of neglect in the public schools, but the Pledge of Allegiance was alive and well at Chick & Ruth's Delly. The American flag hung behind the cashier, near a sign that read "Cashier/Carry Out/Hotel Check In," and every morning at eight-thirty, slightly later on weekends, everyone stood for the pledge. I had been sitting so long, I welcomed the opportunity to shake out the cramps in my legs and persuade my right foot, which had gone to sleep, to rise and shine.

After the pledge, we settled back into our seats and I reached for the last french fry, but Paul's fingers got there before me. "You know," he said, licking his fingers, "after that I'm feeling so patriotic I may have to sing 'The Star Spangled Banner.' "

I covered my ears with my hands. "Please! Tell me when it's over!" Although he tried, Lord knows he tried, Paul couldn't carry a tune in a bucket.

"It's a difficult song, anyway," Ruth commented. "Way out of my range, especially the rockets' red glare part."

"Dad doesn't have any trouble," I said softly. He'd taken me to an Orioles game the previous fall and I'd stood beside him, marveling as he sang the heart right out of that anthem in his rich, full baritone.

Over my head, a bagel danced on the end of the pull cord for the fluorescent light fixture. "What turns so many veterans into homeless alcoholics?" I wondered out loud. "All those guys sleeping on heat grates in Washington, D.C.?"

Ruth got my drift. "That won't happen to Daddy, Hannah. He's got his pension."

Paul signaled the waitress for a refill on our coffee.

"She's right, Hannah. Darlene could steal your father's affection and everything of value that he owns, but she couldn't take that away from him."

"Yes, but there's more to life than money," I said. "Much more."

Sunday and Monday we took turns visiting the hospital. Even Dante, who had Monday off, stuck his head in before disappearing for a reunion with his little family. When I showed up around noon, Daddy was in high spirits, propped up in bed reading a Patrick O'Brian novel. There was no sign of the d.t.'s. That doctor was totally wrong. He got us all spun up over nothing.

Daddy laid the book facedown on his blanket. "Hi, sweetheart."

"Hi, yourself."

"You just missed Darlene."

"Oh?" I said. "What a shame." To be truthful, I was glad I didn't have to deal with Darlene. The way she acted around my father, all kiss-kiss and lovey-dovey, made me gag. After a few minutes of small talk, I was brave enough to ask, "What do you see in her, Daddy?"

"She's fun. She makes me feel young again." He slipped off his reading glasses and looked directly into my eyes. "And that's worth quite a lot in today's market!"

"I'm sure that's true, but as long as we're talking about today's market, there are hundreds of widows out there for every available man. Why not date somebody closer to your own age?"

"Seventy? Ha! I'm seventy years old, sweetheart. I'm running out of time in the life expectancy sweepstakes. I don't want a relationship with someone I'm going to have to worry about losing at any minute." He closed his eyes for a moment and I knew he must be thinking about Mother.

"Darlene could get hit by a bus tomorrow, Daddy. You never know what's going to happen." I pointed to his bandaged head. "You just proved that."

It was the first time I'd heard Daddy laugh since Connie and Dennis's wedding. "I could get hit by a truck?"

"You could get hit by a truck."

He stared out the window where we could see the bare dancing branches of the trees lining Franklin Street. "When your mother died, something inside me died, too." He turned his head toward me and winked. "Darlene's relit the spark." He snapped his fingers. "There's life in the old boy yet!"

I tried not to think about what form relighting that spark might take. "Does that mean you're *serious* about this woman? Is she The One?"

Daddy didn't answer right away, but when he did, his voice was almost a whisper. "Your mother was The One. The only one."

"So, does this mean you're *not* going to marry Darlene?"

"There'll be time enough to think about that when I get out of here."

"Don't rush it."

"What? Marrying Darlene or getting out of here?"

"Either one."

Daddy twisted his long body sideways, winced, then rearranged the pillow that supported his back. When he got settled again he said, "Sometimes I feel sorry for her, Hannah. Did you know that somebody tried to poison Speedo?"

"Speedo?"

"Her dog."

"No! That's horrible!"

Daddy nodded. And she's been getting harassing telephone calls."

"Really? What do they say?"

"Not much in the way of words. Someone breathes noisily for a while, then hangs up. Or, they make a noise like this . . ." Daddy gave a particularly liquid Bronx cheer. "Then they hang up."

"Sounds like kids. Forty years ago I tortured strangers with a very fine rendition of 'Is your refrigerator running?' "

Daddy smiled, then shook his head. "Somehow, I don't think it's kids."

"What makes you think that?"

"Because she's also getting nasty cards and letters."

"Nasty cards?" I sat back in my chair and thought for a moment. When I worked at Whitworth & Sullivan we used to call them Nasty-Grams—the terse communiqués emerging from the office of the office manager slash drill sergeant. But I'd never heard of a nasty card.

"Sick. People are sick," Daddy snorted. "Don't know where they buy these things, but they're sick."

"Like what?"

"I'm almost embarrassed to tell you."

"Daddy, last time I looked, I was forty-seven. I'm a grown woman. I think I can take it."

"First there was an envelope addressed to Darlene in block letters. But the return address was printed on. It said Last Chance Dating Service, and at the bottom of the envelope someone had stamped Application Rejected."

I stifled a laugh. "But that's funny! Surely whoever sent that envelope meant it as a joke."

"Darlene doesn't think so."

"That's it?"

"No. There have been others, and she's been getting cards, too. Cards with twisted greetings like 'Is that your face . . . or are you mooning me?' "

This time I laughed out loud. Daddy shot me a withering glance like I was six years old and I'd just knocked over my juice cup for the third time. I forced the muscles in my face to line up seriously. "Has she argued with anyone recently? A neighbor, for instance?"

He shook his head vehemently. "Ouch!" He patted the bandage where the tape wrapped around his right ear. "Not that I know of."

"How about her own kids?"

"No, they have lives of their own and pretty much keep to themselves." His eyebrows shot up and his face brightened. "You're going to meet them, by the way."

"I am? When?"

"Saturday night. Darlene's having a party. Seven o'clock." He pointed a long finger in the general vicinity of my nose. "Be there or be square!"

"Saturday! But will you even be out of the hospital by then?"

"Of course. Unless something turns up in the test results, I'll bet I can go home tomorrow."

I must have looked skeptical because he grabbed my hand and insisted, "I'm fine! I feel guilty lying here, like I'm taking a bed from someone who really needs it."

My father's predictions came true. On Tuesday morning, Ruth called to report that she'd be picking Daddy up and bringing him home the following day. When the call came, Paul was at work, Emily and Dante were house hunting with Chloe, and I had taken the portable phone to the basement so I could talk to my sister while sorting the laundry. The largest load was soaking in a pink plastic pail: two dozen cloth diapers necessitated by Emily's refusal to pollute the environment with Pampers or Huggies. I had just added the diapers and a cup of Boraxo to the washing machine when the telephone rang again.

"Mrs. Ives?"

"Uh-huh." I twisted the dial to the fourteen-minute soak-and-wash cycle and pushed it in.

"This is Marjorie Kemper, your father's next door neighbor? I don't wish to alarm you, but I know George is in the hospital and, well, there's a van I don't recognize sitting in your father's driveway, and some guy is loading things into it."

"Ohmygawd! What does the van look like?"

"It's dark blue and kind of battered."

"It doesn't sound familiar. Did you call the police?"

"No. First I called Ruth at her store, but the line was busy. So I called you. I wanted to check if you knew this person before I called the police. Sounds like the answer is no."

"You're quite right. Look, uh, Marjorie. See if you can get the license number. I'll be right over."

"Can I help?" she asked. "I can block the driveway with my car. And I have a gun."

The last time I'd seen Marjorie Kemper, she had been wearing a skirted swimsuit and a flowered bathing cap and was doing laps in her backyard pool. I added a gun to the scenario and had to grab onto the washing machine to keep from falling over. "Lord, no,

Mrs. Kemper! Just sit tight, keep an eye on the van, and write down anything you think might be helpful." I was about to hang up when I had another thought. "And keep trying to get Ruth."

By the time I arrived at my father's house, just seconds before Ruth and five minutes before the cops, the van was gone and so was the wide-screen television, the VCR, the DVD player, the stereo tuner, the CD player, and my father's extensive collection of opera CD's. I threw myself into an overstuffed chair, seriously depressed.

"How am I going to tell him about this? Mother gave him most of those CD's! This'll kill him!" With a sick feeling in the pit of my stomach, I stared at the clean spot on the shelf where treasures such as Wagner's *Ring* cycle and Boïto's *Mefistofele* had so recently sat. "Is anything else missing?"

"The silver tea service is OK and I checked the silverware drawer, and it's all there." Ruth had a sudden thought. "Wait a minute!" She rushed upstairs, but was back in less than two minutes. "False alarm! Mom's jewelry is still in its box on the dresser."

"They were after the electronics," one of the officers, the tall one, said.

"Our neighbor got his license number," I said brightly, standing up and pointing out the window in the direction of the Kemper house.

The officer shook his head. "I hate to be discouraging, but that plate was probably stolen."

I leaned against the wall feeling defeated. "Will the insurance cover it?" I asked Ruth.

"I should imagine, but there'll be a deductible." She sighed and sank into the chair I had just vacated. "I can't imagine Daddy living anywhere for long without his opera."

I ran my hand over a shelf which was not even dusty, then jerked my hand away. "Fingerprints?"

"We'll dust for fingerprints, ma'am, but I'll have to be honest with you, I doubt it will do any good. Whoever did it probably wore gloves," the shorter cop said.

His partner nodded. "Whoever got in had a key. Or the door was unlocked. There's no sign of forced entry."

Ruth scowled. "I *always* lock up."

I believed her. Ruth was compulsive about locking up, but the police didn't know that.

"Are you sure?" the short guy prodded.

Ruth nodded her head so vigorously that her long beaded earrings bounced against her neck. She turned to the officer, each word falling from her mouth like a blow. "The doors were locked." She folded her hands in her lap. "I dread telling Daddy. He'll think I'm not taking care of his things."

She looked so pitiful that I decided to spare her that. "Don't worry about it, Ruth. I'll tell him."

When I got to Anne Arundel Medical Center and found my way to Daddy's room on the second floor, he was sitting up in bed, watching television. He beamed at me, then aimed the remote at the TV and clicked it off. "Hi, sweetheart."

"How are you feeling?"

"Peachy! I'm ready to blow this pop stand."

I pulled a chair over and sat down in it. "Daddy, there's something I need to tell you."

"Hold that thought!" Daddy flung off the covers,

revealing legs so skinny I was shocked. "Gang way! Gotta use the head." He slid out of bed and padded across the tile in his bare feet.

While I waited for him to finish in the bathroom, I stared at my hands, wondering how I'd phrase it. Too soon, I heard a flush and Daddy crawled back into bed, pulling the covers taut around his body and tucking them in, like a cocoon, his arms resting on top. "OK. What is it?"

"There's been a robbery at your house."

"A robbery?" His eyes grew wide.

"The TV and DVD. All your stereo equipment." I thought I'd fire that round and let it soak in before dropping the bomb about the missing CD's.

"Nope. I gave Darlene a key."

"What do you mean, you gave Darlene a key?"

"Just that."

"Somebody mention my name?"

Daddy turned toward the door, a grin as wide as the Golden Gate Bridge plastered across his face. "Good to see you, sweetheart."

Blood rushed to my head and I thought I was going to pass out. *Sweetheart! That was what Daddy always called me!*

Darlene set a colorful shopping bag on the bedside tray table and bent to kiss my father lightly on the lips. "So, what am I supposed to have done?"

Daddy looked at me. "I was just telling Hannah that I gave you a house key."

She shrugged. "Seemed only fair since I gave him one of mine."

I stared her down. "Somebody used a key to steal my father's TV and stereo equipment today."

"Well, it wasn't stolen," she said matter-of-factly. "Darryl helped me move it, at your father's request."

I glanced quickly at Daddy, who looked back almost guiltily.

Darlene's face wore a look of triumph. "Since he'll be moving in with me."

Daddy smiled crookedly. "See, you were worried for nothing."

I was certain this plan was a surprise to him, but if Darlene was as calculating as I feared, she probably figured that where the opera recordings went, so went the man. Ruth had lost this round. Score one for Darlene.

"So it seems," I said. I regarded Darlene coolly. High black boots disappeared beneath the hem of a Burberry raincoat made bulky by the addition of a zip-in lining. Her blond hair frizzed out behind each ear and was held in place with silver combs.

"It's the most logical thing. He still needs looking after." She laid a palm on his forehead like a mother checking a child's temperature. "Don't you, Georgie?" She straightened blankets that were already pathologically straight. "And Ruth, well, she has to work, doesn't she?"

"Seems you have this all planned." I turned to my father. "Daddy?"

Darlene smiled at Daddy, stiff-mouthed, as if daring him to contradict her. Daddy tore his eyes from his girlfriend's face and looked at me blankly. He nodded. "It's for the best."

Suddenly he grabbed my hand and squeezed. "You will come to the party, won't you?"

"If I'm invited."

"Of course you're invited," he insisted passionately, still not letting go of my hand. "Tell her, Darlene."

"Sure. Bring Ruth, your husband, Emily. Hell, bring the whole family."

"I can't speak for everyone, of course, but I'll try. Georgina and Scott won't be available. They're taking the kids to his parents in Arizona for the week before Christmas."

Darlene shrugged. Whether we came to her damn party or not was clearly of little or no consequence to her. She picked up the Styrofoam water pitcher and jiggled it, then removed the lid and peered in. "You need more ice, Georgie." She pressed the call button that would summon a nurse, then began straightening the newspapers that lay strewn about the floor.

While she was bending over *The Baltimore Sun*, I walked my hand along the tray table until it touched the bag Darlene had brought. I poked at it. Something solid. With my index finger I peeled down the top of the bag and peeked inside. Absolut. Darlene was bringing our father a bottle of vodka!

I wrapped all my fingers around the neck of the bottle, fighting the very real urge to smash it over the stupid woman's head. "Darlene? Can I see you for a minute? In the hall?"

She looked genuinely puzzled, but shrugged and followed me out the door.

Holding the contraband in front of me, I walked nearly to the nurses' station, seething, before I turned on her. "What's this?" I hissed, waving the bottle under her nose.

"It's a little prezzie for your dad."

I shook the bottle at her again. "Darlene, he doesn't

need this. In case you hadn't noticed, Daddy has a big problem with alcohol!"

She blew air out through her lips. "No, he doesn't! He just drinks a little too much sometimes. Haven't you ever done that?"

I had, but it was a long time ago. The memory of a hangover the size of a satellite map of Hurricane Floyd kept me from doing it ever again.

"Vodka is *not* going to help."

"You're overreacting."

"No, I'm not." I stuffed the bottle deep into my bag. "And I'm not going to let you give this to him."

"Fine. See if I care," she huffed.

I touched her arm, but she drew back as if I'd given her an electric shock.

"Darlene, if you really care for my father, you'll help him take control of his drinking."

She glared at me with narrowed eyes. "A little beer and wine never hurt anybody."

I couldn't believe anyone could be so ignorant. Didn't she read the newspapers? Didn't she watch television? "For an alcoholic, even a little is too much," I said.

"He's had a tough time," Darlene whined. "We both have. We deserve to *live* a little."

I stepped close to her, so close I could tell that she showered with Irish Spring. "Just make sure all that living doesn't kill you." I spun on my heel and hurried away from her down the hall, feeling her cat-green eyes drilling into my back.

chapter

7

AFTER THE ABSOLUT EPISODE, I HAD HALF A MIND to forget calling the police to let them know that Darlene's son, Darryl, wasn't a thief, at least not in the technical sense of the word. Fortunately for Darryl, the regions of my brain where scientists chart charity, compassion, and mercy prevailed in me. Poor schnook couldn't help it that his mother was a professional, uh, girlfriend.

Besides, I would soon learn that I knew a couple of thieves myself, was harboring one, in fact, right under my own roof. Late Wednesday, Emily informed me matter-of-factly that she and Ruth had taken it upon themselves to remove some items from Daddy's house "for safekeeping." When pressed, she confessed that she and her aunt had liberated the silverware, Grandmother Barton's china, Mother's jewelry, and the Waterford crystal that my mother hadn't even had time to unpack before she died.

"Where did you put the stuff?"

"We've decided not to tell. That way, when you're asked, you can truthfully say 'I don't know.' "

"But what if your grandfather notices the things are gone?"

Emily shrugged. "We'll cross that bridge when we come to it, I guess."

I thought the move was risky and I told her so, but I was secretly pleased that they had taken matters into their own hands. We had all noticed things disappearing from my parents' home over the past several months—a pair of sterling silver ashtrays, an Etruscan horse, a crackleware vase, a formal portrait of my father in his Navy uniform. There was no point asking Daddy about them. It didn't take Hercule Poirot to figure out whose mantel that horse was prancing on. In a few days, I would be driving to Chestertown and could visit the horse myself.

I was looking forward to studying Darlene in her natural habitat, which is more than I can say for Ruth. I didn't need the staff meteorologist at WBAL-TV to tell me that a storm was brewing on that front. As Daddy prepared to relocate to Chestertown, he and Ruth moved around the house almost as strangers, inching their way toward an inexorable clash like high-pressure systems moving across the face of a weather map. From the devil's point of view, I thought, things were percolating along nicely; we could just sit back and wait for the eruption and hope that Darlene would not survive the fallout.

Round one went to Darlene when Ruth begged off the party at the last minute, blaming it all on Eric Gannon, her ex-husband, who is notoriously unreliable. If there was any time of year when Ruth needed help, it was the extended Christmas season when the downtown stores were open late and midnight madness often reigned. But Christmas also meant rounds of parties for the freewheeling and fun-loving Eric, who was not inclined to let part ownership in Mother Earth cramp his style.

"No can do," Ruth announced when I stopped by the shop on my way home after some Christmas shopping. Ruth reached under the counter and handed me a holiday bag with silver and gold tissue paper erupting from the top.

"What's this?"

"I must be getting soft in my old age," Ruth said.

"What?"

"Look inside."

I tunneled down through the tissue paper and discovered a gift-wrapped bottle.

"It's peppermint schnapps for Darlene. My peace offering. I don't know what came over me at dinner the other night. I must be menopausal."

I looked up from the bag expecting to see Ruth's self-deprecating smile, but her face was composed and perfectly serious. "I don't think it's hormones, Ruth. We were all on edge. You stepped a wee bit over the line is all."

"I've decided to be as nice as pie, even if it revolts me."

This reminded me of the trouble we'd had with Emily. The more dead set we were against some wholly unsuitable boy she was dating, the more determined she'd be to stick with the relationship. I wondered if the same were true of senior citizens. "Dad's a stubborn old bird."

Ruth nodded. "I know. Anyway, take that to Darlene with my apologies."

"I will, and I'll pop in on Monday with a full report."

"Monday? Why not tomorrow?"

"Ah, well. That's the surprise. Paul has reserved rooms at the Imperial Hotel. He didn't want to drive back late at night when we might be tired and, well, just a bit tipsy." I stepped closer to the counter as two customers entered the shop and began sniffing experimentally at the incense sticks that sprouted from an array of ceramic jugs on the shelf behind me. "Besides, it's *my* turn to be the designated drinker!"

"Are Emily and Chloe staying over, too?"

I nodded. "He's reserved the Parlor Suite for us"—I shot my sister an exaggerated wink—"and the room next door for Emily. Dante has to work this weekend."

"Again?"

" 'Fraid so. It wouldn't be so bad if he didn't have such a long commute."

The ladies behind me had made their selections, so I said a hurried good-bye and breezed out the door, Ruth's gift for Darlene tucked into the shopping bag I'd got at The Nature Company. I took a shortcut through an alley to State Circle, where I stopped at Annapolis Pottery to buy a gift for my author friend, L.K. Bromley, and at Flowers by James to buy a poinsettia for Darlene. I had just gotten home and was wedging the plant behind the driver's seat of my Le Baron when Paul appeared on our stoop, freshly scrubbed, looking *très distingué* in gray slacks, a white open-necked shirt, and a tweed jacket. He cast a critical eye over my jeans and red chenille sweater. "You gonna be warm enough?"

"You kidding? It must be fifty degrees out!" I slammed the car door with a comforting *thrump*. "Besides, I'm going to change."

Paul followed me upstairs and fussed with his tie while I threw on a green, ankle-length wool skirt and a

V-neck sweater, appliquéd with handmade Christmas ornaments. I clipped a jingle bell earring on each ear and pinned a Christmas wreath with teeny blinking lights to the collar of my sweater. I had a necklace of miniature Christmas tree bulbs somewhere, given to me by Sean and Dylan, but picked out by my sister, Georgina. I found the necklace in a box marked "Xmas" at the back of my jewelry drawer, slipped it over my head, then spread my arms wide. "There! How do I look?"

Paul's eyebrows did a two-step. "Like a mail-order catalog on December the first."

I punched him on the arm. "So where's *your* Christmas spirit?"

He fingered his tie, a conservative red with an overall pattern of minuscule Christmas wreaths. He waggled the tail of it under my nose.

"That hardly counts, Paul. It would take a magnifying glass to distinguish those wreaths from garden-variety polka dots."

We rounded up Emily and Chloe (looking Baby Beautiful in a stretchy red headband bow), took our festively attired selves to the car, and were soon whizzing through the tollbooths and over the Bay Bridge. By the time we reached the fork in the road where Routes 50 and 301 split, Chloe was asleep in her car seat. Next to her, Emily sat listening to something on her CD player. If I had ever watched MTV for more than five minutes, I probably could have recognized the tune from the *chee-cha-cha, chee-cha-cha* noises leaking from the earphones she had clamped to her head. I had half a mind to warn her she was going to go prematurely deaf, but thought better of it.

At the exit for Route 213, Chloe awakened, her

chubby face red with the effort of producing something of significance in her diapers. A few miles later, we crossed the old-fashioned drawbridge over the Chester River into Chestertown. I consulted the map I had printed off the Internet and it was a good thing, too, because the left turn onto Queen Street came up so suddenly, we almost missed it. Paul eased the car down the street while I scanned the house numbers. "There it is!" I pointed. Paul slowed the car to a crawl. Darlene's house stood in the middle of the first block, a two-story, double-dormered brick structure that had at one time been painted white, but the paint had softly weathered, giving the house an attractive, antiqued look.

"Well, at least it's not a dump," Emily commented. "I guess she spent all her ex-husbands' money getting into this neighborhood and now she wants Gramp's bucks to keep her in the style to which she's become accustomed." When I turned to scowl at Emily she raised a hand. "Joke!"

Signs along the street indicated that only residents should dare think about long-term parking there. "Where will we park?" I asked as we passed a turning for East Church Street.

"Never fear!" Squinting into the dark, Paul spun the steering wheel hard right and pulled into a driveway that led to the parking lot behind the Imperial Hotel. While we waited in the car, he gathered up our overnight cases and quickly checked us in, then we walked the block or so back to Darlene's with Paul lugging the poinsettia.

I stepped onto the porch and mashed my finger on the bell. I heard it buzz rudely somewhere inside. The door swung open almost immediately to a whoosh of overheated air and a blast of *Mannheim Steamroller Christmas*. Peeping around the door were the violet eyes and the beaming cherry-cheeked face of a woman I'd never seen before.

"Welcome! Come in!" I detected an accent. French, perhaps? When she threw the door wide, I got a full frontal view of a woman, nearly as tall as Paul's six foot one, swathed in purple. A wide silver belt cinched her knit dress together at the waist and a fringed paisley scarf was tied and secured at her right shoulder by an antique silver brooch.

But it was the tiara that captured my attention, an astonishing object of intricately twisted silver wire from which crystal beads dangled and slender lavender feathers trembled in the breeze.

My husband was the first to recover his power of speech. "We're Paul and Hannah Ives," he stammered, extending his hand. "And this is our daughter, Emily, and her daughter, Chloe."

"LouElla." She leaned down to take a closer look at Chloe. "Well, hello, precious!"

I caught Paul with his mouth in mid-gape as he took in our superannuated prom queen's too-black hair, parted cleanly in the middle and twisted into donuts at each ear, like Princess Leia in *Star Wars*.

"Where's Darlene?" I asked, gesturing with the bag Ruth had sent.

"When last seen, in the kitchen." LouElla indicated a square table set in the entrance hall on which gaily wrapped packages were piled like children's blocks, by a not terribly well-coordinated child. "You can leave that there."

There was no room on the table, so I set Ruth's gift on the floor next to a rectangular package wrapped in silver paper and decorated with multicolored hearts. Paul placed the poinsettia carefully nearby, rotating the pot until the plant's best face was forward.

"You can leave your coats in the upstairs bedroom, first door on the right." LouElla clapped her hands together. "But I see you haven't any!"

Paul chuckled. "No, it's unseasonably warm out there."

"But I'd love a place to change the baby." Emily smiled at LouElla. "May I?"

"Of course, my dear," she purred. "There's a bedroom on the left and the bathroom's at the end of the hall."

LouElla's eyes followed Emily as she mounted the stairs. "Just call if you need anything, dear!" Then she turned and glided ahead of us through the hallway and into the dining room, where a tweedy gentleman was fishing with a toothpick for a Vienna sausage floating in a reddish-brown sauce over a can of Sterno. "Dr. McWaters?"

The tweedy guy turned, eyebrows raised, the sausage now teetering precariously on the tip of his toothpick.

"Let me introduce you to the Iveses," LouElla said. She extended her hand in his direction, palm up. "Dr. McWaters is a general practitioner," she announced, giving equal emphasis to every syllable.

Dr. McWaters bent at the waist. "Guilty!" he said. "And it's Patrick."

The doorbell buzzed and LouElla twitched like a startled rabbit. "Whoops! Another customer!" She twirled smartly on one Ferragamo toe and wheeled out of the room.

"I see you've met LouElla Van Schuyler," the doctor observed.

I snagged a carrot stick. "Who is she?"

"One-woman welcome wagon." He dropped his used toothpick into a silver bowl, one that looked vaguely familiar. I inched my way closer to it. "Drinks table is in the kitchen." The doctor gestured to his left with a glass of white wine.

"And our hostess, too, I presume?"

He nodded.

"I'll look forward to talking to you later, then," I said, not wanting to appear rude.

On our way to the kitchen, Paul and I passed through a well-organized pantry with a wall of glass-fronted shelves to the right and on the left, a zinc sink which might have been used in the preparation of the extravagant flower arrangements that filled Darlene's house. "How many silver bowls with silver dollars set into their bottoms do you know of?" I asked my husband.

"What are you talking about, Hannah?"

I grabbed his arm, stopping him in mid-stride. "Those toothpick holders look very much like Mom's little silver dishes."

"You mean your father's little silver dishes."

"Why do you have to be so logical?"

Paul shrugged. "Occupational hazard."

The pantry opened out into a large kitchen that extended a dozen or so feet from the back of the original house, almost certainly a modern addition. In the daytime, a wall of windows offered a panoramic view, I would learn later, of Darlene's colonial-style garden. A handful of guests milled around a table strewn with bottles of wine, hard liquor, and an odd assortment of glasses. Olives, slices of lemon and lime, cocktail onions, and maraschino cherries were neatly arranged on clear glass saucers. Mixed nuts filled two more of my mother's little silver dishes.

I located Daddy at once, lounging by the television, talking to a young woman dressed somberly in black with hair dyed to match. Darlene stood on his left, her back to him, engaged in an animated conversation with a twenty-ish guy dressed in blue jeans, high-top leather boots, and a short-sleeved University of Maryland T-shirt. As we entered Darlene looked up, smiled slightly, then returned to her conversation. *Well, hello to you, too,* I sneered, *and welcome to my home.* The only friendly face in the bunch belonged to a Chesapeake Bay retriever who lay comfortably on a beanbag bed, his head resting heavily on his paws as if the red bow tied around his neck had grown too heavy. The dog's eyes were moving, following the to-ing and fro-ing of the guests like a tennis match.

I knelt in front of the dog. "Hello. You must be Speedo." I stroked the silky blond hair between his ears. Daddy's sob story about the harassment Darlene had been experiencing had failed to move me, but Speedo here, that was a different matter. Why would anyone want to hurt a harmless animal?

Paul found the drinks and poured us each a glass of red wine. He watched while I took a sip. "Drink up, Hannah. I have a feeling this is going to be a long evening."

I gestured with my glass. "Do you suppose the girl in widow's weeds and Biker Boy are Darlene's kids?"

Paul studied the tableau, his eyes darting from one face to another as if searching for a family resemblance. "Good bet," he said at last. "Check out the noses."

I had been thinking the same thing. "And the chins. Well, wish me luck. Here I go!"

Paul closed his eyes. "I'm not sure I can bear to watch."

I left Paul to carry on alone at the drinks table and swished over to confront Darlene.

"Hello, Darlene."

"Hello, Hannah." An introduction to her companion didn't seem in the offing, so I extended my hand to the young man. "Hello. I'm Hannah Ives, George's daughter. And you are . . . ?"

"Darryl Donovan."

"Ah," I said. "I thought you might be." After a prolonged silence during which I took two sips of my wine and listened to the mourning dove on Darlene's bird clock *who-WHO-who-who-who* seven, I asked, "Tell me, Darryl. What do you do?"

He shrugged. Clearly he'd learned the niceties of social intercourse at his mother's knee.

"Darryl manages tables at McGarvey's," Darlene supplied.

Darryl snorted. "What Mother means to say is that I'm a waiter."

"Really?" Another sip of wine slid down my throat. "I must have seen you there, then."

"I think I would have remembered." Darryl cast a sly eye at my décolletage, which, I must admit, pleased me enormously. He was practically undressing me with his eyes. If Darryl had actually managed to charm me out of my sweater, though, he would have been in for a shock. The plastic surgeon had done a masterful job of rebuilding my breast, but I didn't think *Playboy* would be renewing my centerfold contract anytime soon.

Over Darryl's shoulder I watched as Paul was way-laid on his way to join us by an attractive, silver-haired woman dressed in a red plaid suit. "Is your sister here tonight?" I inquired.

Darryl grunted. "She's the one talking to your dad."

"Deirdre's working on her Ph.D. at the University of Maryland," Darlene added. The proud mother wore a long-sleeved, scoop-neck cocktail dress in a stunning shade of turquoise with a matching pashmina artfully looped around her neck. As she reached out to touch her son's shoulder, the pashmina shifted. What I saw nearly stopped my heart; I had to press my hand to my chest to get it going again. Knocking about in her cleavage on the end of a pure silver chain was my mother's favorite jade-and-silver necklace. There was no mistaking it; Daddy had had it made in Japan by a jeweler working from an original design. When I could breathe again I said, "That's a lovely necklace, Darlene."

She reached up to caress it. "Thank you. Your father gave it to me." She smiled, revealing even white teeth. "An early Christmas present."

No wonder it was hard to breathe. Rage was tak-ing up the space in my chest normally reserved for my lungs. Lucky for Daddy that all these people were around, because I felt like picking up one of Darlene's country French kitchen chairs and clobbering him with it. "Well, I'll let you get back to your conversa-tion," I seethed, then turned on a furious heel to seek out the moral support of my husband.

I found he'd migrated back to the dining room, where he was hovering over the cheese board, still talking to the woman in the red plaid suit. Before I could tell him about the necklace he said, "Hannah, I'd like you to meet Darlene's friend, Virginia Prentice." He turned a dazzling smile on Virginia. "My wife is George's daughter. The middle one."

Virginia, who I guessed must be around seventy, grinned at me with a crimson mouth carefully outlined in a darker shade of red. "Are your sisters here, Hannah?"

"I'm afraid not. Georgina's in Arizona with her in-laws and Ruth had to work tonight."

Virginia shifted her drink so that she was holding her plate and her glass in the same hand. She selected a jumbo shrimp and dredged it through a puddle of cocktail sauce. "Too bad they're missing the party!"

I speared a crab ball for myself. "Ruth sent along a bottle of schnapps, although it'll never be noticed among all that loot. Honestly, Virginia, I've never seen so many hostess gifts!"

Virginia wrinkled her eyebrows. "Hostess gifts?" She brightened. "Oh, you must mean the stuff on the hall table. Those aren't hostess gifts, my dear."

"They aren't?"

"You look so surprised. Surely you know!"

"Know what?"

"Those are wedding gifts."

"Wedding?" Paul slipped a steadying arm through mine and clamped it firmly to his side.

"Your father and Darlene are getting married at the courthouse in Annapolis a week from next Friday."

"New Year's Eve?" I croaked.

"Oh, yes. On New Year's Eve, just before midnight."

Paul's grip on my arm tightened. "Well, we knew they were thinking about it, of course, but we didn't realize it was so . . ." He paused, and I could feel him staring at the side of my face as if checking to see if it would crack and explode. ". . . So imminent."

"I think it's sweet, don't you?" Virginia waggled her fingers in the air. "Then they'll slip away on their honeymoon, driving into the next millennium together."

I was sorry that I had eaten that crab ball because I was in grave danger of throwing it up all over Darlene's clean oak floor and tasseled Oriental carpet.

"Have you met our daughter, Emily?" Paul asked.

"I may have." She sipped her drink, something clear on the rocks with a twist of lime. "What does she look like?"

"She's not hard to spot," Paul offered. "Not with our granddaughter grafted to her hip."

"My, yes! Cute little thing," Virginia burbled. "They're in the living room, I think, looking at the tree."

I certainly didn't have an overwhelming desire to look at Darlene's tree, but at least if I did I knew I wouldn't see anything of my mother's on it. As far as I knew, all the family Christmas decorations were either hanging on our tree or still packed away in boxes at my house. I decided to find Emily, if only to get out of that dining room, which was suddenly filled to overflowing with Darlene's laughter as she swanned in on Daddy's arm. It was either that manic cackling or me.

But Paul had other ideas. "It's time," he said, "to greet the happy couple." His teeth flashed shark white in the candlelight. "Shall we?" He tipped an imaginary hat to Virginia, then dragged me across the room to a table where Daddy was fixing three cups of eggnog, one each for himself and Darlene and another for a white-haired guy on his right. The Bobbsey Twins, Darryl and Deirdre, had wandered off somewhere.

Paul came straight to the point. "I understand congratulations are in order, Captain."

Daddy refused to look at me directly and the lobes of his ears changed from pink to red, almost as red as the white-headed guy's sweater. The left side of his mouth turned up in a crooked grin. "Yes." His arm snaked around Darlene's shoulders. "We both realized rather suddenly that we weren't getting any younger, and with the millennium almost upon us, we thought it might be fun to start out the new century together."

Perma-grin firmly in place, like Br'er Rabbit, I lay low.

Daddy shifted his weight from one foot to another and said, "Have you met Darlene's neighbor, Marty O'Malley?"

Mr. O'Malley raised a hand. "No relation."

My laugh was forced, but I welcomed the change of topic. "You must get that all the time!"

Although they were approximately the same height, the man whose hand I was shaking bore absolutely no resemblance to Baltimore's newly elected mayor, Martin O'Malley. Marty O'Malley the mayor was broad-shouldered, muscular, and dark-haired, while Marty O'Malley the neighbor was slim, solid, and straight as a tree, with a generous head of pure white hair and an infectious grin. I'd doubt we'd catch Baltimore's new mayor wearing red-and-green striped suspenders, either.

"Oh, I do, I do," Marty said. "All the time. And when I show up at restaurants, I get all kinds of grief, as if I'd gotten my reservations under false pretenses!" He waved a Heineken at me. "I can't help what my parents named me. Besides"—he leaned closer, until his mouth was almost touching my ear—"the mayor's thirty years my junior, so it's *he* who should be apologizing to *me* for the inconvenience!"

"What do you do, Mr. O'Malley?"

"Nothing, my dear. Absolutely nothing." He cackled. "I'm retired."

Virginia Prentice, accompanied by a youngish woman in a silver, bead-encrusted sheath, joined the growing knot of people clustered in front of the drinks table. "Nonsense! You're the busiest person I know, Marty."

Marty ran his thumbs up and down the inside of his suspenders. "Not during the winter, I'm not. Been reading a lot, though, Virginia."

"Have you read *The Perfect Storm*?" Virginia wanted to know.

The young woman, who was introduced as Eileen, shivered inside her silver sheath. "No, and I don't intend to. I might never go sailing again! No, I'm reading that new book by Phyllis Talmadge, *Flex Your Psychic Muscles*."

Marty puffed air noisily out through his lips. "Who believes in all that crap? Might as well waste your money on the psychic hot line."

Eileen bristled. "*I* believe in it."

"I looked for that Talmadge book in the Compleat Bookseller the other day, but they were all sold out," Darlene complained.

"I bought my copy from Amazon dot com," Eileen said.

"No, thank you!" Marty's eyes narrowed. "I prefer to support the independents."

"But the Internet is so convenient," Eileen insisted. "In a couple of days—bingo! It appears in your mailbox."

"I get my contact lenses by mail," Darlene said.

"That's different," said Marty. "That's medical. I'm retired and I get my vitamins, blood pressure medicine, you name it, by mail."

Virginia waved an opal ring in front of Marty's face. "I got this ring yesterday. Only sixty-nine ninety-nine."

Marty caught her flailing hand and squinted at the ring. "You should own stock in the Home Shopping Network, Virginia. Didn't you just buy a necklace and some fancy no-fat cooking grill?"

Virginia reclaimed her hand and turned it back and forth so that the stone caught the light.

"Weren't you afraid someone would steal it out of your mailbox?" Daddy inquired, eyeing the ring.

Virginia shook her head. "Pshaw! Not in Chestertown!"

"Pshaw? Pshaw? You sound just like my great-aunt Matilda," said Marty.

Virginia blushed to her silver roots.

I decided to stick in my oar. "I try to buy everything locally. By the time you pay for shipping and handling on that mail-order stuff, you eat up all the money you might have saved."

It wasn't until she spoke that I realized that LouElla had been standing just behind me, listening to the conversation. "The CIA was always rifling through my mail. That's why I had to get a post office box."

"LouElla!"

"Well, it's true."

Darlene ladled herself another eggnog. "I don't know about the CIA, LouElla, but my mailbox was so stuffed with junk mail that I had to get a bigger one."

Marty seemed to be the expert in these matters. "I *told* you not to order all that stuff from mail-order catalogs. All it takes is one order and—*ka-ching!*—you're on every mailing list from here to the planet Pluto."

Daddy had been staring, apparently bored, at a spot just over my left shoulder, but he suddenly joined the conversation. "I heard that the DMV even sells their mailing list."

"There oughta be a law," said Eileen.

While Darlene argued cheerfully with LouElla over the United States government's peculiar interest in the contents of her, LouElla's, mailbox, I took the opportunity to drift away. I cornered Deirdre next to the fruit punch and introduced myself. "I guess we'll be seeing more of each other now."

She topped off her cup with bourbon poured from a silver pitcher. "I guess."

"We don't know very much about each other, do we?"

"No."

So much for breaking the ice. Deirdre seemed as cold and inflexible as the molded ice ring bobbing about in the punch bowl. I didn't have time to wait for the bourbon to loosen her tongue, so I tried again. "Frankly . . . Deirdre, is it?"

She nodded almost imperceptibly.

"Deirdre. I'm glad Daddy's found someone to share his life. He's been so lonely since our mother died."

Deirdre stared at me over the rim of her cup. Her lower lip seemed stuck to it.

"Has your mother told you much about us?"

Deirdre swallowed. Holding her cup in both hands she said, "Not much. We've never been very close."

"Maybe now that you're living nearby?"

"I doubt it. Frankly, Hannah, I'm only here because I'm curious. About your father. About the lot of you." She set her empty cup down on the table. "But I'm disappointed that your sisters weren't able to attend."

"We didn't have much notice."

Deirdre squinted at me in puzzlement. I explained

about Ruth and Georgina. "But surely you've met my daughter, Emily?"

"Oh, yes. She was talking to my brother in the living room." One corner of her mouth turned up in what I took to be a smile. "He was putting the moves on her. Chip off the old block."

"Your father was a womanizer?"

She hooted. "Hardly! I meant Mother!" She leaned toward me. "You realize, don't you, that if your father marries my mother he'll be number four."

"Daddy doesn't seem to mind." I shrugged.

"Mother doesn't have much luck with husbands."

"What happened to your father, Deirdre?"

"He died of a heart attack when I was eleven."

"I'm so sorry."

"It was a long time ago."

"How soon before she remarried?"

"Not long. Mother disappears into her relationships, like she's standing in front of some flowered wallpaper wearing a flowered dress. She can't seem to define herself in terms other than wife. Widow is a role she doesn't like to play." Deirdre's eyes darted to the left. "Is it, Mother?"

Darlene's voice screeched like a clarinet tuning up in my ear. "What on earth are you going on about, Deirdre?"

Deirdre's eyes sparkled in the candlelight. "Nothing much, Mother."

"Impossible girl!" Darlene tugged on my arm, drawing me toward the food table, effectively dismissing her daughter. "Your father wanted me to ask you something, Hannah."

"Yes?"

"We wanted to borrow the silverware for the party,

but when we went to look for it, it wasn't in the drawer."

I nearly choked on my chocolate-covered strawberry. "There were lots of things they hadn't had time to unpack before Mom got sick," I said, which was true as far as it went. Mom and Dad had lived in the house less than three months when she died. The basement was still full of boxes.

Darlene stared. "He can't find the crystal, either."

"As I said, Darlene, tell Daddy to check the boxes in the basement." I swallowed my revulsion at seeing Mother's necklace bobbling on Darlene's incomparable chest as she breathed. Did she know the necklace had belonged to my mother? Did she care?

Heat from the nearby radiator swept over me in waves—the scent of the candles, the ripe aroma of the gorgonzola, Darlene's heavy perfume. A pounding began in my ears. Any second I would pass out. "Excuse me," I mumbled. I waved my glass vaguely, then scuttled into the living room where I leaned against a bookcase, breathing deeply, and watched Emily work her magic on Darryl. I thanked my lucky stars that Dante wasn't there to observe what was going on, although I rather suspected that the jealousy gene was completely missing from Dante's particular strand of DNA.

Freshly diapered, Chloe lay asleep on a flowered chintz sofa, her little body tucked in by a needlepoint pillow. The music ended; when nobody seemed to care, I moved to change it. I was pawing through a pile of CD's Darlene had stacked on a nearby end table— many of which I recognized—and was just tipping Mozart's Greatest Arias into the carrier drawer of the CD player when LouElla materialized at my elbow.

From over my shoulder, she studied the plastic jewel case I was holding. "He is alive, isn't he?"

"Who?"

"That chap." She pointed with a purple fingernail to a picture of the conductor, resplendent in his tails.

"I should think so," I said.

"Good." She pushed a button and we both watched while the CD was sucked inside. "Because I don't like listening to dead people."

This place was getting seriously weird. "Excuse me," I said, desperate to escape. But LouElla followed me into the dining room. While I gulped down some punch, she positioned a shrimp on her plate next to a precarious tower of carrot and celery sticks cross-stacked over a glob of sour cream onion dip like a well-laid campfire. "Your father is a handsome man, Hannah. Darlene is a lucky woman."

"Are you married, LouElla?"

"I was, many, many years ago." She slid a mushroom cap into her mouth and chewed thoughtfully while staring into the corner of the dining room where my father and Darlene were still pinned by Virginia and Dr. McWaters. "Look at him! Except for the bandage, you'd never know he'd been in an accident, would you?" LouElla laid three well-manicured fingertips on my arm. "Poor man. First your mother, then the accident . . ."

Bearing up pretty well, I thought, watching Daddy practically slobber all over Darlene. Aloud I said, "He totaled his car."

"What's he driving, then?"

"A rental. A dark blue Taurus. He's ordered a Chrysler PT but it won't be delivered for another three months."

I found myself wishing the good doctor were giving Daddy advice on the dangers of immoderate drinking, but I suspected that both men were enabling each other well into their fourth or fifth cocktail. LouElla nattered on about a conspiracy between the oil producers and the auto industry to put the nation's railroads out of business and I nodded appreciatively, but my attention wandered. Suddenly, reflected in the window behind LouElla, Darryl passed behind me and into the kitchen and I saw my chance to escape. "I've got to go check on the baby," I said. I gestured toward my father. "Keep an eye on him while I'm gone, will you?"

LouElla nodded, the crystal globule in her tiara glittering in the candlelight. "Don't you worry, my dear."

Eager to hear what Emily had to say about Darryl, I retreated to the living room, but Emily was nowhere in sight. I flopped down on the sofa next to Chloe, who was still sleeping like . . . well, like a baby. I touched her face gently. If I could just close my eyes for a minute maybe all this would go away. Maybe when I opened them again it would be just me, Chloe, Emily, and Paul, and my father would walk through the door, smiling, holding my mother's hand.

I felt the cushion next to me shift, and I opened a damp eye to find Emily facing me, her legs tucked under her and her arm stretched along the back of the sofa. "What's wrong, Mom?"

I had a hard time focusing on her face through a sheen of tears. "It's just too hard! Our first Christmas without your grandmother is bad enough, but this?"

Emily handed me a paper napkin with holly berries on it. "I know. Daddy told me about the wedding."

I handed the napkin back. "I'm not going to cry! I refuse to let that woman get to me!"

Emily tucked the napkin into her sleeve as if not really believing she wouldn't just have to hand it back to me shortly. Next to me, Chloe stirred, her little mouth working as if tasting something sweet. I laid a hand on her chubby leg. "I'm very glad your father made arrangements for us to stay in Chestertown tonight, Emily. I wouldn't relish the drive home."

"Sure you want Chloe and me, too? I mean, we wouldn't want to cramp your style."

Her face wore such a serious look that I had to laugh. "Don't be silly. This is supposed to be a *family* weekend."

I downed what was left of my punch in three short gulps. I found myself looking forward to the cool night air, the short walk back to the Imperial Hotel, a hot bath, snuggling down into the scrumptious antique bed in room 309 with Paul.

My head went all balloony. "Let's find your father and blow this joint," I said. A few minutes later I liberated my husband from the animated attentions of a stubby matron wearing a top that glittered like Times Square. "Let's get out of here," I whispered.

"Don't you want to bid a fond good night to the happy couple?"

"Not particularly."

"Hannah!"

I bounced my forehead three times against his chest. "Oh, all right, but my heart's not in it. I suppose we should remind Daddy that he's agreed to join us for lunch at the hotel tomorrow."

"Isn't Darlene coming, too?"

I shook my head. "Noon is too early for Her Majesty, it seems."

Paul crooked a finger under my chin and tilted my

face toward his. "You're up to some mischief, aren't you? I can see it in your eyes."

"Unless you call trying to talk him out of a disastrous marriage mischief, no." I widened my eyes in mock innocence.

Paul threw back his head and roared. I began to giggle. Sometimes it's an advantage having a husband who can read you like a book, just as long as it's not cover to cover.

chapter

8

AT ONE END OF DARLENE'S FRONT PORCH TWO GUYS were arguing football in a haze of Marlboro Lights, so Paul and I waited at the upwind end for Emily to bundle Chloe in her pink bunny snowsuit. My farewells to our host and hostess had been far from satisfactory. A tepid smile and a limp hand from Darlene and from Dad, a boozy kiss that went wide of the mark—my cheek—and landed squarely on my ear. I filled my lungs with the cool night air, heavily scented with the dusky smell of wood smoke that was curling from a hundred nearby chimneys. I'd had a bit more to drink than was good for me and was counting on the night air to clear out the cobwebs. I wondered how my sisters, especially Ruth, would react to the news of Daddy's impromptu wedding. Perhaps I'd send each of them an e-mail and stay out of town until the fireworks were over.

When Emily appeared, Paul plucked Chloe from her arms, hoisted the baby to his shoulders, and trotted down the sidewalk ahead of us. Emily and I followed at a more leisurely pace.

"So," I said, "what did the charming Darryl have to say?"

Emily linked her arm through mine. "Reminds me of somebody I used to date. Jimmy, remember? The Harley freak?"

"How could I forget?"

Emily chuckled. "Darryl's harmless enough for a self-centered prick. He kept twitching his pecs. Guess I was supposed to swoon at his feet."

I jiggled Emily's arm encouragingly. "So, what did he *say*?"

"Not much. His dad keeled over from a coronary, his stepdad died in a plane crash. Darryl didn't know much about husband number three, the Tinsley guy, except to say that he lived in Fall River, Massachusetts, and was in real estate."

We turned into the parking lot of the Imperial Hotel, where our car was still parked. Through a wide gateway, the parking lot gave way to a courtyard and garden where evergreen shrubs twinkled with thousands of white pin lights. Wreaths of fresh holiday greens adorned both sides of the double door. When Emily and I pushed our way through into the lobby, Paul already stood at the elevator opposite the reception desk punching buttons.

"If there's anything you need, just let me know." The young desk clerk, probably a Washington College student, smiled at us from behind the counter. As we stepped inside the elevator and the door closed on her fresh-scrubbed face I waved. "We will!" I was already picturing the Parlor Suite with its red swag drapes, lace curtains, pink-and-white striped wallpaper, reproduction Victorian lamps, and the double bed with its ornate Victorian headboard. Most of all the bed.

Once inside our room, I peeled off my holiday regalia, draped it over an antique chair, and crawled beneath the comforter, just for a moment, to wait for Paul to get out of the shower.

The next thing I knew, Paul was snoring, open-mouthed, beside me and morning sunlight was kissing the railing of the verandah just outside our window. I peeked at my watch. Nearly ten o'clock! Without waking Prince Charming, I stepped out of bed, rummaged through my overnight bag for the copy of *Longitude* I was reading, and headed for a long soak in the tub. Through the wall I could hear the TV playing in Emily's room next door; she'd be watching cartoons with Chloe, pretending not to enjoy them.

I was up to the chapter about sauerkraut kicking scurvy overboard on James Cook's second circumnavigation when Paul tapped on the bathroom door. "Sweetheart?"

"Ummm?"

"Mind if I come in?"

"Uh-uh."

"Is that an uh-uh *yes* or an uh-uh *no*?"

I was feeling limp, like an overcooked noodle. "That's a come-in-quickly-and-close-the-door-behind-you." I didn't want any of the delicious steam to escape.

Paul slipped his narrow body through the doorway. Wearing only his briefs, he stood in front of the sink and peered into the mirror. "You better get a move on, sweetie." He grabbed a washcloth and wiped the mirror free of condensation, then began to shave.

I rolled over lazily, rested one arm and my chin on the edge of the bathtub, and watched as he pulled the razor down each cheek then raised his chin and cleaned the lather off his neck with practiced, upward strokes. "What time is it?" I asked as he rinsed the razor under the hot water tap.

He grabbed a towel and patted his face dry. "Almost noon."

"Yipes!" I stood up so fast that my head swam and I had to grab onto the wall for support. "We're going to be late!"

Paul tossed me a clean towel. "Here. You dry off and I'll go pick up Emily and Chloe and be downstairs in time to meet your dad. Take your time."

Time! I turned in a personal best, maybe even an Olympic gold medal performance for hair drying and makeup application. When I breezed into the restaurant fifteen minutes later, radiant in my favorite black slacks and red sweater, my family was waiting for me.

But two chairs at the table were empty. "Where's Daddy?" I asked as I headed for one of them.

Emily shrugged. "He'll be along."

I checked my watch. "But he's twenty minutes late."

Paul stood and pulled out my chair. "And so, may I remind you, darling, were you."

I plopped myself down. "Oh. I see your point."

Paul handed me the menu. "I've ordered you some coffee."

"Thanks." I decided on a mushroom phyllo, then sipped my coffee and watched Chloe push Cheerios around on her high chair tray with a plump finger. Emily poured orange juice from her glass into a bottle, screwed on the nipple cap, and handed it to Chloe. The sun shone, cars passed by on High Street just outside the window, my family was around me . . . what could be wrong? But when fifteen more minutes had

passed, my third cup of coffee did little to calm my growing dread. I rummaged through my purse, extracted
my cell phone, and handed it to Paul. "Here. You call
him."

"Why me?" he asked. "I don't even know Darlene's
number."

I opened my address book and read it off to him. He
dialed and after a long minute, he mashed his thumb
down on the End button. "No answer."

"That's odd. Somebody should be there!"

Paul shrugged. "Sorry."

"Here, let me try," I said, taking the phone from
him. "Maybe you got the number wrong." I punched in
Darlene's number and waited. After the tenth ring, I
hung up. "Not even an answering machine." I laid the
phone on the tablecloth and rested my chin on my
hands. "Do you suppose he forgot?"

Emily spooned applesauce into Chloe's mouth. "Not
likely. He told me he was looking forward to it." She
studied me with serious eyes. "Maybe he's too hung-
over, Mom."

I pushed my plate away, my lunch barely touched,
knowing that Emily was probably right but a little annoyed at her for saying so. "I'm going over there." I
sent Paul my I-dare-you-to-try-and-stop-me look.

Paul folded his napkin and laid it next to his plate.
"All right, but I'm coming with you."

Emily looked up from wiping applesauce off Chloe's
chin. "Did you ever think you might be interrupting
something?"

I rolled my eyes toward the ceiling, trying to wipe
that picture out of my head. I stood up. "I certainly
hope so!"

"We'll be here when you get back," Emily said. She waved a spoon. "Don't think you're going to stick me with the bill."

As I passed behind her chair, I patted the top of Emily's head. "Don't worry, we'll be back soon."

I believed it when I said it, I really did. But ten minutes later, standing on Darlene's front porch, repeatedly ringing the doorbell and listening to Speedo's urgent barking from the entrance hall just behind the door, I forgot my promise. Darlene's Porsche was still parked on the street, but Daddy's car was nowhere to be seen.

Paul parked his buns on the porch railing. "Hannah, they must have gone somewhere in your father's car. Be reasonable!"

While Paul sat there, relaxed, both hands stuffed in his pockets, I peeked through the front window. The Christmas tree lights still blazed, lamps on the end tables burned softly, and I could see the red and green glow of the indicator lights on the stereo system. Plates with bits of food still on them and half-empty glasses covered every surface. Clearly the party had gone on long after we left.

I turned around to face my husband. "Look for yourself, Paul! If they went somewhere, don't you think they would have cleaned up first?"

"Not necessarily."

I tapped on the window with my knuckles and was startled when Speedo lunged into view. The dog leapt onto the sofa, settled his big paws on the windowsill, and pressed his wet, black nose against the glass. I tapped on the window again. "Hey, boy!"

Speedo went berserk. He jumped off the sofa, raced

in a tight circle about the room, scrunched up two scatter rugs with his windmilling paws, then leapt onto the sofa again, barking furiously.

"Hey, boy, what's wrong?" I laid my hand flat on the window where Speedo's nose had left a smeared impression. I turned my head to look at my husband. "Something's wrong in there, Paul. I just know it."

Paul was beside me in two long strides. Shading his eyes with his hand, he peered through the window, which did nothing to calm the frantic dog, who began to scrabble at the windowpane, toenails clicking on the glass. Paul straightened, walked to the front door, and turned the knob. "Locked." He gave the doorbell another try, listened, then rapped loudly with the knocker. Speedo relocated himself behind the front door and began to howl.

"I'll try around back." I scampered off the porch and dashed around the side of the house, through a wooden gate, and into the garden. I careened around the patio table, exclaiming as I scraped my thigh against the arm of one of the chairs. Still swearing and rubbing the sore spot, I stepped onto the neatly laid brick patio and peered through the double French doors into the kitchen.

The screen on the TV Daddy had been lounging in front of the night before was dark. Like the living room, dirty dishes were piled on every flat surface and open bottles of alcohol, including a bottle of schnapps—Ruth's?—stood like soldiers on the long kitchen counter. The light over the kitchen table still burned, but the candlesticks on the table were empty. My heart did a flip-flop in my chest. "The candles burned down to nothing," I said as Paul caught up with me. "Nobody blew them out."

I jiggled the door handle and gasped when the door swung slowly inward. I pulled it closed just as Speedo thundered into the kitchen. When the dog sat politely on the other side of the door and simply whined, I said, "I'm going in."

"Hannah! What if they're asleep?"

"If they are, then we'll wake them up. If they're gone, then what they don't know won't hurt them." And before he could persuade me to change my mind, I pushed open the door and eased myself into the house.

What I saw then made Speedo hang his head: A prizewinning pile of dog poop had been deposited squarely in the middle of Darlene's highly polished floor. I scratched behind the dog's drooping ears. "Poor Speedo. It's not your fault. Nobody let you out today!" Cold fingers squeezed my heart and I looked at Paul. "This is not good."

Although sunlight flooded the kitchen, cheerful with its glossy white woodwork and blue-and-white gingham curtains, it did little to lighten my mood. "Let the dog out, Paul," I said.

Paul held the door wide, stepped out onto the patio, and slapped his thigh. "Come on, Speedo. That's a good boy." But Speedo refused. I was standing under the overhead rack where copper saucepans and frying pans hung in a gleaming row when Speedo startled me by dashing past, through the pantry and into the dining room. I followed, catching sight of the dog's tail as he disappeared around the curve in the staircase that led to the second floor. With my heart thudding, only partly from the exertion of racing up the stairs two at a time, I finally caught up with Speedo, sitting, four feet firmly planted, waiting politely by the bathroom door. My pulse drummed in my ears. I tried to breathe normally, and failed. The last time I'd followed a crazed dog there'd been a body at the end of the trail. I didn't relish a repeat performance. So, when Paul appeared at the head of the stairs I wimped out and waggled my hand toward the door. "*You* open it."

Paul reached for the knob, then swiveled his head in my direction. Our eyes locked and I knew he was reading my mind—*dog, door, death*. Life with Hannah is never dull. I clutched Speedo's collar and held my breath as Paul turned the knob and . . . slowly, slowly . . . pushed open the door.

I was kneeling beside Speedo, my arms wrapped around his neck, my cheek pressed against the comforting warmth of his fur, so I didn't see anything unusual at first.

Then Paul stumbled backward. "Sweet Jesus!"

With one hand grasping Speedo's collar, I slowly rose until my eyes were level with Paul's shoulder and I saw what he saw, a scene that is etched indelibly in my brain like a VCR frozen on Pause. "Who is it?" I asked.

"I think it's Darlene."

The naked body in the bathtub bore little resemblance to the Darlene I knew. It was the head that confused me, covered with thin graying hair that erupted from a nearly bald landscape of scalp in untidy tufts. But the nose and the chin . . . that patrician profile was unmistakable. Darlene's eyes were closed and she lay in the tub peacefully, as if she were asleep.

"Is she dead?" I whispered.

"I think so." Without touching the tub, Paul squatted

on his heels and placed two fingers on Darlene's pallid neck, just under her left ear. He nodded.

"Jesus!" And then I noticed something strange. "There's no water in the tub!"

"I know." Paul pointed to the plug, an old-fashioned rubberized disk on a chain. "It probably leaks." Paul straightened his knees. "Come here, Hannah." He pointed at something in the bottom of the tub. "What do you make of that?"

My breakfast was staging an encore, the acid combination of coffee and orange juice biting the back of my throat. I took a tentative step forward, then another. At the bottom of the tub, lodged between the drain hole and a smooth and still shapely foot, was an empty wineglass. "She must have taken something to drink into the bath with her." Without thinking, I reached out to retrieve the glass, then pulled my hand back in horror.

I had drawn close enough to see her breasts, to notice that they bore the sunken scars of several incisions. Darlene had undergone biopsies, maybe even a lumpectomy. Tears stung my eyes. I felt profoundly sad for this woman, this pathetic object in a cold, hard bathtub who, only hours before, had been a living, breathing human being.

Contracting cancer is a life-changing experience, I knew firsthand. Maybe that's what had turned Darlene so cold, calculating, and get-it-while-you-can. I was nothing at all like Darlene, but because of the cancer I suddenly felt a certain kinship to her.

"Oh, cover her up!" I wailed. "A towel. Anything!"

Paul shook his head. "Better not mess with the scene."

I wiped my eyes with the hem of my sleeve. "I wonder how she died," I sniffed. I was no expert, except for what I saw on TV during twice-daily reruns of *Law and Order*. Nothing about the body indicated foul play, at least not to me. Darlene's face was composed and her eyes were closed. She could have been napping. There were no bruise marks on her neck. No stab wounds. No bullet holes. No blunt force trauma.

"She just *died*, Hannah. Maybe a heart attack, or a stroke."

"But, what happened to her hair?"

Paul pointed to a wicker footstool under the window. On it, Darlene's familiar blond hairdo lay in a damp heap, like a slumbering cat.

I stood there with Paul for what seemed like hours, tears cooling on my cheeks, the *drip drip drip* of the bathtub tap thundering like a bass drum in my ears. I studied the mildewed grout between the bathtub and the tile, the way the curtains were drawn back from the window with black ribbons tied in precise bows, the wallpaper where corseted Victorian ladies fussed with their hair, powdered their cheeks or adjusted their garters. I willed any one of them to speak up and tell us the story of what happened in this room. Finally, Paul grabbed my hand and pulled me out into the hall where Speedo waited obediently, his head on his paws. But not before I had noticed my father's red toothbrush still in the holder over the sink, and his Norelco shaver dangling from the end of a cord plugged into an electrical outlet in the fluorescent light fixture over the medicine cabinet.

I rooted in my purse for the cell phone and dialed 911. Story of my life.

While we waited downstairs in the kitchen for the

ambulance to arrive, Paul used a spatula and a wad of paper towels to clean up after Speedo. But all the time I was filling Speedo's bowl with kibble and his dish with fresh water I was wondering: *Where in bloody hell is my father?*

chapter

9

CAPTAIN YOUNGER OF THE CHESTERTOWN POLICE Department wanted to know the same thing. While his officers secured the scene upstairs and we waited for the Kent County medical examiner to arrive, Younger, dressed in dark blue uniform trousers and a light blue shirt, shotgunned us with questions.

The man was good. Almost before I realized what was happening, he had pried open the family closet and the skeletons had come rattling out in all their sordid splendor.

During the interview I sat stiffly on a two-cushion sofa next to Paul, our shoulders touching. Through the French doors I could see Speedo snuffling joyfully about in the patches of parsley, sage, rosemary, and thyme in Darlene's immaculate garden. I wondered if I'd ever again experience such pure, mindless joy.

"Your father was living here, then?" Younger asked.

I nodded. "Most of the time."

"So, where is he?"

"Captain Younger, I honestly don't know."

The Kent County medical examiner turned out to be a nurse from the local hospital. When she showed up, followed by the Maryland State Police crime lab, things got busy and Captain Younger let us go.

Halfway back to the hotel I grabbed Paul's arm. "Holy Mother of God! I forgot to call Emily!" We found our daughter waiting inside, pacing the long central hallway from the front door of the hotel to the reception desk in the back, holding Chloe and frantic with worry. "I didn't know what to do," she complained. "I finally let them clear the plates away."

After we explained what had happened and arranged with the hotel to stay another night, Paul suggested we go back into the restaurant and order some lunch, although it was well past two o'clock by then.

I had forked up the last bite of a poached pear tart when a white police cruiser with a splash of red on its rear quarter panel pulled into a parking space on High Street just outside the dining room window. I watched, chewing thoughtfully, as Captain Younger uncoiled himself from the driver's seat, adjusted his sunglasses, slammed the door of the cruiser, then stepped onto the porch. "Oh, oh," I said.

Paul eased himself out of his chair. "Best to get it over with." He waylaid the officer at the door to the dining room, just as he passed by.

We invited Younger to join us for coffee. While I filled his cup, he pulled up a chair, moved some glassware, dirty dishes, and the salt and pepper shakers aside, then dealt some items out on the tablecloth in front of us. They looked like greeting cards encased in plastic sleeves. "What do you know about these?"

I started to pick up one of the cards, then withdrew my hand, waiting for his permission to touch them.

"It's OK," he said. "Have a look."

I used my fingertips to slide the cards around the tabletop. I must have had a question mark on my face because Younger suddenly said, "We found them in a pigeonhole in her desk, tied in a bundle with white string."

Each plastic sleeve held a greeting card, open and flat. The illustrations and writing on the face of each card seemed tame enough, but if you flipped the sleeve over, you could read the ugly sentiment inside.

When it comes to describing you,
One word says it all . . .

Bitch!

Emily leaned toward me, reading the card over my shoulder. "Well, she *wasn't* a very nice woman." She smiled at the officer, then picked up another card and read aloud,

Consider this a personal invitation . . .

Go fuck yourself!

"Emily!"

"*I* didn't use the F word, Mother, the card did." She flapped it at me.

I tried to look serious. "Daddy mentioned that somebody was sending Darlene poison-pen mail. This must be some of it."

The jeweled ring in Emily's eyebrow shot up. "You don't think Darlene was *murdered*, do you?"

I looked into the officer's intelligent eyes and said, "Somebody *did* try to poison her dog."

Emily gasped. "Speedo?"

I nodded. "Daddy told me about it."

Paul was examining a postcard of Arlington Cemetery on which someone had scrawled, "Wish you were here." He laid down the card and stared at the officer. "What's going to happen to Speedo?"

"One of the neighbors showed up. Virginia Prentice? She volunteered to keep the dog until Mrs. Tinsley's kids decide what to do with him."

That was good news. I fell back into my chair and prayed that he'd run out of questions and head back to the police station soon. Fat chance.

"Mrs. Ives, do you have any idea, any idea at all, where your father is?"

I shook my head. "Maybe he went home?"

"Nobody's seen him in Annapolis."

I spread my hands, palms up, and shrugged.

"Places he hangs out?"

I shook my head.

"We do need to talk to him."

"Captain, if I knew where he was, I'd certainly tell you." I met his gaze squarely. "We want to find him just as badly as you do. I'm worried about him." I explained about Mother's recent death and Daddy's even more recent engagement to Darlene. "If she died in her bath and Daddy found her body . . ." I paused and took a deep breath. ". . . There's no telling what he might have done."

Paul reached for my hand, squeezed it, and didn't let go. "How can we help you find him, Captain Younger?"

As Paul told Younger about Daddy's accident on the Bay Bridge and described the rental car, I watched a range of emotions play across the officer's face. I could see the wheels turning, almost hear Younger thinking, *This must be the unluckiest guy alive.*

But my radar was down. That wasn't what he was thinking at all. "Where would your father have been at approximately one-fifteen last night, Mrs. Ives?"

"I don't know. We left the party around ten." A wave of nausea and dread washed over me. "Why? Is that when she died?"

"We don't know when she died; that'll be determined by the Office of the Chief Medical Examiner over in Baltimore."

"Then why do you ask?"

"We had a hit-and-run last night. Somebody ran down an elderly gentleman out near the intersection of routes two-thirteen and three-oh-five."

I gasped, my head swimming. If I hadn't been holding Paul's hand, I might have keeled over. "My father?" I croaked.

He shook his head. "No. He was a local waterman, on his way home from a late-night card game."

"*Was?* Do you mean he's dead?"

"I'm afraid so."

A nightmare scenario flashed through my head. Daddy, drunk as usual, discovers Darlene dead and drives off in a haze of alcohol and grief. An old man, crossing the road, frozen in the glare of oncoming headlights. A cry. A sickening thud. I opened my mouth to proclaim Daddy's innocence when Paul squeezed my hand again, hard. "Perhaps if you talked to the other guests. My wife and I didn't know many of them, but . . ." Paul looked at me. "What was that strange lady's name, honey?"

"LouElla," I said. "LouElla Van Schuyler."

"Yes," Paul continued. "Check with LouElla. She appears to know everybody."

Captain Younger smiled cryptically. "And everybody in town knows LouElla." He gathered up the plastic-covered greeting cards, tucked them into a folder, and stood to go. "Don't worry," he said. "We'll put out a broadcast. We'll find him."

I received this promise with mixed feelings. With Paul's arm around me, I watched Captain Younger climb into his cruiser, ease it out of park, and merge his vehicle smoothly into the traffic moving north along High Street.

"Look at this!" Emily's voice was muffled.

When I turned, Emily was kneeling on the dark carpet next to Chloe's high chair. She struggled to her feet holding one of the greeting cards by the edges between both hands. "It must have slipped out of its sleeve."

Emily dropped the card onto the tablecloth.

Do me a favor . . . (Paul read before opening the card with the tip of a knife)

Eat shit and die!

"Well, what do you know," said Emily. "Maybe she did."

chapter

10

BY MONDAY MORNING I'D ORGANIZED THE IVES family troops. I remained in Chestertown, moving into a smaller room on the second floor of the hotel. I instructed Paul and Emily to drive to Annapolis at a horn-provoking crawl while scanning the highway on both sides for skid marks, tire tracks in the grass, or breaks in the guardrail. Ruth agreed to hold down the fort at Daddy's house on Greenbury Point. And although it seemed crazy, I even notified the couple who had bought my parents' old place in Seattle to be on the lookout for him.

Daddy hadn't been seen since midnight on Saturday.

He hadn't telephoned.

He hadn't e-mailed from some anonymous cyber-café.

Even if Darlene's death had sent Daddy off on a drunken binge, I couldn't believe that he would fail to get in touch. I knew that something must have happened to prevent him from contacting us, and I feared the worst.

I spent the morning zigzagging through the streets and alleyways of Chestertown—down High, along Water, up Canon to Cross, back to High and up to Spring—searching for my father's rental car, checking behind hedges, and peering into ditches. In the parking lot behind the Old Wharf Inn I spotted a dark blue Taurus with Maryland plates parked behind a boat hauled up on carpet-padded jack stands. With my heart banging against my rib cage, I combed the waterfront all the way to the bridge, praying I wouldn't catch sight of anything floating in the Chester River wearing Daddy's familiar blue sweater and gray wool pants. But I saw nothing except a wayward crab pot float, and when I returned to the parking lot, a grizzled fellow carrying a paint can was just climbing into the Taurus.

Around noon, I found myself opposite the police station, an L-shaped brick building with two police cars parked at an angle out front. Hoping that there might be some news, I went inside.

A Coke machine nearly filled the waiting room. On the wall to my left were two armless chairs and a potted plant, flanked on one side by the Maryland state flag and a Lions Club gumball machine and on the other by a water cooler. I stepped up to the window on my right, leaned my arms against the counter, and waited, studying the various notices and framed certificates that hung on the wall.

"Hello?" I ventured at last.

A serious-looking woman, astonishingly pretty in spite of the oversized eyeglasses that threatened to slide off her nose, appeared almost immediately. "Can I help you?"

I asked for Captain Younger and learned that he was out working a case. I wondered if it were *my* case. "Can you tell me if anybody's located my father, George Alexander?"

She shook her head. "Let me check with Chief Hammett." She disappeared through a door into an adjoining office. I heard the murmur of voices, and then she returned, followed by a policeman in his mid-forties who reminded me of a young Rod Steiger.

He had no news.

I gave Chief Hammett my cell phone number and told him where he could reach me, smiled a good-bye, then stood on the steps of the police station for several minutes, staring numbly at the fields beyond the railroad tracks. With his rental car nowhere to be found, I didn't know what made me think that Daddy was still in Chestertown, I just knew it, is all, the way I sometimes knew that he was on the telephone by the way it rang. I smiled as I recalled the discussion at the party about that book, *Flex Your Psychic Muscles,* and decided that I'd distract myself by wandering over to the bookstore to see what all the hype was about.

As I strolled east on Cross Street toying with the idea of actually hiring a psychic to help locate our father, I found myself outside Play It Again, Sam, a retro, fifties-style coffee shop where a young professional couple sat on a sofa in the window drinking lattes and sharing a biscòtti. I stared, unabashed, as she nibbled coyly on the pastry, then offered him the end she had just bitten. Although the couple in the window was decades younger than my father and Darlene, something about this little mating ritual reminded me of watching Darlene feed my father crackers and brie. I felt a chill, hugged myself for warmth, then hurried on.

At the bookstore I discovered that Virginia was

right; *Flex Your Psychic Muscles* was on back order. I browsed the collection of books by local authors, selected one on the history of Chestertown, paid for it with my credit card, and wandered back out onto High Street, turning the pages as I walked. In front of me was the courthouse and, according to a centerfold map, Court Street would be to my right. Court intersected with Church Alley, I discovered, which dumped you back onto North Queen Street, just half a block from Darlene's.

I tucked the book in my bag and headed in that direction, curious because I could see from where I stood that the east side of Court Street was lined with quaint eighteenth-century, one-story shops that had been converted into law offices.

As I turned the corner into Church Alley, I ran smack dab into Virginia, walking Speedo on a leash. At the sight of me Speedo went bonkers, dancing on his hind legs and pawing the air like a palomino. Finding Darlene's body together had clearly been a bonding experience.

"Speedo! Sit!" Virginia ordered.

Speedo ignored her. Virginia hauled back on the leash, but Speedo only pranced around in a tighter circle, barking joyfully.

"Looks like you have your hands full." I chuckled.

"Speedo!" Virginia's breath came in short gasps. "Damn dog!"

"Let me try," I said, taking the leash from her hands. Soon Speedo was sitting at my feet, happily panting drool all over my running shoes. I smiled at Virginia. "You're sweet to take the dog," I said.

"I need my head examined," she said, tugging at the hem of her lightweight jacket which had ridden up during the struggle. She looked up. "Any news about Darlene or your father?"

I shook my head. "We've looked everywhere for Daddy. Nothing. And as for Darlene, we'll just have to wait for the police."

"Deirdre is making arrangements to have her cremated, after . . ."

We both must have been thinking the same thing: after the autopsy. I shivered. Bone saws, Y-incisions. It didn't bear thinking about. "Is there to be a funeral?" I inquired, realizing with a pang that Daddy might miss saying good-bye.

Virginia shook her head. "Darlene wants . . . wanted her ashes scattered among the azaleas at Longwood Gardens."

"They'll let you do that?"

Virginia shrugged. "Who's to stop you?"

Who indeed? I nodded toward the dog who was lying spread-eagle on the pavement with his muzzle resting on my shoe. "Where are you heading, Virginia?"

She pointed to her right. "That way," she said. "I live on Lawyers' Row."

I must have looked puzzled.

"Otherwise known as North Court Street," she added. "It's only to confuse the tourists."

"Well, whatever it's called, let me walk you and Speedo home." I tugged on Speedo's leash until he reluctantly got to his feet.

Virginia smiled, bowed, and with a broad sweep of her arm, indicated I should lead the way. We walked back the way I had come along Church, passing a row of modest, two-story colonial homes, recently renovated and variously covered with aluminum siding in shades of vanilla, sand, or pink with darker, contrasting shutters. Number 108 on the west side of the street was a particular standout in pale lavender, with shutters the color of ripe plums and a red door. Behind it, a tall white picket fence stretched for a hundred feet before ending at the back of somebody's garage. On the other side of the fence, a broad-brimmed straw hat bobbed. I couldn't see who was underneath.

Speedo stopped, raised a hind leg, and relieved himself against a sugar maple tree whose roots extended under the pickets, causing the fence to buckle. Virginia and I looked at each other and pretended not to notice. Instead, I waved my free hand toward a row of three nearly identical houses. "Which one is yours?"

"The green one." Virginia turned and headed toward the house on the end nearest us. In front of it, brown grass sprang from cracks in a sidewalk bordered by a privet hedge from which unruly tendrils shot out in all directions. I yearned for my pruning sheers. The hedge turned a corner at Virginia's driveway and we followed it for a few yards before I handed the end of Speedo's leash back to Virginia. I was surprised to see that Virginia's house lay backyard to backyard with Darlene's. The steep-pitched roof of Darlene's garden shed poked out above a chest-high stone wall that separated the two lots.

"I didn't realize you and Darlene were neighbors," I commented.

"Oh, yes." Virginia opened a gate and released Speedo, leash and all, inside. "We would probably have been even better neighbors if it hadn't been for that wall." She shrugged. "But it was already here when I moved in," she said, almost apologetically.

"As inherited walls go, that one's fairly attractive." Four rosebushes were espaliered equidistantly along the wall, two on each side of an ancient wooden gate covered with ivy. In summer the bushes would be heavy with blooms. "Did you plant the roses?"

"Oh my, no!" She laughed. "I'm terrible with plants. Have a brown thumb, if you want to know the truth."

Speedo, dragging his leash, loped joyfully around the pocket-sized yard.

"Would you care to come in?" Virginia asked.

With psychics on my mind a lot lately, I concentrated on sending hot tea messages in her direction. "I'd love to."

Virginia reached for the doorknob, turned, and called, "Speedo!"

Speedo, in the midst of a full-blown squirrel alert, ignored her. He dashed off after the poor creature who barely escaped with its tail by scampering up the ivied wall and frisking over the fence.

"Speedo!" The dog skid to a halt, dirt flying, his nose inches away from the wall. He sat there mournfully, gazing up at the spot where the squirrel's tail had last been seen. "Speedo!"

At first Speedo didn't seem to hear, then he got to his feet, turned, and trotted in our direction. "Beastly dog," Virginia muttered. "I'll be glad when Darryl comes to collect him."

"Where does Darryl live?" I asked Virginia.

She held the door wide until Speedo, with me close behind, had both entered the house. "Up near Glen Burnie, I think."

Virginia's kitchen radiated sunshine. To my left, a pleasant breakfast nook, painted yellow, was built into an alcove under a window. Frilly country curtains printed with concentric, multicolored rings like the Olympic flag were tied back with wide red grosgrain ribbon. Piled on the painted tabletop were a number of magazines and mail-order catalogs. To my right was a serious stove with two overhead ovens and six gas burners. "Are you a gourmet chef, Virginia?"

"Not a bit of it." She pulled the back door closed behind her. "Another thing I inherited from the previous owners." She indicated the breakfast nook. "Have a seat, won't you?"

I moved aside a pair of scissors, a pad of lime green Post-it notes, two plastic mailers from L.L. Bean, a flat, square carton from Harry and David, and a Jiffy bag from Amazon.com. Virginia lifted a stainless steel kettle from the stove, strolled to the double sink, and filled it from the tap. She set it on a front burner and twisted the knob, adjusting the flame from boil to incinerate. While she rummaged in the dishwasher for some clean cups, I browsed through the catalogs spread out before me. In addition to L.L. Bean, there was Ross Simon, TravelSmith, Signals, J. Jill, Orvis, White Flower Farms, Boston Museum of Art, and, hanging out in an awfully good neighborhood, a Sears Roebuck catalog.

"Christmas shopping?" I asked.

Virginia smiled a sad smile. "A bit. Mostly I just enjoy looking at them."

I picked up the catalog from White Flower Farms where spring bulbs of every variety were offered for sale. "I thought you said you weren't a gardener?"

"I'm not." She crossed the black-and-white checker-board linoleum, took the catalog from my hand, and riffled through it. "My husband was."

Something about the way she said *was* made me look up.

She put the catalog down and looked at me directly. "Harry died five years ago."

"I'm so sorry."

She stood before me, her fingers neatly laced together. "It was sudden and rather horrible, but I'm pretty much over the shock of it now."

"Did you and Harry have any children?"

Her face took on a look of such infinite sadness that I wanted to snatch back my words. Her eyes, her face, her hands—everything about her body grew still.

"I had a daughter," she said. "But she died, too."

To my relief, the teakettle screamed, rescuing me. Virginia hurried over to the stove where she bustled about preparing the tea. She lowered a tea bag into each cup, then looked up. "Earl Grey OK?"

"Perfect!"

"Milk?"

"No, just tea. I'm a purist."

"I am, too. That's why I use bone china. Real bone china."

She set a cup in front of me and I sipped at it gratefully. In a moment, a plate of Pepperidge Farm cookies appeared at my elbow. I stuffed one in my mouth. Milanos worked better than a foot anytime.

"How long have you known Darlene?" I mumbled, my mouth still full.

"Since I moved here from Tiverton." She looked thoughtful. "About two years."

"Tiverton?"

"Rhode Island."

The only thing I knew about Tiverton was that it was near Bristol, Rhode Island, where they build boats. I'd visited Bristol with Connie when she'd been shopping for a sailboat, not long before she'd bought *Sea Song*. On the other hand, everything was close to everything else in Rhode Island.

Virginia settled onto the bench opposite me. Silence grew in the space between us until it loomed so large I felt I had to break it. "How long did you stay at the party last night?"

Virginia must have known where I was going with that question because she set her cup down, smiled at me sympathetically, and said, "Your father was still there when I left at eleven."

"Who else was still there?" I wanted to know.

She wrinkled her nose in disgust. "That Darryl person."

"I gather you don't like him."

"Whatever gave you that idea?" She laughed, then her face grew serious. "In the short time I've known him, I've grown to like your father a lot, Hannah. But that Darryl I never liked. Never liked him at all."

I thought about the untidy hair. The insolent attitude. The belligerent scowl. "He *is* a little hard to warm up to," I admitted.

"And he's a sponge. Always borrowing his mother's car, loafing around her house . . ." Virginia's cup clattered against its saucer. "He'll never pay your father back."

"Pay my father back for what?"

"George has been lending Darryl money."

"How do you know that?"

"I saw them at the ATM at Commerce Bank. Your

father took out a wad of money and handed it over to Darryl."

"Maybe Daddy was sending Darryl to buy him something?"

Virginia puffed air out through her lips. "If you believe that, I've got a gen-u-ine Rolex watch for twenty-nine dollars that might interest you." She leaned toward me across the table. "They're freeloaders, those Donovans, the whole lot of 'em."

Whether Darlene was or wasn't a freeloader hardly mattered now. "Deirdre, too?" I wondered aloud.

"Ice would not melt in that girl's mouth."

We sat in companionable silence for a while, drinking tea. Clearly Virginia had no use for the Donovan clan. I wondered why. Was *she* in love with my father? They were about the same age, Daddy and the widowed Virginia, and with her bone-white hair, porcelain skin, and sea-green eyes, she was certainly attractive in a much less flamboyant way than her late neighbor. Could she have cared enough about Daddy to eliminate her rival?

Virginia's eyes flitted to the back door, her lips parted, and she gasped. "Oh, no! Can't I have a moment's peace?"

After two brisk taps, the door was pushed open by a broad hand with familiar purple fingernails, followed almost immediately by LouElla's cherubic face. Her ebony hair was braided and twisted into a luxurious nest on top of her head. A robin could have set up housekeeping in it. "Virginia?"

Virginia rose and headed toward the door. "Oh, hi, LouElla. Won't you . . ."

But LouElla had already pushed her way into the

kitchen, crossed to the stove, and stooped over to pat Speedo on the head. From a cord around her neck a straw hat hung down her back. I realized who the gardener behind the picket fence must have been. Confirming my suspicions LouElla said, "I was working in my garden when I saw you walk by."

"I was looking for my father when I ran into Virginia," I said.

It wasn't until I spoke that LouElla seemed to notice me. In her crepe-soled gardening shoes, she squeaked over to the table and waved a hand indicating I should scoot over. She plopped down next to me on the bench. "Terrible what happened last night. Terrible! Terrible!" She patted my hand. "Don't worry about your father, my dear. I'm sure he'll turn up hale and hearty!"

I wished I could believe that. I felt drained, increasingly discouraged by my inability to help my father at a time when he needed me the most. "I'm really worried," I said. "I've searched for him all morning. I've been everywhere. There's no sign of him or his car. It's like he disappeared off the face of the earth!"

LouElla turned her pleasant face to mine, her eyebrows neatly arched as if painted on with a stencil. "Even if aliens got him, sweetheart, they'll beam him back unharmed." She patted my hand again reassuringly, then closed her eyes momentarily. She smiled a closed-lip smile then turned to me again. "I was abducted by aliens once. In Vermont." She sighed, as if the memory were a pleasant one. "Don't believe everything you hear, my dear. It didn't hurt one little bit."

LouElla was an enigma. Just when you thought she was making sense, she'd fly off into never-never land.

Virginia floated a halfhearted attempt to get rid of her neighbor. "Are you in a hurry?" Her eyebrows shot up hopefully.

LouElla beamed. "Goodness, no. I've got all the time in the world."

Virginia caved. "Would you like some tea, then?"

LouElla bobbed in her seat and clasped her narrow hands together. "Oh, tea would be delightful!"

From a glass canister, Virginia selected a tea bag at random and dropped it into a ceramic mug, tag and all. I noted that LouElla wasn't getting a bone china cup, and I wondered if Virginia had picked a disgusting flavor like chamomile or licorice in hopes of discouraging a long visit, but when she brought LouElla's mug over I could tell from the scent that the tea was one of my favorites, Lemon Lift.

LouElla had already helped herself to a cookie; several crumbs clung to her frosted plum lipstick. "I left the party around twelve-thirty," she announced, unasked, "and the only people left were your dad, Darlene, and her children." She raised a painted eyebrow. "Are you staying in town, dear?"

"I'm going home in the morning."

LouElla touched my hand where it rested on the tabletop. "He's a good man, your father. A good man."

A tear rolled unbidden down my cheek. "I know, and he means well, but he doesn't always show good judgment."

"He's still grieving for your mother, isn't he?"

"We all are. It hasn't even been a year. After the funeral I prayed he'd find something to interest him, but I had something in mind like woodworking or stamp collecting! Not a girlfriend. Not so soon."

LouElla perched next to me like a 1970's talk-show host: ultragroomed, wearing a three-piece double-knit pantsuit in pink and tangerine. I couldn't believe she'd just spent hours working in her garden. If it'd been me, I'd have grass stains on my knees, streaks of dust on my face, and black dirt under my fingernails. No doubt LouElla had worn gloves. "That often happens with widowers," LouElla continued in a Doctor Ruth sort of voice, "coming out of a longtime, happy marriage." She wagged her head. "They jump at the first woman who comes along, hoping to recapture their happiness."

"Daddy took off with the first thing that sat next to him on a barstool," I complained.

LouElla stared at me, silently nodding. In demeanor she was so much like Doctor Ruth or Dr. Joyce Brothers that I just couldn't help confessing to her.

"Has he always drunk heavily?" she asked.

"No, not until after Mom died. Up until then, he'd been a social drinker. After the Navy, he worked as a consultant to the aerospace industry. There was a lot of entertaining with his job, so drinking kind of went with the territory." I ran my fingers through my hair, separating strands that were damp with the sweat beading up on my brow. "Lately we were beginning to worry that it was getting out of hand." I accepted a tissue from Virginia and used it to blow my nose. "When Daddy went into the hospital after his accident, they ran some tests to see if he was an alcoholic. He must have been fine, though, because the doctor let him go."

LouElla shot a quick glance at Virginia, who jumped right into the conversation. "I hate to tell you this,

Hannah, but the doctor *didn't* check your father out of the hospital. He checked himself out."

I couldn't believe that this woman who was practically a stranger knew more about my father than I did. "How do you know that?"

Virginia chewed on her lips, then said, "Darlene told me. She said the doctor wanted to keep him for a while, but that it was an unnecessary expense and he was perfectly fine so she was going to take him home."

I thought back to that day in the hospital, to the bottle of vodka in Darlene's hand, and to Daddy's remarkable "recovery." I realized that if Darlene weren't already dead I would have killed her myself.

"If you want my opinion, he should have stayed there a few more days." LouElla gave me a knowing look. "And not just for the head injury, if you know what I mean." I felt my face flush with embarrassment. It was one thing to suspect your father of being an alcoholic, and quite another to realize that everyone in town must be talking and tut-tutting over it, too. I shoved my teacup toward the center of the table, suddenly certain that I'd never want to eat or drink anything again. "I'd better go."

LouElla clapped both hands to her cheeks. "Oh! I nearly forgot why I came!"

Virginia had taken my empty cup and was heading toward the sink with it. She glanced back at LouElla. "What might that be?"

LouElla rose and ambled to the center of the kitchen where a shaft of sunlight settled on her for a moment, highlighting her hair and giving it a reddish cast. I wondered if she colored it herself—a packet of "midnight blue," perhaps, followed by a "summer berry" rinse. "Look, Virginia," she said. "I know you're not a dog person, but I am. I would love to take Speedo off your hands for the time being."

Virginia's eyes widened in surprise. "You would?"

"I really, really would." LouElla knelt in front of the dog. "You'd like that, wouldn't you, Speedo, old boy." But Speedo was sound asleep, his back legs twitching as if chasing squirrels in his dreams. "If you're worried about it," she addressed Virginia, "I have experience. Who did they call on when the CIA station chief in Athens was murdered in a drive-by shooting?"

I thought I could guess, but why spoil LouElla's pleasure. Virginia simply stared.

LouElla stood tall. "Me. Why, me, of course."

"How did you help?" I asked, sublimely naïve. "Did you bring the terrorists to justice?"

LouElla's eyes sparkled. "No, I adopted his dog, a German shepherd named Bonzo."

Virginia smiled as if everything were normal and her whole kitchen hadn't slipped into some parallel world where grass is red and the sky is green and fish are plucked out of the clouds. The woman actually looked grateful. "I'd like you to take the dog, LouElla. Thank you."

LouElla clapped her hands together. "There! Then it's settled." She reached for the leash which Virginia had draped over the kitchen doorknob. "C'mon, Speedo."

Speedo opened one eye, rose to his feet, and shook himself with extravagant pleasure. LouElla clipped the leash to the dog's collar and led him toward the door. "We'll come visit you, Virginia. Won't we, Speedo?"

Speedo's whole body wagged. "Well, bye," she caroled.

When the door had closed behind LouElla and her new charge, I turned to Virginia. "Why did you let Speedo go home with LouElla?" I couldn't believe it had escaped her notice that LouElla was a bit . . . eccentric.

Virginia waved me back toward the table, a steaming kettle of water in her hand. After I sat down, she poured hot water over the cold, soggy tea bag in my cup. "Let me tell you about LouElla." She set the teakettle down on a braided mat. "LouElla's right, I'm not a dog person. I much prefer cats."

"You have cats?" I hadn't seen any around.

"They've been hiding out since Speedo came to stay. Jennyanydots is cowering under my bed upstairs, and the last time I saw Bustopher, he was in the basement curled up on top of a heating duct."

"I'm a cat person, too," I admitted, "although I'm between cats right now. I'm just waiting for the right one to adopt me." I dunked my tea bag up and down thoughtfully. "But you were going to tell me about LouElla."

"Yes, well, LouElla might have been married at one time, because she had a son. But no one ever saw her husband and she never talks about him. When she came to live in Chestertown, her son was six. They were very close, as close as a mother and son could be. But, just before high school, Sammy got sick." She rested her elbows on the table. "Two years ago, just about the time I moved here, he was diagnosed with a brain tumor. They tried chemotherapy, radiation, surgery . . . everything. Eventually, there was nothing more they could do, so the doctors sent him home to die."

My heart ached with sympathy for that strange woman and her son. I thought of my mother's death in the coronary care unit of University Hospital in Baltimore. She hadn't even had the luxury of coming home before she was taken away from us.

"As you can imagine, LouElla was pretty torn up about it. We all urged her to put Samuel in a nursing home, but she wouldn't hear of it. She rented a hospital bed and a Porta Potti. A truck used to come by each week with fresh oxygen tanks. She spoon-fed the boy, she bathed him, she did everything for him. Lord, how that woman worked to save that child!" Virginia gazed out her window in the direction of LouElla's backyard. "LouElla was trained as a nurse, of course."

I thought about all the things LouElla claimed to have done. It wouldn't have surprised me to hear that she'd been trained as an astronaut and was volunteering to help resupply the space station.

"Samuel died only six months ago, Hannah, so I thought that if she wanted to keep Speedo, it might give her something to do."

I had witnessed for myself the effort that LouElla had put into being official greeter at my father's engagement party, and thought that a person like that with time on her hands could be dangerous. "So you think Speedo will be safe with LouElla?"

"Of course!" Virginia snorted. "LouElla throws herself wholeheartedly into everything. By the time Darryl shows up, if ever, Speedo will be winning blue ribbons at the Westchester County Dog Show."

The thought of Speedo holding still long enough to allow himself to be groomed or perform for the judges made me laugh. "I'm sure you're right." I looked at my watch. It was nearly two o'clock. "I'd better be going, Virginia. Thanks so much for the tea and cookies." I stood, determined to leave this time.

As I opened the door, Virginia laid a hand on my shoulder. "I'm sure your father will come home soon, Hannah."

"From your mouth to God's ears," I said.

As a card-carrying sun worshiper, the short days of December had never much appealed to me. December twenty-first was no exception as darkness fell early, bringing a premature halt to my fruitless combing of the grounds of Washington College for any signs of my father or his car.

On my way back from the campus, I stopped at a convenience store and bought a few items I could nuke into a reasonable facsimile of supper in the little kitchen that adjoined my room—a Stouffer's turkey tetrazzini and a spinach soufflé. After I scraped the last bits of spinach from the corners of the cardboard tray and licked my fork clean, I took a long, hot bath, then crawled into bed with the remote. It had taken me a little time to find the TV. In an attempt to maintain Victorian verisimilitude, the decorator had hidden it in an antique wardrobe opposite the bed.

I grazed through the channels, watching a few minutes of an old Clint Eastwood film, then switched to a popular sitcom after Clint's bullets started flying.

When the local news came on at eleven, there was nothing, thank goodness, about Darlene's death or my father. At this point I was certain that no news was good news and that any news would be bad news.

Sometimes I hate being right. In the morning, just as I was finishing my continental breakfast of croissants, juice, and coffee, Paul and Captain Younger showed up almost simultaneously—Paul to take me home and Younger requesting a few moments of my time. From the look on Younger's face, I suspected he was going to need more than a few moments.

"Did Mrs. Tinsley have high blood pressure, do you know?"

I glanced at Paul, then back at the officer. "I don't know. She could have, I suppose. Why? Did she die of a stroke?"

"Does your father have high blood pressure?"

"No, he doesn't. Definitely not." I couldn't figure out where this conversation was going.

"Anyone in your family have high blood pressure?"

I shook my head.

"Your sister Ruth, for instance?"

I was mystified. Was this guy a policeman or a doctor taking a medical history? "No," I said. "As far as I know, *nobody* in my family has had trouble with high blood pressure. Why do you ask?"

"Mrs. Tinsley died of an overdose of clonidine."

I shrugged and looked at Paul, who shrugged back at me. "What's clonidine?" Paul asked.

"It's a blood pressure medication."

"Maybe Darlene had high blood pressure, then, and nobody knew it."

Captain Younger shook his head. "Dr. McWaters has been her family physician ever since she moved to Chestertown. He told me she'd just had a checkup. The woman was healthy as a horse. Had the blood pressure of a twenty-five-year-old."

"Maybe she took the clonidine by accident?" I offered brightly.

"It hardly seems likely."

"On purpose?" I said before I realized how ridiculous that must have sounded. A woman about to marry the retiree of her dreams doesn't usually go around committing suicide. I raised a hand. "I withdraw that."

I wondered how easy it would be to lay one's hands on some of the drug. "Is clonidine a prescription medication?"

"Yes, ma'am."

I was just about to ask Captain Younger why he mentioned my sister Ruth when I remembered the bottle of schnapps sitting open on Darlene's kitchen counter. Someone must have told him the schnapps had been a gift from Ruth. I took a deep breath. "The schnapps! You don't think my sister . . ."

"Mrs. Ives, there was enough clonidine in that bottle to knock out everyone at the party. Clonidine is particularly dangerous in combination with alcohol."

"But . . . but . . . Ruth would hardly be so stupid as to doctor a gift meant for Darlene and then tell everybody about it!" I set my half-eaten croissant down on a napkin. "Besides, when my husband and I came to Darlene's on Sunday morning, that bottle was sitting right out on the counter, wide open. Anybody could have put something into it." I grabbed Paul's hand for support and he squeezed it back, hard. "It would be pretty safe to do that, you see. Everyone knew it was Darlene's favorite drink. I can't imagine anybody else wanting to drink that stuff, can you? It's positively vile."

Younger jotted something down in his notebook with a ballpoint pen, then tucked the notebook back into his pocket. "By the way, we've found your father's rental car."

My heart flopped. "Where?"

"In a satellite parking lot at BWI, the Blue lot." Anticipating my next question, he raised a hand. "But we checked with all the airlines and there's no indication that he flew anywhere."

I folded my hands and sat silently. I studied my ragged fingernails, promising myself for the umpteenth time to stop gnawing on them.

"Have you heard from him, Mrs. Ives?"

"No, I haven't. Not a word, and I'm really worried."

Younger looked so skeptical that I suspected he'd order a wiretap the minute he got back to his office. "If he does contact you, you will get in touch with me, won't you?"

"Of course."

"You have my number?"

I patted my pocket where I could just feel the outline of the business card he had given me. "I certainly do."

On the drive home, with Paul a captive audience, I tried to sort it out. Darlene, celebrating her upcoming marriage to our father, had waited until the last guests had gone home, then poured herself a congratulatory glass of peppermint schnapps and taken it into the bath.

Wait a minute! Where would Daddy have been?

That was easy. Passed out on the couch.

OK. So, Darlene tucks Daddy in, steps into the bath, takes a drink and shortly after that, goes to sleep and never wakes up. Later, Daddy comes to, looks around in confusion, realizes the party's over, and stumbles upstairs to the bedroom. No Darlene. Then he looks in the bathroom . . .

By the time we reached the spot on the bridge where my father had rear-ended the truck, I was fighting back tears of frustration. I'd looked everywhere, talked to everyone. If the police couldn't find my father, how on earth could I?

It was almost noon when we got back to Annapolis. Pinned to the fridge was a note from Emily saying that Dante had taken her and Chloe house-hunting. Presumably Chloe's opinion on her nursery was required. Paul was supposed to attend a departmental Christmas luncheon. He had invited me along, but I said I wasn't in the mood. He offered to stay home and keep me company, but I urged him to go on alone and he reluctantly agreed.

After the front door closed behind him, I nuked some cider in the microwave, stirred it with a cinnamon stick, slipped some Mozart into the CD player, threw myself into a chair in the living room, and stared at the Christmas tree. If Mozart, hot cider, and the beauty of a well-decorated Christmas tree failed to cheer me up, I was in trouble.

In my absence, the elves had been busy. Scattered among the gaily wrapped packages I had arranged beneath the tree myself were several surprises. A box the size of a small suitcase, wrapped in gold-and-silver paper, caught my eye. Maybe just a peek?

I eased out of my chair and bent over for a closer look at the tag. "For Emily, with love always, Dante." Sweet. I hoped their love *would* last forever. I sat on the floor and retrieved some smaller gifts that had been shoved to the rear when Dante set the box for Emily in front of them. Cuff links for Paul. Earrings for Emily. A key chain for the paper boy. The vase I'd chosen for L.K. Bromley. I fingered the ribbon on Ms. Bromley's gift and wondered if she'd be at home. If so, this might be the perfect time to deliver it. Bromley's intelligent, eccentric company would be a tonic for my worry over Daddy.

I called ahead and she met me at the door of her apartment in the Ginger Cove retirement community wearing blue jeans, a pink turtleneck sweater, and a man's white shirt buttoned up the back like a smock. An orange bandanna covered her short, gray hair. She held a paintbrush in one hand. "Excuse my appearance," she apologized. "I hadn't forgotten you were coming, Hannah, but I wanted to work a bit more on this painting. Come on in. Let me show you."

I handed Ms. Bromley her present, an oblong package wrapped in silver paper and tied with a fancy gold ribbon. I'd bought the wrapping as a kit at the grocery store. "Merry Christmas, Ms. Bromley. This is to put under your tree."

"How thoughtful, Hannah. Thank you, although I don't have much of a tree this year, as you can see, just this little bush." She accepted the package and placed it on a small, round table underneath a white-painted branch resembling reindeer antlers from which red-and-green glass ornaments hung. "But this will certainly look jolly underneath it."

Ms. Bromley led me to an easel set up in her dining

alcove, which was surrounded by windows on three sides. She pointed with the wooden end of the brush. "There! What do you think?"

She had painted some exquisitely lifelike geraniums in a Mexican earthenware pot. "I love it," I said, truthfully.

"That's good, because the painting's for you! Merry Christmas."

"Oh, I couldn't! That's way too generous!"

"Of course you can. It's the least I can do after all you've done to catalog my books."

I felt guilty, because I hadn't set foot in the St. John's College library for at least two weeks. I still had a month's worth of work to do before the extensive collection of mystery novels Ms. Bromley had written over the course of a fifty-year career would be completely processed into the library's Special Collections section.

I perched gingerly on the arm of a chair and admired the painting. Suddenly the pottery vase I had bought for my friend—I thought she might use it as a paintbrush holder—seemed woefully inadequate.

Ms. Bromley used a rag to squeeze excess paint out of her brush, then turned to me. "Come talk to me while I clean up."

I followed her into the modest kitchen and watched while she lathered up with soap and scrubbed her hands using a fingernail brush shaped like a pig to coax the paint from beneath her fingernails. She dried her hands thoroughly on a towel, then beamed at me. "So, what's new with you?"

I thought the last thing in the world I wanted to do was to wipe that cheerful smile off her face. "Well, you know me," I said. "Never dull. Can we sit down?"

She looked at me with dismay. "Such a long face! I think you need some coffee. Decaf or regular?"

Normally I would have chosen decaf, but under the circumstances, I thought I could use something stronger. "High-test."

Ms. Bromley started the water gurgling through the filter, then invited me to join her on the living room sofa. "OK. So what is it?"

"Do you want the bad news first, or the bad news?"

The corners of her mouth turned up slightly. Clearly she expected me to follow this quip with a joke. I took a deep breath. "The bad news is that my father just got engaged to a totally unsuitable woman."

"And . . . ?"

"And the bad news is that she's dead."

Ms. Bromley's eyes grew wide. "My goodness! How did she die?"

"The police think she was murdered. An overdose of clonidine."

Ms. Bromley sank back into the goose-down cushions. "Clonidine? Hmmm. I know about clonidine. Hard not to, living in a place like this."

I explained about Darlene's normal blood pressure readings, about the peppermint schnapps, and about the empty glass the police had found in the bathtub.

"So, any one of the guests at the party could have slipped the medicine into the bottle, right?" She blinked. "Any fingerprints?"

"There could have been a hundred fingerprints on that bottle." I turned on the sofa to face her, tucking a foot between me and the cushion. "But what really worries me now is that my father has disappeared."

I told her about the suspicious hit-and-run and that the police had found my father's car at BWI. She looked thoughtful. "Nobody knows your father better than you do. If you want to find him, I'd advise going to the last place he was seen and try thinking like he would."

While Ms. Bromley went to fetch the coffee, I considered her suggestion.

"Do you have a recent picture of your father?" she called over her shoulder.

"I don't think so." I heard the rattling of the cups as she arranged them on a tray. "Wait a minute! Emily had one of those disposable cameras and was using it to take pictures of Chloe at the party. There may be a snapshot or two of Dad on the roll."

"Perfect! And if they were taken at the party, he's likely to be wearing the same outfit as when he disappeared."

After she served the coffee, Ms. Bromley excused herself and went to the bedroom that I knew served as her office, returning in a few minutes carrying a familiar volume, the *Physicians' Desk Reference*. With the book balanced on her knees, she leafed through it to a series of color photographs. "Here we are." She stabbed at the page with a stubby finger, its cuticle outlined with a trace of red paint. "Look here. This is clonidine. Have you ever seen any pills like these before?"

Still holding my cup, I scooted closer to her. Clonidine hydrochloride seemed to come in three sizes. The 0.3 tablet was slightly oval and a light brownish-pink. The next size down was the 0.2 pill, a pale burnt orange tablet about the size of an Advil. The smallest, 0.1, was a taupey color. I tried to memorize the markings in case I should ever see them again.

After we'd finished reading the complete description

of the drug in all its gobbledegooky glory, Ms. Bromley snapped the book shut and laid it on the floor next to her feet. I picked up my coffee, took a sip, and sloshed the warm liquid around in my mouth, enjoying the taste of fresh ground beans, natural sugar, and half-and-half before swallowing. "I see you didn't give *all* your reference books to the library." I peered at her over the rim of my cup. "I thought you'd retired old Charlie to the Florida Keys, Ms. Bromley." Charlie Mackey was one of Ms. Bromley's several sleuths, a Cleveland-based bookstore owner with a checkered past. "Don't tell me . . ."

She smiled at me slyly. "You never know, Hannah. The other day I read the most interesting article . . ." She waved the thought away. "But we can talk about that later. What you need to do now is get that film developed and get yourself out to the airport."

I hated going through Emily's things, and she would have hated it, too. Five years ago there would have been a sign on her door—*Danger: Nuclear Fallout Zone*—and I wouldn't have dared to go in without her permission. Back then, she'd have thrown a tantrum, and the next thing we knew, she'd be calling from a truck stop in Des Moines, Iowa, begging for bus fare to get herself back home.

Even though Emily had mellowed considerably with age, marriage, and motherhood, I still stood outside her room and thought about it for several long minutes before opening the door. Fortunately I didn't have to do any rummaging because the camera was sitting on the Ikea desk Emily'd used since junior high. Then the desk had been littered with cosmetics and bottles of nail polish in colors named "Sludge" and "Acid Rain," but now it held a pile of clean, neatly folded baby clothes, a box of hypoallergenic baby wipes, a tube of zinc oxide ointment, and several paperback books. I picked up the instant camera and decided it was worth sacrificing the three pictures remaining on the roll. The new Emily would certainly understand.

I usually took my film to Ritz Camera in the Annapolis Mall, but in my present mood, I didn't think I could tolerate the relentless Christmas cheer being cranked out over the sound system while I waited the hour or so it would take to have the film developed. So I drove to the Giant Mall on Riva Road instead, dropped off the film at MotoFoto, then walked a couple of doors down to House of Hunan for some serious comfort food: hot-and-sour soup. An hour later, with my mouth still tingling, I picked up the finished photos and took the packet to my car. I started the engine, turned on the heat, and relaxed against the seat.

For some reason, I was almost afraid to look at the pictures. I had brought along a waxed paper bag of those crunchy doodads you're supposed to sprinkle on top of your hot-and-sour soup, so I munched on one, then another, fingering the packet of photos between bites and chiding myself for being such a coward. Finally I ran out of doodads and excuses. I tore open the packet.

Most of the pictures were of Chloe. I lingered over the pictures of my granddaughter longer than I ought, but I'm a grandmother; it goes with the territory. There was Chloe looking darling in a red headband with poinsettia trim; Chloe grinning at the camera, her chin covered with chocolate. In a third picture, Dante held

Chloe up in front of our tree and I realized, with a pang, how much Chloe took after her father, especially when she screwed up her cute little nose like that.

I sorted the pictures into three piles on the passenger seat. Of the twenty-four pictures that had been exposed, ten were of Chloe, one was of me with my eyes shut (pitch that one!), and the rest were photographs taken at the party. Among the party shots, there were two of Paul, one of Chloe napping on the sofa, and several of Daddy himself. I selected a particularly fine close-up of Daddy standing next to Darlene in her kitchen. Darlene's artificial curls rested lightly on his shoulder and the happy couple, surrounded by guests, smiled directly into the camera. I shivered. Was I looking at a picture of one ghost or two? I stared out my windshield at the crowds of holiday shoppers, fighting the urge to rest my head against the steering wheel and bawl. Not knowing she had only a few hours more to live, Darlene looked radiant. I promised myself I would try to remember her that way rather than as the pathetic heap of wrinkled flesh that I'd found in her bathtub only a few mornings ago. Sad to think that those curls were now separated from their owner, resting in a sealed plastic evidence bag somewhere with the cops or at the Office of the Chief Medical Examiner in downtown Baltimore.

I tucked the photo of Daddy and Darlene into my purse, stuffed the others back into the packet with the negatives, and closed the packet up in my glove compartment.

With no clear plan in mind, I drove across the parking lot, waited for the light to change at Riva Road, turned left, and took the exit to 665 heading toward Baltimore.

As the car hummed north along I-97, Ms. Bromley's words lingered in my ears: *Pretend to be your father. Think like he'd think.*

Officer Younger told me that Daddy's rental car had been found in the Blue long-term parking lot. I made the twenty-minute drive in fifteen, pulled up to the turnstile, punched the button for a ticket, and drove into the gigantic parking lot. *Now what, Ms. B.?*

For ten minutes, I meandered around the lot looking for a parking space, cursing all holiday travelers and their children and their children's children. A shuttle bus squealed to a stop in front of me and I waited, tapping the steering wheel impatiently, until everyone had gotten off. I followed a man dragging a small suitcase to his car parked near the chain link fence paralleling the road. After he drove off with a friendly salute in my direction, I pulled into his slot, parked, and stepped out of the car. I locked the door and leaned against a fender.

OK, Daddy. Where did you go?

There weren't many options. He could have walked across the busy highway to the Green lot, but what for? A few lots away was the Park 'n' Go. Nothing much of interest there, either. If Daddy'd been ambitious, he might have trudged to the Holiday Inn or to the gas station convenience store about a mile down the road, but that didn't seem very likely.

As I waited there, thinking, another airport shuttle bus pulled up at a kiosk two rows away. *Daddy must have taken the bus!* Barring LouElla's alien acquaintances, there were no other options. I made a dash for the vehicle, but it pulled out just as I got there, so I sat down on the bench, panting, to wait for the next one. In less than five minutes, another bus showed up.

The doors swooshed open and I climbed aboard, settling into a seat behind the driver, an attractive woman in her early thirties with café-au-lait skin and thick fringed eyelashes. Before the bus could get underway, I showed her the picture. "I'm looking for my father. He may have been here last Saturday night or Sunday morning. Have you seen him?"

The driver glanced at the picture and shook her head. "Nope."

"How many bus drivers are on duty at any given time?"

She shrugged. "Dunno." Keeping those lovely lashes trained straight ahead, she eased the bus into gear and pressed down on the accelerator.

"What's the best way to get in touch with them?" I asked as the bus lurched forward.

"Most of the guys are on duty right now." She took the bus up to ten miles per hour, then began to slow as she approached the next kiosk. "Why don't you just ask around?"

"Thanks," I said. When the bus ground to a halt, I hopped off and sat on the bench in the kiosk, waiting for the next bus to come along.

I showed Daddy's picture to every bus driver who stopped at my kiosk. No luck. When the lady with the fringed eyelashes came by again, I hopped on her bus for a ride to the terminal.

"Any luck?" the driver asked.

" 'Fraid not."

At the next stop, while she waited for the passengers to heave themselves aboard and stow their luggage in the racks, she said, "Too bad, and Christmas comin', too."

I had to agree.

She stretched in her seat to glare at someone in the rearview mirror. "Can't block the doorway!" she yelled. "Move that bag."

I got out with the passengers heading for flights on American Airlines, walked through the automatic doors, and just stood there in the Christmas chaos. Someone speaking Cantonese or Swahili announced a gate change, and I nearly got run over by two elderly ladies pushing a luggage cart and a mother with twins in an oversized stroller. A family of six bore down on me with a baggage cart the size of a Volkswagen. I leapt out of the way just in time to keep from being crushed against the red tile wall. "Merry Christmas!" I warbled as they rumbled by me without the slightest twinkle of Christmas in their eyes.

At Pier C I found a spot out of the traffic and leaned back against the wall near the sunglasses concession, watching the holiday insanity going on all around me and trying not to hyperventilate. *What would Daddy do?*

He would have suggested to that ponytailed punk slouched against his suitcase that he straighten up and get a haircut; helped that elderly woman with her shopping bags; patiently explained to that violinist that busking wasn't allowed, then given him an extravagant wink and dropped a dollar into the hat at his feet; hurled a few *expletives deleted* at that tour group of boisterous teenagers blocking the aisle so that nobody could get by . . . and then he'd have a drink.

But nobody'd seen Daddy at the various bars and restaurants around the airport; in case he'd opted for less intoxicating fare, I checked Starbucks, Cinnabon, and Roy Rogers with equal lack of success.

On a hunch, I followed a pathway of lights set in

the floor to an elevator that took me to the observation deck. I watched two Southwest planes take off, their skins glowing orange and tan in the setting sun. I felt soothed, somehow, by the all-consuming roar of the jets and by the wind, surprisingly warm for this time of year, as it lifted my hair and howled past my ears. But I didn't feel the presence of my father anywhere there.

I knew it would be a waste of time to check the airlines and the rental car agencies; the police had been there ahead of me with powers of persuasion far greater than mine. In a funk, I walked all the way to the end of the International Pier and realized Daddy could have taken the light rail all the way to Baltimore, getting off at any one of a number of stops. That got me so depressed that I looked around for a place to sit down, but nobody had thought to install any benches. No benches! This made me just as mad as it would have made my father. I leaned against the wall and pouted. Then I paced back and forth in front of the fare machines.

When I stopped fuming long enough to actually look at a fare machine, I threw up my hands in frustration. Even if you knew where you were going, the damn thing was so complicated that even I would have lost patience with it in five seconds flat. There was no way Daddy'd ever have been able to put in the right amount of money, punch the right button, and produce a usable ticket.

So, what did he do?

I walked down a level and strolled back along the sidewalk to the baggage claim area, watching curiously as courtesy vans for the various rental cars agencies and local hotels cruised by. Blue-and-yellow SuperShuttles to Washington and Baltimore pulled up on a regular basis. Buses for the satellite parking lots passed me, and taxis came, one after another, and a few limousines. *Holy cow!* I thought. *You can go anywhere from here!*

When the bus to the BWI train station shuddered to a halt in front of me, my heart did a flip-flop. Daddy loved trains. As much as trains had been modernized since he was a lad, he was fond of saying, thank God no one had engineered out that comforting, soothing *clack-a-tah, clack-a-tah, clack-a-tah.* I stood there like a dummy, staring at the bus. Would Daddy have taken a train? From the BWI train station one could catch an Amtrak train to anywhere on the eastern seaboard. A man could easily lose himself in New York City or Boston or Philadelphia.

I hopped aboard the courtesy bus and rode the short distance to the train station, where a substantial queue of people jostled each other in their eagerness to board the bus I had just gotten off. I wandered into the station, which was small and nearly square, with enough molded gray plastic seats to accommodate about twenty people. To my left stood a coffee wagon; straight ahead lay the ticket counter.

I grabbed a train schedule and took a place in line behind a blue-jeaned student carrying a ragged backpack. From the schedule I realized Daddy could have gone anywhere from here, all the way from Boston to Fort Lauderdale with transfers west at any number of cities in between. He could be halfway to California by now. I made a note to ask the police: Had he used his credit card? The ATM?

When the student left the window, tucking his ticket into a back pocket, I stepped up and showed Daddy's picture to the blue-shirted agent, who glanced up from his electronic keyboard only long enough to give it a cursory glance and say, "Sorry, miss."

"Look again? Please?"

He met my gaze. "Nope."

Disappointed, I turned and surveyed the room. Under the automated schedule board, self-serve ticket machines lined the wall. Behind me were the rest rooms and on the opposite wall, some vending machines. I decided that if Daddy had done any waiting in this room, he would have bought some coffee, so I joined the line at the coffee wagon.

When it was my turn, I ordered a medium coffee and showed the woman who handed it to me Daddy's picture. She studied it for a while, holding the snapshot in one hand while absentmindedly wiping the counter with her other. "Nope. Don't ever recall seeing that guy." I winced as she laid the picture down on the damp counter in front of her, thought for a minute, then tapped it with a lacquered fingernail. "But that woman there. I've seen her before."

I was beginning to wonder what on earth Darlene had been doing at the BWI train station when I looked more closely and saw that it was LouElla's face the server was pointing to. In the photograph, LouElla stood behind Darlene, just to her left, and was talking to Dr. McWaters. I tried to steady my breathing. "Are you sure?"

She chuckled. "Who'd forget *that* hairdo!"

"When did you see her?"

"Oh, I don't know. Couple of days ago." Her eyebrows suddenly disappeared behind a fringe of bangs. "Wait a minute! I remember now. It was after lunch, because she complained that the coffee was too weak, so it must have been last Sunday, the day the coffee machine broke down."

She pushed the picture toward me. I picked it up carefully, wiped the back on my slacks, and returned it to my purse with thoughts tumbling around in my brain and crashing into each other at one hundred miles per hour. *What the hell was LouElla doing here on Sunday afternoon? Taking Daddy to the train? Following him?*

I didn't realize I'd spoken out loud until the woman answered me. "Damned if I know."

BY THE NEXT MORNING, I HAD DECIDED TO TAKE
the direct approach and simply ask LouElla about it.
But I'd forgotten that Emily and Dante were house-
hunting again, this time in Port Royal, Virginia, and I'd
volunteered to watch Chloe.

By nine o'clock, Chloe had finger-painted with warm
oatmeal on the high chair tray and played how-many-
times-will-Grandma-pick-up-the-bottle-if-I-throw-it-
on-the-floor, but I was distracted and knew I couldn't
rest until I had talked to LouElla.

I tried to telephone to let her know we were coming,
but the operator told me that her number was unlisted.
LouElla probably didn't want the CIA to get ahold of it.
So I wrestled the car seat into the back of my Le Baron,
strapped Chloe into it, and took off for Chestertown.

Luckily I found a parking spot on Church Lane di-
rectly under a plum tree and opposite the Geddes-Piper
House which also served as the Historical Society of
Kent County. I unbuckled Chloe, threaded her legs

into the circular openings in a Gerry pack, and eased her onto my back, one strap at a time.

At LouElla's, I rang the bell, but nobody answered. Maybe she was in her garden. I walked around the corner and along Court Street, peering through the slats in the fence that surrounded her backyard.

LouElla was there, kneeling on a thick pad of newspaper, digging up a small garden plot with her trowel. As I watched with my eyes glued to the one-half-inch gap in the fence, she took an object from a box, stood it upright in the hole she had just dug, and patted the earth snugly around it.

"Mrs. Van Schuyler?"

LouElla looked up, then around, confused about where the voice was coming from.

"It's me. Hannah Ives. I'm over by the fence." I waved my hand high in the air.

LouElla stood and beamed in our direction. "Oh, my! How delightful to see you! Delightful!" She wiped her hands on a wide blue apron and plodded over to the fence. I stepped back as one blue-violet eye loomed large between the slats in front of me. "And Chloe! This is my lucky day! You must have come to see my garden."

A gloved hand shot over the fence with an index finger pointing southward. "There's a gate down at that end. Meet me there."

With Chloe in the backpack playing Vidal Sassoon with my hair, I made my way to the gate and waited while our hostess undid a series of locks. After a minute of ominous clicking and clacking, the gate swung open. "Come in, come in."

LouElla stood on a flagstone path that curved away from us toward the back of her house, where it joined a twelve-by-twelve-foot patio. Speedo lay on the patio in a spot of sun in front of a sliding glass door that led inside. When he caught sight of me, he scrambled to his feet and wagged his tail energetically. Chloe hooted with delight.

LouElla spoke directly to Chloe. "And I have something to show *you*, precious." She crooked her finger and led us over to the plot of ground she had been working on. I stood over the freshly turned earth, completely robbed of my power of speech. Eight Barbie dolls, bare-chested and variously coiffed, stood in a row, buried in the dark soil up to their waists. In a box nearby, at least a dozen more Barbies lay, awaiting planting. What exactly did LouElla expect to reap, I wondered, particularly since Ken seemed to be nowhere in the vicinity?

"Da-da-da," said Chloe.

I swiveled my head to look at my granddaughter. "You took the words right out of my mouth, Chloe.

"Golly, LouElla," I said at last. "You must be very proud."

LouElla nodded.

"But tell me, why did you put the dolls out in the garden?"

"They *like* to be outside," she said reasonably.

"Oh." I digested this information while Chloe beat on my head with the flat of her hands like Ricky Ricardo at the Tropicana. "But, why are they buried up to their waists?" I inquired.

"Because otherwise they'd fall over."

I had to double over myself to keep from laughing. Chloe used this as an opportunity to lean sideways out of the backpack, reaching for Speedo's wet, black nose. Here was a disaster in the making. "Help me with the backpack, would you, LouElla?"

Soon Chloe was sitting stiff-spined on the patio, her legs in a V with Speedo lounging beside her, seemingly unconcerned that his short friend had grabbed a fistful of fur and might begin any minute to suck on it rather than on her Tinky Winky doll.

I gazed around the garden. Except for the Barbies, it was perfectly normal looking. Rows of perennials stood tall along the fence—I recognized rhododendron, yarrow, and spiderwort—and annuals would undoubtedly fill the beds in front, adding splashes of color in summer. Ground ivy provided a blanket of green, and in the corner nearest the house stood a dogwood, underplanted with azaleas, ferns, and hosta. Each bed was neatly edged with oyster shells.

LouElla was saying something. "Do you get it?"

"Get what?" I asked dreamily.

"The theme, dear."

I shook my head, uncomprehending.

She touched an oyster shell with her toe, then pointed to a set of wind chimes hanging from a polished disk in the dogwood tree. "Silver bells and cockle shells . . ." She lifted one dark eyebrow expectantly.

A light bulb went on over my head. "And pretty maids, all in a row?" I finished.

Her laughter tinkled, like the wind chimes.

Something magical was going on and I hated to break the spell. I cocked my head, listening as the wind played a tuneless lullaby on the chimes, then, remembering why I had come, I pulled myself together. I had just opened my mouth to ask about BWI when LouElla shrieked, "Chloe!"

I turned in time to see Speedo's tail and the diapered end of Chloe disappear through the sliding glass door. It was a race to see who could reach the house first, LouElla or me.

My overpriced jogging shoes with a recognizable logo won out over her sensible crepe soles. I burst into Lou-Ella's spotless kitchen to find Chloe and Speedo doing a do-si-do under the kitchen table, Speedo on his paws and Chloe on her chubby hands and knees. "Chloe!" I watched in amusement as my granddaughter pulled herself up to a standing position by holding on to a table leg. "You little rascal! I didn't know you could do that!"

LouElla stripped off her gloves, laid them carefully on top of the table, then removed her apron and hung it on a hook next to the back door. "Rascal, indeed! You can't turn your eyes away for a minute! But, now that we're inside, would you like some refreshment?"

I was thinking that a stiff shot of bourbon would be nice, but LouElla was offering milk, orange juice, or water. I took o.j. While LouElla fetched two glasses from a cupboard near the sink, I scooped up Chloe and sat down at the table. LouElla opened her refrigerator, and the light shone on spotless shelves, almost completely devoid of food. My refrigerator hadn't been that clean since the day it was delivered. I worried if LouElla was getting enough to eat and regretted having said yes to the orange juice.

While LouElla poured juice for the two of us, I popped the question. "Something very odd happened yesterday, LouElla. I was looking for Daddy, showing his picture around the airport, and when I got to the train station, the woman at the coffee wagon said she recognized you. She said you'd been at the train station last Sunday afternoon."

LouElla continued pouring, the hand holding the juice carton steady as a surgeon's. "That's easily explained, my dear. I *was* at the train station on Sunday afternoon." She turned toward me, a glass of juice in each hand. "I was investigating your father's disappearance. I often did such work while on undercover assignment for J. Edgar Hoover and it pays to keep my hand in." She set the glasses on the table, then pulled out the chair opposite me and sat down. "He had a lot of confidence in me, you see." She leaned across the table and whispered, "My code name was 'Medusa.' "

I could think of a lot of names old John Edgar might have called this woman, had he known her, but "Medusa" wasn't one of them. "It's kind of you to take an interest in our troubles," I said.

"I'm concerned about all God's creatures," she assured me. "That's why I wanted to adopt Speedo. Poor Virginia doesn't need to be worrying about caring for a dog just now. She's had enough troubles of her own."

Virginia had seemed fairly calm and composed to me, so I wondered what her "troubles" might be. "She mentioned that her husband and daughter had died," I said. "Such a shame."

"Oh, but that wasn't the worst of it. Dear me, no."

I swiveled away from the table and jounced Chloe on my knee as she was threatening to play junior magician by yanking the tablecloth out from under the glassware, sugar bowl, and salt and pepper shakers. I stared at LouElla. "Why? What happened?"

LouElla leaned close and looked right and left

before she whispered, "Virginia's daughter took her own life."

I gasped, thinking about Emily. Losing my daughter under any circumstances would be more than I could bear, but by suicide? "How terrible! Why did she do it, do they know? Was she distraught over her father's death?"

LouElla shook her head. "This happened *before* Harry died. Virginia thought she'd never get over it, and then Harry . . ." She paused and took a sip of her orange juice. "I'm not sure how much of this I should be telling you."

I considered telling LouElla that I had worked for J. Edgar, too, and that my code name was "Minotaur," but I was afraid she'd think I was mocking her. The woman might be slightly daft, but she certainly wasn't stupid. "Have no fear," I said. Using a zipping motion, I drew my fingers across my mouth. "What you say will go no further than this table."

With a sly look at Chloe, as if the baby might be concealing a listening device in her diapers, LouElla continued, "Remember that British agent who died of a poisoned umbrella tip?"

I didn't, but I nodded sagely.

"Well, that's what got Harry, too."

I shook my head. "Poor Virginia."

"Poor Virginia, indeed," she agreed. "He collapsed and died right on her kitchen floor."

"Could it have been a heart attack?" I asked.

"There are heart attacks and then there are *heart attacks*." LouElla took the empty glass from my hand and walked to the sink with it. While her back was turned, I stood and jiggled Chloe on my hip, inching my way over in the direction of the living room. Through the open door I could see a well-worn sofa, a threadbare carpet, and faded drapes, all in gaudy floral patterns that warred with one another. Like the kitchen, the room was scrupulously clean.

As I passed the pantry, I stole a look inside. Familiar red-and-green boxes of pasta, large bottles of spaghetti sauce, row upon row of Campbell's soup, and boxes of whole wheat crackers stood in orderly ranks on the shelves. Not much variety, but I needn't worry. LouElla wouldn't starve.

But it was the case of chocolate-flavored Ensure that made me gulp and look quickly away. She must have fed the nutritional supplement to her gravely ill son. How could she bear to keep such a poignant reminder of his suffering around? I felt as if a black cloud had descended on this house. No, not on this house. On this block. On Chestertown's own little Bermuda Triangle, where so many hearts needed healing, and not the least among them was mine.

RUTH'S ATTITUDE DIDN'T HELP ANYTHING WHEN Captain Younger showed up at Mother Earth on Thursday morning, just before Christmas. I was going to lunch at McGarvey's where I planned to have a word with Darlene's son, Darryl. According to Virginia, he had been one of the last people to see my father the night of the party. Perhaps Daddy had said something to his future—ugh!—son-in-law that might give me a clue to his whereabouts. I had hoped to drag Ruth along with me, but Ruth was short-staffed and the little bundles of incense sticks she'd done up as stocking stuffers seemed to be selling like Pokémon, so she nixed the plan. I was heading out the door on my way to the restaurant when I saw Captain Younger double-park his cruiser on Main Street directly outside the shop, and switch on the flashers.

I rushed outside to meet him, slamming the door behind me so hard that the bells hanging there nearly jingled themselves off their bow. I caught Younger before he could open the cruiser door. "Officer Younger! Do you have news? About our father?"

Younger tucked his sunglasses into a breast pocket and squinted at me through the open window. "I'm afraid not. I was hoping to see your sister Ruth."

My heart went into free fall thinking about the bottle of schnapps. Surely he wasn't going to arrest her? "She's in the store," I said. "I'll tell her you're here."

While Younger uncoiled himself from the driver's seat, I hurried inside to warn my sister. "Batten down the hatches, Ruth. The Chestertown police are here."

"Oh, glory hallelujah." Ruth rested her forehead for a moment against the top of the cash register. "Just what I need."

Captain Younger entered the shop, glanced around, and greeted us cheerfully. "Morning, ladies." I relaxed. He didn't seem in a hurry to arrest anybody. He examined a few of the New Age greeting cards Ruth had displayed in a rack near the door, turning them over to check the manufacturer before sliding them back into place. I could practically hear the gears grinding and meshing in his head—he must have been comparing them to the poisoned pen cards that Darlene had received.

He acknowledged me with a nod. "Mrs. Ives." His eyes Ping-Ponged from me to Ruth as if trying to detect a family resemblance. It's there if you're looking for it: a determined chin, a certain twist to the mouth when we smile, and an upward tilt of the eyes. Ruth is a slightly older (and grayer) version of me.

Ruth stepped from behind the counter. "I'm Ruth." She held her hands clasped behind her back. Evidently she didn't intend to shake his paw. "Hannah says you want to talk to me?"

Younger's eyes slid from me to Ruth. "Is there someplace we can go?"

Ruth shrugged. "I have an office in back, but it's no bigger than a phone booth. Why can't we talk right here?"

Younger shook his head. "Privately?"

"There's nothing you can say to me that Hannah can't hear."

"Very well, Mrs. Gannon—"

"It's *Ms*." The way she buzzed the "*s*" like a "*z*" was embarrassing.

"Very well, *Mizz* Gannon." Clearly two could play that game. He took a notebook from his pocket, licked his thumb, and flipped the pages over one at a time until he found what he was looking for. "I wonder if you would describe for me the bottle of schnapps you gave Mrs. Tinsley."

Ruth looked at the ceiling, the furrow deep between her brows. "Let me think. I got it at Mills . . ."

"The liquor store down the street?"

Ruth nodded. "I remember there was a choice between a bottle with mint leaves on the label and one with candy canes. Being that it's Christmas, I'm pretty sure I picked the candy canes."

"Hiram Walker," Younger said.

"If you say so. I don't remember."

Younger made a check mark in his notebook, then turned to me. "Does that agree with your observations?"

"The bottle Ruth gave me to take to the party was gift-wrapped. I don't know what it looked like underneath the wrapping." I sent a *so sorry* look in Ruth's direction, hoping that I wasn't getting her in trouble. But I hadn't seen the bottle before Darlene unwrapped it. Besides, who knew how many bottles of schnapps Darlene might have had lying around the house, with or without candy canes on the label? The bottle I saw standing open on her kitchen counter might not even have come from Ruth. I wondered if that had been the bottle with the clonidine in it.

Younger shifted gears. "How did Mrs. Tinsley and your father get along?"

"Daddy thought the sun rose and set on that woman. He was positively smitten," I told him.

"Did they argue?"

I shook my head so emphatically that my silver and brass earrings chimed. "Absolutely not. Quite the opposite. They—"

Ruth interrupted me. "They were so lovey-dovey it made me want to puke."

"Ruth!"

"I'm not as circumspect as Hannah," Ruth observed, stating the obvious. "I see no need to candy-coat the situation. That woman had our father wrapped around her little finger. She was an opportunistic bitch. End of story."

Younger stared at Ruth intently. "Would it be fair to say that you're not particularly sorry that Mrs. Tinsley is out of the picture?"

"You could say that."

"Do you know anybody else who might feel the same way?"

Ruth laced her arms over her bosom like a pretzel. "Not really. But she was married three times. There could be a long line."

"You might talk to her children," I suggested. "Deirdre lives in Bowie. Darryl's up in Glen Burnie somewhere, but he works as a waiter at McGarvey's. Down the street and to the left," I added, ever helpful, just in case the officer wasn't familiar with Annapolis. "In fact, I'm heading over there now."

Captain Younger grunted. He consulted his notebook, then skewered Ruth with his eyes. "I understand you've been house-hunting."

I opened my mouth to ask what house-hunting had to do with bottles of peppermint schnapps when Ruth surprised me. It was a subtle thing, just a small step backward, then a hand laid almost too casually at the edge of the counter. "I was."

"Was?"

Ruth nodded. "I made an offer on a house in Bay Ridge, but the deal fell through."

"There was a contingency clause in the contract," I volunteered. "The sellers pulled out at the last minute." I glanced over at Ruth, trying to gauge her reaction, hoping I wasn't playing fast and loose with the truth.

Younger pressed on. "Ever hear of Tidewater Credit?"

Ruth seemed to deflate before my eyes. She reached for the stool she keeps behind the counter, then sat down heavily on it. "Yes. They're the outfit that refused to loan me the money."

"Ruth?" This was news to me.

Ruth took a slow, deliberate breath. "I was going to tell you, Hannah, but I was so embarrassed." She went eye-to-eye with Captain Younger. "Somebody's stolen my identity. My credit is so screwed up right now it'll take me years to get it straightened out." A tear leaked from the corner of her eye and she quickly brushed it away. "When I checked with the credit bureau to find out why my application for a loan was denied, I found out I'm over twenty-seven thousand dollars in debt on credit cards I didn't even know I had. It's so bad that

I've had to ask Eric to handle any new accounts for the store."

That *was* bad. My sister hated asking her ex-husband for anything, even the time of day. I reached her in two steps, folded her into my arms, and squeezed tight. "You aren't responsible for those debts," I soothed. "We'll get you a lawyer. It'll all work out."

Ruth, who rarely cried, fell apart like a dime store toy. "No, it won't!"

I rubbed her back with the flat of my hand. "Yes, it will. You'll see."

Over Ruth's shoulder, I noticed Captain Younger fiddling with a miniature Japanese garden as if the answers to life's big questions—such as, what is it with women anyway?—were written large in the sand. I reached behind the counter and yanked a fistful of tissues out of the box Ruth kept there, then waited with the officer for my sister to dry her eyes.

"Ms. Gannon?"

Ruth blew a honking B-flat into the tissue, then waved the used wad in the air. "Sorry, Captain Younger. It just makes me so angry."

"Ms. Gannon, were you aware that over the past six months unpaid bills for accounts in your name with Visa, MasterCard, and Discover were piling up in a post office box in Edgewater?"

I've known her all my life, so I could tell that Ruth's surprise at this news was genuine. "What?" she exclaimed.

"We're trying to find out who rented the post office box, but whoever applied for it seems to have used a fake ID."

"In Edgewater?" Ruth seemed bewildered.

"But how can that be?" I asked. "Edgewater's on the other side of the South River. Ruth lives in downtown Annapolis, not Edgewater!"

"It's ridiculously easy to get a post office box," Younger continued. "All you need is a driver's license and a major credit card."

"But it can't be so easy to get a credit card in somebody else's name." I paused and looked at Captain Younger for reassurance. "Can it?"

"I'm afraid so." A corner of his mouth twitched. "Think back. How many offers for credit cards have you found in your mailbox lately?"

I didn't need to think. "Tons. Back in September I remember getting two or three a week. Gold cards, platinum cards, cards with my favorite football team on them. Some promising zero-percent APR until the next millennium, all that B.S."

"What did you do with them?"

"What do you think? I threw them away."

"Torn up? Shredded?"

I shook my head. "No, why?"

Captain Younger stared at me. The last time I'd seen a look so painfully patient it was worn by the guy trying to explain to me why my precious Le Baron was going to fall apart on the interstate if I didn't have five hundred seventy-five dollars' worth of work done on the transmission right away. "All someone needs to do," Younger informed us, "is intercept that credit card offer, fill it out with a change of address, and then when the card is delivered to that address, take it out on a shopping spree."

"And never pay," I added helpfully.

"Right." Captain Younger turned to Ruth. "So, who would have had access to your garbage?"

"Just about anybody, I suppose." Her shoulders drooped.

"Wait a minute!" A thought had hit me like a two-by-four square on the forehead. "Nobody would even need to get their hands dirty, Ruth. Think about it! Who had access to your *mail*?"

"Daddy, and . . ." She turned to look at me, her eyes wild. "Darlene Tinsley had a key! Darlene and that no-good son of hers!" She spun on Captain Younger. "You can check with the Annapolis police about that. Darlene and her son stole some things from my father's house, but since they had a key, they were never charged with breaking and entering." She began to sputter. "Son of a bitch!"

Younger stood patiently, waiting for Ruth to run out of expletives deleted before continuing to grill her. "So you see my problem, Ms. Gannon. If you suspected that Ms. Tinsley was responsible for ruining your credit . . ." He ran a hand over his thinning hair. "It would give you a very good motive for slipping something into her schnapps."

Ruth closed her eyes and shook her head. "I had absolutely no idea."

It seemed time for me to jump in. "How could Ruth have suspected *Darlene* of being responsible for her financial problems? From what you've just said, it could have been anybody."

"Your sister may have guessed." He slipped his notebook back into his pocket. "An officer of the law, of course, requires probable cause before taking action. The same rules might not necessarily apply to a private citizen."

"That's ridiculous! Ruth would never kill anybody!"

If she lives to be a hundred, Ruth will never learn to

leave well enough alone. She hopped off her stool and stood tall before us, her spine rigid with determination. "That's where you're wrong, Hannah. If I ever find out who is responsible for losing me that house, for crippling my business, not to mention tarnishing my good name, I'll personally wring his scrawny little neck." She looked directly at Captain Younger. "And I don't care *who* knows it!"

After that, it was all I could do to keep Ruth from shanghaiing me to mind the store while she dragged Captain Younger off to McGarvey's to point out the despicable Darryl so he could clap the cuffs on him. With Darlene dead, Ruth had narrowed her list of possible card fraud suspects down to one. I pointed out reasonably that any larcenous neighbor or enterprising garbage man could have pawed through Daddy's trash and stolen the credit card offers addressed to her, but Ruth was unmoved.

When three teens breezed into Mother Earth shopping for crystals, Captain Younger made a quick escape, tossing a final "Shred 'em" over his shoulder as he disappeared through the door. Two minutes later I escaped as well, promising Ruth that I'd run Darryl down and put the thumbscrews to him. One of us needed to get the goods on Darlene Tinsley's baby boy. If not the policeman, then it might as well be me.

Some claim that McGarvey's Saloon on the Annapolis waterfront serves the best fish-and-chips in town. I'm partial to the Irish version of the British classic that's served at Galway Bay on Maryland Avenue, but in a pinch, McGarvey's will do, and at six ninety-five, you can't beat the price.

In spite of the trying morning, I managed to work

up a respectable appetite in the three minutes it took
to walk from Mother Earth to the restaurant. Having
skipped breakfast probably had a lot to do with it,
though. I pushed through the double glass doors and
loitered near the bar, waiting for a table to open up in
the bright, atriumlike no-smoking section. The hostess
seated the couple standing in line ahead of me, then
turned to me. "Just one?"

Just one? Must women always travel in pairs? She
made me feel so guilty about dining alone that I fought
back the urge to quip, *No, my dear. My Latin lover will
be joining me shortly and look out, 'cause he's hot!*

The hostess led me to a table near a live ficus tree
that flourished under a skylight. When she handed me
the menu I asked, "Is Darryl Donovan working today?"

"He comes in at two."

I checked my watch. Fifteen minutes to go. I studied the menu, although I already knew what I wanted,
and entertained myself by watching the fellow behind
the raw bar shuck oysters. He would cradle the oyster
in a steel mesh glove and pry open the shell with a
skillful twist of a sharp, stub-bladed knife. One every
five seconds without losing any fingers! Impressive.

The waitress took my order for fish-and-chips without writing it down, and returned in a few minutes with
my glass of iced tea with extra lemon. I was sprinkling
powder from a pink packet into my tea—it dissolves in
cold liquids better than sugar—when somebody called
my name.

"Hannah?"

I looked around, puzzled, not seeing anybody I recognized.

"Over here." Deirdre was standing by the door, wagging her hand at me. I realized that I hadn't seen her

since the engagement party. Her short black hair was pulled into a tufted ponytail at the nape of her neck, and she wore faded black jeans, a black sweater, and her mother's décolletage.

I motioned for Deirdre to join me and when she reached the table, I stood up and extended my hand. Hers was cold and slightly damp. "I'm so sorry about your mother, Deirdre."

"Thank you." She dragged a chair out and sat down opposite me, resting her forearms on the table. "I'm glad I ran into you, Hannah. I wanted you to know that I don't believe for a minute that your father had anything to do with my mother's death."

"Thanks."

"I suspect he really loved her," she continued.

"I know." Thinking about Daddy brought tears to my eyes, so I concentrated on scrunching the paper sheath down accordionlike on my straw, and quickly changed the subject. "Are you here to see your brother?"

She nodded. "I need to talk to him about getting a lawyer. I was surprised to find out that Mother didn't have a will." The waitress appeared and Deirdre ordered a hamburger with french fries. She turned to me apologetically. "I don't usually eat like this, but I'm feeling pretty sorry for myself." I watched my own therapeutically engineered fish-and-chips being carried toward me on a tray and silently agreed. Between Deirdre's lunch and mine there would be enough bad cholesterol on the table to last us both until Easter.

"Have you heard from your father?" Deirdre seemed genuinely concerned.

I shook my head. "It's a damn roller-coaster ride. I'm just feeling good about his car being found at the airport, thinking that he must be OK if he's able to fly off somewhere. But then I start worrying that whoever poisoned your mother might have kidnapped Daddy and left him lying in a ditch somewhere." I rotated my plate until the McGarvey's-style circular fries were closest to Deirdre. "Have one."

She shook her head. "No, thanks. I'll wait."

I took a deep breath and let it out slowly. "It occurred to me that the killer might have driven Daddy's car to BWI to cover his tracks."

"You must be terribly worried."

"I am."

Deirdre ran an index finger absentmindedly around the rim of her water glass. "I don't know why it surprised me that Mother didn't have a will. Typical of her, really. Always thinking of herself."

Remembering the surgical scars I had seen on Darlene's body I thought I'd send out a probe. "She couldn't have been expecting to die. She was in good health, after all."

"Everybody should have a will."

"Do you?" I asked.

"No, I . . ." Darlene blushed. "I see your point." She took a sip of water, then glanced in the direction of the kitchen as if checking on the status of her order.

"It seems odd," I said at last, "to be having this conversation with you. Particularly since it was here that it all began."

"What began?"

"Daddy met your mother."

Deirdre scowled. "Mother met her last husband in a bar, too." One eyebrow shot up and she peered at me slyly. "A bar where Darryl was working. Coincidence? I think not." Before I could reply, Deirdre snorted. "It wouldn't surprise me if Darryl didn't get some sort of finder's fee."

"That's pretty harsh."

"Hannah, I was embarrassed by my mother. I couldn't even bring guys home from college without her coming on to them."

"Surely you exaggerate."

She shook her head. "Dad died of a heart attack when I was eleven. Mother started dating only weeks after the funeral."

The waitress had arrived with Deirdre's hamburger. Deirdre deluged her burger with catsup, then mashed the bun down on top, twisting it to spread the catsup evenly. She took a bite, chewed thoroughly, then continued. "At first, she'd leave us alone in the house, expecting me to look after Darryl. Then one of the neighbors complained to child welfare so she started bringing her dates home." Her laugh was hollow. "Less than a year later, she married again. It would have been sooner, but the guy was still married and they were waiting for the divorce to come through." She chewed thoughtfully on a fry. "Carson was nice enough, I suppose. He moved us all into a big house on Narragansett Bay." She took a drink of water. "Odd what you remember. He helped us with our homework. Like I said, a nice man. Everything was hunky-dory until he got killed in a plane crash."

I was beginning to feel a little sorry for Deirdre and her brother. "That's really sad," I said. "Just when you think you've picked up all the pieces, something comes along to knock them right out of your hand."

"Well, Mom didn't waste much time crying over the broken pieces. She went looking for Lynwood instead."

"Lynwood?"

"Lynwood Tinsley. Of her exes, she was married to Lynwood the longest. Broke up his marriage, too, in order to do it." Deirdre dredged a fry through the catsup that was leaking over the edge of her burger. "I don't think Lynwood was all too happy with Mother," she said. "I never knew him all that well, but I think he got more than he bargained for. Mother would give these big parties, invite everybody, drink a little too much, and strut her stuff. Well, you've seen the outfits she wears."

I nodded.

"Lynwood kept his rage all bottled up. My theory is that it turned in on him. Killed the poor cuss."

"Cancer?" I asked.

She nodded. "Colon."

"Too bad."

Deirdre shrugged. "Lynwood was never a part of my life. He never helped me out financially or anything." She dusted her fries with salt. "I've been on my own since I turned eighteen."

I thought about the small fortune we'd spent educating Emily at Bryn Mawr. Deirdre was working on her Ph.D. That meant a prior B.A. and probably a master's. Where had the money come from? "How on earth did you manage?" I asked.

Deirdre wiped her chin with her napkin. "Scholarships. Part-time jobs. Actually, Lynwood was willing to help out with college fees, but Mom said absolutely not. She had this theory that the only things we appreciate are the things we have to work for." Deirdre grimaced. "She'd rather spend Lynwood's money on cruises."

I wondered if Darlene had truly appreciated the

men she had worked so hard to catch. "You've come a long way on your own, Deirdre. Didn't Darlene tell me you're working on your Ph.D.?"

"Uh-huh. In biology."

I nibbled around the circumference of my fried potato while I wondered if students working in biology labs had access to drugs like clonidine hydrochloride. "Did Darlene give Darryl money for college?" I asked.

"Hah!" Deirdre grunted, her mouth half open. Straight white teeth hovered over both sides of the hamburger bun then slammed shut. "Not him, either. Mother held on to every freaking penny. Why do you think Darryl works here?" She bit down on the bun.

Good question. I peeked at my watch. Deirdre's little brother was nearly twenty minutes late for his two-o'clock shift. Maybe, courtesy of Ruth, he'd come into sudden wealth and quit the job. "It's well after two, Deirdre. You don't suppose that Darryl's won the lottery and told McGarvey's to shove it?"

"That's a laugh! Last month he hit me up for half his rent." She turned in her chair, spotted our waitress leaning against the raw bar, and waved her over. "Have you seen Darryl?"

The waitress tucked our check into a plastic service wallet. "He was supposed to work today, but I just heard he's coming in late. His car broke down."

"Damn him! He *knew* I was coming. Jerk's avoiding me."

"Dessert?" the waitress asked helpfully.

Without consulting me, Deirdre said, "Just the check." She seemed in a hurry to leave.

Deirdre pawed through the saddlebag that served as

her purse and came up with a worn leather billfold. I would have given my collection of *National Geographic* magazines to see what else was in that purse. I laid a ten-dollar bill on the table and said, "I'll walk out with you. Do you want to make a pit stop first?"

Deirdre studied the bill. Maybe math wasn't her strong point.

"Is ten enough?" I asked.

"Sure. Fine." She added a ten of her own to my ten on the table, laid the check on top of them both, closed the bill server, and said, "Yeah, I could use the rest room. I've got a long drive."

I hoped Deirdre wouldn't realize I lived close enough to downtown to simply walk home to wash my hands. Although I thought it would probably be a complete waste of time, I followed Deirdre up the steps to the second floor. She disappeared immediately into a stall, leaving her purse propped up next to one of the sinks. "Watch my bag, will you?" The stall door creaked closed and I heard the squeak of the latch being thrown.

I stared at the purse, not believing my luck.

I don't know how it is with guys, but women like to *blah-blah-blah* in rest rooms. In elevators we just stand there, eyes glued front, and never open our mouths, but in rest rooms those same mouths are flapping a mile a minute.

From inside her stall, Deirdre announced, "Darryl's counting on being on easy street now that Mom's dead."

I eased Deirdre's purse open with two fingers while keeping one eye on the door to her stall. "Was your mother well off, then?" I peered into the yawning

mouth of the saddlebag and saw the billfold, a calcula-
tor, two lipsticks, a jumble of used tissues, a wad of
credit cards held together with a rubber band . . .

"She was quite comfortable. Not rich, but comfortable."

"I was just wondering," I said, "because of the
Porsche."

"Oh, that!" She chuckled. "Lynwood's pride and joy.
He bought it used and spent every night and weekend
restoring the damn thing!"

To the *lub-lub-lub* of toilet tissue coming off the
roll, I plucked out Deirdre's credit cards and thumbed
through them quickly. American Express, Visa, and
MasterCard, all in the name of Deirdre Kay Donovan.
Another Visa card belonged to Darlene Tinsley. That
was interesting.

I thrust my hand quickly to the bottom of the bag,
feeling around to see if I could find any pill containers,
but all I unearthed was a small bottle of Motrin and a
flat, round dispenser of birth control pills. *Rats!* If
Deirdre'd had any clonidine, or credit cards in my sister's name, she must have left them at home.

The toilet flushed with a roar. With the palm of my
hand I hit the button on the blow dryer and was rubbing my hands briskly under the hot air when Deirdre
emerged from the stall. She picked up her purse and
slung it carelessly over one shoulder. "There'll be some
money, of course, once we sell the house. But most of
Mom's money came from her widow's benefits under
Lynwood's pension plan."

I finished pretending to dry my hands by patting
them on my jeans. "Did she have any life insurance?"

Deirdre sniffed. "The policy was taken out years
ago. It's hardly enough to bury her."

"Inflation," I said, "is a terrible thing."

Deirdre shot me a look I couldn't read and I thought maybe I'd stepped over the line. "I know what you're thinking," she said as she ran her hands quickly under the hot water tap. "You're thinking Darryl killed Mother for her money."

I nodded. "Or?"

"Me?" Deirdre's laugh carried well over the howl of the hand dryer. "Believe me. Twenty thousand dollars in equity in a house that needs fifteen thousand dollars in repairs before I can even put it on the market isn't worth spending the rest of my life in jail for!"

"Does Darryl know that?" I asked.

Deirdre's face grew serious. "I honestly don't know."

chapter
14

WHEN EMILY LEFT HOME FOR GOOD, WE GOT OUT of the habit of giving barrelloads of Christmas presents, agreeing to hold the line at one or two, max. We'd made pacts with our siblings, too: a gift apiece and cash for the kids. I was always a little sad about that. It's hard to get sentimental over cash, after all, unless it has James Madison's picture on it.

We'd held the line this year, too. Sort of. Wrapped up under the tree was a hand-knit sweater for Paul, something in a small box from Aurora Gallery for me, and a half dozen gifts for Emily and Dante. But Santa had really turned the sack upside down for Chloe. It was all my fault. When I enter a store I must have GRANDMA written large on my forehead because the sales staff attach themselves to me like refrigerator magnets. How could I resist that green-and-white-striped dress with holly berries appliquéd on it? Or that fuzzy, cross-eyed bear? Or that wind-up turtle that bumps crazily into the furniture?

But what choked me up so badly that I had to hide

them in a closet, behind the overcoats, pushed way out of sight, were three gaily wrapped boxes intended for my father. I had been steeling myself for our first Christmas without Mother, but being in limbo about Daddy was just too much.

Yet I had to hold it together, if not for myself, then for my family. On Christmas Eve, with still no Daddy, I prepared our traditional supper of oyster stew, French bread, and salad. We left for the Naval Academy chapel early enough to get prime seats in the first row of the balcony. The Christmas Eve candlelight service was a tradition, too; maybe it'd help keep me centered.

We went as a family—at least, what family I had left. Connie and Dennis were still honeymooning, of course. Scott and Georgina had returned from Arizona, but they had to spend Christmas Eve in Baltimore where Georgina was accompanying the All Hallows choir in the Vivaldi *Gloria,* not to mention assisting Santa in his squeeze down the narrow chimney of their home in Roland Park. I suspected they'd be up till all hours, assembling the dollhouse they'd bought for Julie.

We sat in a row—Paul between Ruth and me, with Emily at the end of the pew next to Dante, who was cradling Chloe. *Once in royal David's city.* I shivered as the sweet, pure soprano voice, bright and clear as the night sky, filled the chapel from the baptistery to the great dome nearly one hundred feet overhead. Christmas had truly begun.

Chloe zonked out in the middle of "Lo, How a Rose." In the dim light I smiled at my slumbering grand-daughter. She *was* a rose, a perfect little rose. As we sang the old, old song, I gazed down at the tall evergreens that flanked the altar. Each was decked with white pin lights and white-and-gold Chrismons—handmade jewel-encrusted ornaments signifying Christian symbols such as IHS, Alpha, and Omega. Poinsettias in profusion, both red and white, decorated the altar and the ledges of the baroque cases that housed the organ pipes. *Joy to the world, the Lord has come!* The deep rumbling of the great pipes resonated with my bones, notes so low that I felt, rather than heard them.

As the service progressed, I stared at the Tiffany window over the altar: Christ walking on the water. *Please, don't take my father! You have my mother. Isn't that enough?*

It worried me that I had almost forgotten the sound of my mother's voice. With my eyes closed I tuned out the scripture reading and concentrated on trying to bring back her soft, slightly nasal, Cleveland-bred accent. *Open your heart and your mind,* Mom seemed to be saying, *and God will tell you what to do.*

Something was seriously wrong. Daddy would never have left us alone during the holidays, not willingly, this Christmas of all Christmases, our first without Mother. If he hadn't contacted us, it was because he couldn't. That meant he was either dead or incapacitated.

I ran over it again and again, trying to put myself in Daddy's shoes. Much the worse for drink, he finds Darlene dead in her bath. He panics and drives to the airport, where he gets aboard . . . what? . . . and travels . . . where? Once there, he drowns himself in alcohol and despair. My father could be living on the street, one more faceless, hopeless, homeless veteran.

Find him, Hannah.

I had survived breast cancer. A car crash. A sinking

boat. I had to believe there was a reason for that, some purpose for which I was spared. I wasn't able to save my mother. Maybe it wasn't too late to save my father.

As the service of Lessons and carols unfolded, I closed my eyes and let the music wash over me. Memories made bittersweet by the tragedies of the past year flitted in and out of my consciousness like butterflies.

Suddenly I was aware that everyone around me was standing and I leapt to my feet to join in the singing. *We three Kinks of Borry and Tar, Trying to smoke a rubber cigar. It was loaded and ex-plo-o-ded* . . . I was back in Virginia Beach, huddling with Ruth in a drafty hallway, peeking through a crack in the door, determined to catch Santa as he came down the chimney. I glanced at Ruth. She had her eyes closed, too. Perhaps the same irreverent lyrics were running through her head.

Lully lullay, Thou little tiny Child. My mother's favorite carol. It transported me to the Uffizi Gallery in Florence where I stood hand in hand with Mother, awed, before Fra Filippo Lippi's "Madonna and Child with Two Angels." A tear escaped and rolled down my cheek. When I looked up again, Christ's stained-glass face smiled for me. It wasn't a miracle—the illumination came from a spotlight trained on the window from outside the chapel—but the smile was for me.

Oh, come all ye faithful. The overhead lights were extinguished, plunging the sanctuary into darkness. Ushers advanced and lit tall candles, then carried them down the center aisle. As the flame passed from worshiper to worshiper, the light from nearly two thousand candles made the chapel glow with a honey yellow light. I could feel the warmth of the flames, smell the burning tallow. *Silent night, holy night.* Paul's arm slid around my shoulder and pulled me close as he touched his candle to mine, and the flame passed on. "I love you," he whispered into my hair. And I cried for my mother, for my father, for Christmases past, but most of all, I cried for myself.

Christmas Day, 1999. Daddy had been missing for a week.

Just about the time Chloe was ripping through the contents of her Christmas stocking, we received a holiday phone call from Connie and Dennis, who were sunning themselves on the deck of their sailboat off The Baths at Virgin Gorda. "The sea's rough today," Dennis told me in a tinny voice that faded in and out with the satellite connection. "We're bobbing about like a cork."

Not half as rough as what's going on here, I thought. But I didn't say a word. Connie would be royally pissed when she found out we'd kept the bad news from her, but after agonizing about it, we had decided not to tell them about Daddy. There wasn't a thing they could do about it from the British Virgin Islands, and it would only spoil their honeymoon.

Besides, Dennis probably believes I'm an accident waiting to happen. He's pulled strings for me before, and once or twice he's had to bail me out, quite literally. Connie and I would still be clinging to a mast in the middle of the Chesapeake Bay singing old Girl Scout songs if Dennis hadn't steamed to our rescue with the U.S. Coast Guard in tow. I'd leave Dennis out of it this time. When Mr. and Mrs. Dennis Rutherford returned to Maryland, all this mess would be behind us. Or so I hoped.

It was Georgina's turn to host Christmas dinner. Under the circumstances, I'd encouraged her to take a leaf from my book. Last year I'd wimped out big time by making reservations at the Maryland Inn. But my sister Georginia was a domestic goddess. With her depression properly medicated, she was able to resume a punishing schedule of Christmas season services and still turn out a feast for five thousand.

Eleven, rather. Although there should have been twelve.

Georgina's dining room table had been stretched to the walls and covered with a Vera tablecloth in a holiday motif that hid the fact that her extra leaves were made out of plywood. The table had been set with her best silver, china, and crystal. I could tell Julie had laid the silverware. She preferred the fork on the right, near the right hand that would use it, and treated any suggestion to the contrary with disdain.

Sean and Dylan had made place cards by folding three-by-five index cards into tents and printing our names on them in block letters with crayon. Mine said "Aunt Hannah" and had a Christmas wreath sticker affixed in the right-hand corner, its red bow covering the *h*. Carrying the ice cube bin, I walked around the table dropping ice cubes in glasses. "Aunt Ruth" was written in purple and decorated with a Christmas tree. "Mommy" was pink, with an angel. At the head of the table, I stopped, choking back a sob. "Granddaddy" had a rocking horse.

When Georgina came to check on my progress a few minutes later, I asked, "Why did you set a place for Daddy?"

Georgina smiled sadly. "I keep hoping he'll walk in the front door." We stood side by side, staring silently at his name tag. Georgina was working with a psychiatrist who was helping undo, step by step, the damage inflicted on her and on our father by a previous therapist. She had a ways to go before the rift between them could be completely healed, but I took this gesture as a positive sign.

Georgina shuddered, then began rummaging in the buffet for some hot pads which she arranged in two cloverleaves in the center of the table. "Thanks for helping, Hannah."

"You're welcome." In truth, I hadn't done much. I'd brought the jellied cranberry sauce, still ribbed from the can, and the sauerkraut. Over the years she had lived in the city, Georgina had become a true Baltimorean, and a true Baltimorean wouldn't dream of serving turkey without sauerkraut on the side.

Soon the table groaned with bowls of mashed potatoes, green beans, baby peas, sauerkraut, stuffing, and gravy. Parker House rolls steamed under a napkin in a basket. We stood dutifully behind our chairs, knowing the rules, waiting for everyone to assemble. Paul arrived with the chilled wine, brandishing a corkscrew. Ruth bustled in from the kitchen with a casserole dish of caramelized sweet potatoes sandwiched between two pot holders. She set the dish on a hot pad in front of me.

I leaned over and took a good whiff. "Yummy!" I said. "Thank goodness they've repealed the law that says sweet potatoes have to be cooked with pineapple chunks, coconut, and miniature marshmallows."

Emily gave me a look just as Dante said, "But I *like* them that way, Mrs. Ives."

I rearranged the salt and pepper shakers, feeling my face grow red.

Scott held the kitchen door for Georgina, who glided in with the bird, twenty magnificent pounds of it, golden brown and glistening on a platter. She paraded the turkey around the table, then set it in front of Scott.

Scott stood at the head of the table and looked around uncomfortably. We waited, Julie tipping her chair back and forth on its hind legs.

Paul cleared his throat. "Shall I?"

Scott shrugged.

Emily slipped Chloe a roll to distract her from banging on the tray of her high chair with a spoon.

"I don't mind," said Ruth, but we all knew it had to be either Scott or Paul.

"Where's Granddaddy?" piped up Sean.

"He's on a trip, honey," Georgina said.

Dylan pouted. "Dumb trip."

Emily laid her hand on top of Dante's. "It should be the oldest."

"Right," I agreed.

"Me, then," Paul said. He grabbed my hand, squeezed, then extended his other hand to Ruth on his right. Ruth gathered up Sean's hand and Sean took his mother's. Soon the circle was complete and Paul bowed his head. "Bless this food to our bodies and us to Thy service."

"And bless Daddy, wherever he may be," I added, my chest tight.

Paul smiled at me crookedly, as if apologizing for the simplicity of his efforts. After all, it was Daddy's job to say the grace. He wrote special ones for every occasion. Last year, he'd blessed the food and his joy at forty-nine years of marriage to our mother.

I swallowed hard. No, not twelve places at the table. There should have been thirteen.

TWO DAYS AFTER CHRISTMAS, WE COULDN'T FIND
Tinky Winky. That precipitated a crisis of major pro-
portions, second only to the threat of global thermo-
nuclear war. In less than forty-eight hours, Chloe's
new toys had lost their attraction and she began crying
for "Dink," her purple Teletubby friend. The last time
I'd seen the little guy, Chloe and I had been at
LouElla's.

I apologized for leaving Tinky Winky behind and
volunteered to fetch him the following morning. I had
already mapped out my day. I was calling the Salvation
Army in every major city, beginning on the East Coast,
and after that I'd contact homeless shelters and food
wagons, trying to find my father.

By the way Emily goggled at me I could tell she
thought all that telephoning would turn out to be a
waste of time, totally. But she was in a let's-humor-
Mother mood. "That's OK, Mom. I don't mind going to
LouElla's. I feel kinda sorry for the woman. No family,
no real friends. And it *is* the holidays. I'll take her a

basket of fruit and cheese and stuff." She paused. "Besides, it's Boxing Day."

"What?"

"Boxing Day. In Britain the landowners deliver gifts to their tenants each December twenty-sixth."

"Today's the twenty-seventh." I shook my head. "All that money we spent on college . . ."

"I majored in English," Emily said with a giggle, "not math."

Wondering if the only thing to show for my efforts would be a colossal telephone bill, I took a breather from my so-far-fruitless efforts on the telephone to rummage in the basement storage area for an old Easter basket. While Emily drove to Graul's Market, I salvaged some tissue paper and ribbons from the plastic bag of Christmas trash and used them to line and decorate the basket, finishing off the handle with an elegant red-and-green plaid bow. Emily returned with an assortment of cheeses, crackers, and hard salami, which she plopped into the basket. I contributed a jar of artichoke hearts and marinated mushrooms from my pantry, and Emily added two apples, several tangerines, and a grapefruit from a box Dennis had had shipped to us from Harry and David. Et voilà!

Emily and Chloe drove off in high spirits to deliver the basket. I imagined they'd be singing "Ninety-nine Bottles of Beer on the Wall" by the time they got to the Bay Bridge. Although she chided me for fussing, I insisted she take my cell phone.

Almost two hours later, while I was caught in an automated answering system death loop with a homeless shelter in Washington, D.C., our call-waiting tone cut in. I toggled the switch. "Hello?"

Emily was talking so fast that I couldn't understand

a word she was saying. My antenna shot up. "Slow down, Emily! What's wrong? Has there been an accident? Are you OK?"

On the other end of the phone, I heard Emily take a deep, shuddering breath. "I think I've found Gramps!"

I was certain I'd misunderstood. "What did you say?"

"You're going to think I'm absolutely crazy, but I think he's at LouElla's."

This didn't make sense at all. I clicked my brain into reverse. LouElla had invited me into her house just the other day. Surely she wouldn't have done so if Daddy had been there. And then I remembered. LouElla didn't invite me in, Chloe did, by crawling into the house after Speedo.

"Mother? Are you there?"

"Em, are you sure about this? I was just there!"

"I know! That's why I thought it was odd when LouElla answered the door with Tinky Winky in her hand. She didn't want to let me in, even when I offered her the basket. But then she noticed Chloe out in the stroller and just melted. She invited us into the kitchen and we were playing with Speedo when I heard the most incredible thing!"

"What?"

"You know that Thomas Hampson CD that Gramps likes so much? Well, I heard it playing kinda softly when I came in and I thought, wow, that's really nice and I got a little choked up because it's Gramps's favorite CD and all and I was, like, really missing him. Then it got to 'On the Road to Mandalay,' and I swear to you that Granddaddy was singing along!"

As Emily's story unfolded, my heart began to pound. "Are you sure it was your grandfather?"

"You think I wouldn't recognize his voice? It was Gramps. Definitely. Remember how he always does that funny warbly thing with the *f*'s in 'flying fishes play'?"

"Where do you think the music was coming from, Emily?"

"Upstairs."

A plan began to take shape in the muddle of gray cells that passed as my brain. "Where are you now?"

"In the car. I'm parked on North Court Street, so I'll be able to see if LouElla leaves her house."

I was relieved to hear that. No matter what role LouElla may have played in all this, even if it turned out that she hadn't murdered Darlene and kidnapped Daddy, she might still be dangerous. "Does she suspect you heard the singing?" I asked my daughter.

"I don't think so. Once I figured out it was Gramps I acted real casual, picked up Chloe, collected Tinky Winky, told LouElla we had a party to go to, and got the hell out." At the end of this recitation, Emily was breathless. "What should I do, Mom? Call the police?"

I had to think about that. I knew we should call the police, but I didn't want them to be the first to find Daddy. I was afraid they'd arrest him. Besides, they'd have to get a warrant. With no more to go on than a few snatches of an old music hall tune, the judge might laugh them right out of court. And there was always the possibility that Emily was mistaken, but, *oh heavenly days*, I hoped she wasn't.

I made an executive decision. "Sit tight, honey, I'm coming right over." I started to hang up, then had another thought. "If LouElla is watching, she'll think it's strange if you don't actually leave, so drive away now and meet me at the Feast of Reason on High Street."

"Where?"

"It's a little restaurant just across the street from the Imperial Hotel. It's got a statue of a chef and some copper pots in the window."

"OK."

"And Emily?"

"Yes?"

"Let's both be thinking about a good way to lure LouElla out of her house."

I scribbled a note for Paul, pinned it to the refrigerator where I knew he wouldn't miss it, then broke every speed limit posted between downtown Annapolis and the Bay Bridge. At the tollbooth, I discovered I'd left home without my purse, so I had to search the ashtray, tear up the carpet pads, and borrow ten cents from a driver one car back before assembling enough loose change to get me across the bridge.

Once in Chestertown, I squealed left onto Queen Street, where yellow crime scene tape still streamed like banners from the pillars of Darlene's porch, reminding everyone of the tragedy that had so recently taken place there. I turned right on High and, by a miracle, found a place to park in front of an antique store, well out of sight of LouElla's.

Inside the Feast of Reason, Emily and Chloe waited for me at a table near the cold drinks cooler under a series of colorful Heather King vegetable prints. Emily cradled a steaming cup of tea in her hands, and Chloe was working on a bottle of orange juice.

I sat down at the table opposite my daughter. "OK. Let's brainstorm."

She smiled uncertainly and raised a naturally lush, unplucked eyebrow. "I think I've figured out a way to get LouElla out of her house long enough for you to search it." Emily paused for a moment, driving me nuts because the best idea I'd come up with during my hour-long drive was to pound on LouElla's door and shout, *"Fire! Fire!"*

I stared at my daughter. She wore a smile, the mischievous one, and her cheeks were flushed. I braced myself for a far-out suggestion.

With a quick glance at a customer who was taking his time in front of the dessert case, Emily leaned across the table and whispered, "I'll go back, tell her that I've found some fleas on Chloe and that I think she'll need to get Speedo treated."

I nodded, impressed. LouElla seemed inordinately fond of Chloe. Anything that would prevent our little charmer from visiting LouElla would deeply concern her.

Emily continued. "LouElla's house is so spotless I know she'll freak. So I'll offer to take her to the vet's to get Speedo dipped."

"What if she won't go?"

"Then we'll think of something else."

"What if you can't get in to see the vet?"

She patted the cell phone. "I checked. I found one who's available. I actually made an appointment. We may have to wait a bit but that's even better, isn't it? Just so long as *you* can get into the house."

All of a sudden I remembered the locks LouElla had installed, even on the backyard fence. "She's got locks on all the doors. How am I supposed to get in?"

"I'll think of something when I get inside," Emily said. "Just try the front door."

"How will I know when it's safe?"

"You sit here and finish my tea." She pushed her

cup toward me with two fingers. "After I get LouElla and the dog, I'll drive by the window." She pointed toward the front of the store. "Then go for it!"

I helped Chloe back into her sweater, then watched through the window as she and her mother disappeared around the corner, slightly stunned at the role reversal that had just taken place.

I nursed Emily's lukewarm tea for five minutes, worrying. I asked for more hot water, added it to the tea bag in the cup, and made it last for ten. I talked to the girl behind the counter for three minutes about the trip she was planning to take to Guatemala next summer. I paced for two. After what seemed like hours, Emily drove by in her father's car. There was no doubt about it. Speedo's head hung out the left rear window, his tongue and ears flapping in the winter breeze.

I grabbed my coat and waited near the door until the car had passed through the stoplight at High and Cross. When I could no longer read the license plate, I tossed a quick "thank you" over my shoulder, then hurried down Court Street to LouElla's.

Trying to look nonchalant but quaking in my shoes, I stepped up on the tiny porch. What if the door was locked? In that case, I decided, I *would* call the police. I grasped the knob on the front door and turned. To my delight, the door swung open. I promised myself I would ask Emily later about how she managed it, but right then, the only thing that concerned me was getting myself inside LouElla's house.

I stepped into a dark entrance hall and closed the door behind me. I took a deep breath and held it, listening as the silence deepened around me. To my left was the familiar living room; to my right, a small office.

Emily had said that the music seemed to have been coming from the second floor, so I looked around for a stairway, but didn't immediately see one.

Just ahead of me a large green plant blocked a door that could have led to a staircase. Using both hands, I knelt and muscled the plant aside, shoving it the final few inches with my foot. I opened the door to reveal a yellow raincoat, a blue Polartec jacket, and a red parka with a fur collar that might once have belonged to LouElla's son, all heavy with the odor of mothballs. Definitely a closet.

I closed the door, carefully replaced the plant, straightened my spine, and shouted, "Daddy!" I listened, straining my ears, but the house was as quiet as a funeral parlor. Feeling guilty, I tiptoed into the office that, from its proximity to the kitchen, might once have served as a dining room. A small wooden desk sat in an alcove formed by a bay window. I imagined LouElla sitting there in the hard, straight, ladder-back chair, writing letters to the editor of the Chestertown *Gazette* or to her congressman. I stood in front of her desk and peeked out the window.

LouElla's house had been built at the intersection of two lanes. From this spot, she had a clear view of everything going on in her neighborhood; no one coming up Court Street ahead of me or down Church Alley to the left would escape her notice.

On top of the desk in front of me lay a record book of some kind, bound in black with red leather trim and held open by rubber bands. It lay open to a new page, at the head of which today's date, December 27, was written in bold capital letters. LouElla had recorded today's observations: the temperature that morning at six A.M., 31 degrees; and 0723, the time the sun rose. LouElla's newspaper had been delivered at 0645 precisely. As I browsed down the entries I mused that Chestertown's lawyers better not try any creative billing. LouElla had their comings and goings well documented—P.L., whoever he was, had come to work at 0905 and left precisely at 1023. I noticed he came back again at 1100, probably after a coffee break. The book was nearly full, so I slipped off the rubber bands and turned quickly to the front where events as far back as last summer were recorded. In addition to the weather and temperature, other odd notations at the top of each page caught my eye: 23jb on July 10, 18jb on the eleventh. LouElla collected minutiae. Fascinating, if you had the key.

I closed the logbook and slipped the rubber bands back in place, hoping LouElla didn't pay as much attention to how she left her papers as she did to the sunset. I turned away and began searching the rest of the house, but as quietly as I tried to move, my own footsteps were deafening as I made my way from LouElla's office toward her kitchen. There had to be a staircase around here somewhere!

I paused in the hallway, considering my next move. Could this be one of those old houses where the staircase pulls out of the ceiling? I walked, head tipped back at a painful angle, checking the hallway and likely spots in the kitchen, but there was nothing overhead but plain white ceiling.

I bumped into a counter. On it, a Crock-Pot simmered. I lifted the lid and sniffed. Beef stew. Nearby, two loaves of bread had been left to rise, covered with a checkered dish towel. My stomach rumbled.

Why was I tiptoeing about? Emily could keep LouElla

busy for hours and hours. "Daddy!" I called again. I stopped, not breathing, praying for a response. I tried calling a little louder. "Daddy! It's Hannah!" My voice sounded muffled, as if I were shouting into a padded box. There was no response but the sound of the furnace roaring to life.

I began methodically opening doors. The pantry door I recognized; next to it, a door led to a dry, dusty basement. To the right of the stove, there was another door. *Bingo!* Feeling half jubilant and half foolish, I peered up a stairway into the dark.

The staircase was steep with walls on both sides. I felt around for a light switch, and nearly cheered when a single bulb in a cheap glass globe cast a shadowy light from directly above me.

I took two steps and called again. "Daddy!" I crept up, placing each foot carefully on the uncarpeted treads, not that there was anybody to hear me. I was now certain that Emily's imagination had gotten the better of her. Maybe Thomas Hampson wasn't singing alone; maybe it was that other CD she heard, the one where he sings duets with Jerry Hadley. I paused and leaned against the wall, vowing that if I got out of this house alive, I'd make Emily swear that this breaking and entering would be our little secret.

At the top of the stairs, the late afternoon sun strained to penetrate the gloom of the hall through a narrow slit in a pair of dark velvet drapes. Doors lay to my right and to my left.

I eased open the door on my left and entered a pleasant bedroom decorated with rose trellis wallpaper. A cream-colored rug and dark plum draperies complemented a pink bedspread; lavender throw cushions had been propped against the headboard. At the foot of the bed sat an oversized laundry basket that had been lined with a pink quilt. I smiled, warming up to this odd woman who took such good care of an orphaned dog. A small bathroom adjoined the bedroom. I peeked in. I honestly didn't know you could buy porcelain in that color: a bathtub, sink, and toilet, all in lavender, harmonized with the purples in a Monet water lilies shower curtain. I slid open the door to the medicine cabinet and glanced in quickly. Advil, Scope, nail polish remover, Band-Aids, deodorant, bleaching cream, a fiber laxative, tiny paper cups—nothing remotely resembling clonidine.

Feeling uncomfortably like a voyeur, I backed out of LouElla's room and, with no great expectations, tried the door across the hall. Surprisingly, it was locked. I put my ear to the panel and listened. Nothing. "Daddy!" I shouted. I banged on the door with my fist. "Daddy! Are you in there?"

I stood outside the door considering my next move. I remembered what Virginia had told me about LouElla's son. This must have been Sammy's room. Maybe she'd kept it just the way it was the day he died, the painful memories locked away behind this door.

I struck the door with my fist, almost in frustration. Locks were always an interesting challenge; should I have a go at picking this one? I had already started downstairs to assemble some makeshift tools when, thinking it was my imagination, I heard creaking, like bed springs. "Daddy?"

There was a thud, and then silence. "Daddy? Is that you?"

A voice, hoarse and slightly groggy as if trying out its vocal chords the first thing in the morning, croaked, "Hannah?"

Ohmygawd! I began pounding on the door. "Yes, it's me! Open the door!"

I waited, my ear pressed to the wooden panel. The next time Daddy spoke, it was directly from the other side of the door. "I can't. It's secured."

Secured? LouElla had locked Daddy in! I put my eye to the keyhole but was blinded by sunlight hitting my eye like a laser beam. I blinked and stood up. "Do you have a key?"

"I'm so glad you've come to visit me."

Visit? Daddy was really disoriented. I grasped the doorknob, jiggled it back and forth, and rattled the door until it shook on its hinges. "Just a minute. I have to find a key." I prayed LouElla hadn't taken the damn thing with her. I imagined a whole ring of them, tied to her belt with purple ribbon so that she clanked like a jailer whenever she walked. If I couldn't find a key, the hell with picking the lock. This was an emergency! I would do an Emma Peel and kick-box the door until it splintered away from its hinges.

I threw open the drapes and searched the hallway. *Ta-da!* On a brass cup hook screwed into the chair rail near the door hung a single, old-fashioned key. Sick with relief, I grabbed it, fitted it into the keyhole, and turned.

The tumblers fell into place and the door swung open.

Daddy stood in front of me wearing only his underwear and a broad grin. The deep lines had been erased from his face and he looked rested, better than I had seen him in years. I closed the gap between us in less than a second, grabbed him around the waist, and held on to him tightly. Now that I had him, I wasn't about to let go. "Thank God I've found you!"

Placing his broad hands on my shoulders, Daddy held me at arm's length and smiled into my face. "I didn't know I was missing." His voice was husky, but not from alcohol. Suddenly he blushed, grabbed a thin blanket off the bed, and wrapped it around his waist.

A pitcher of ice water sat on a table. I poured him a glass, then thought better of it. I sniffed the water, thinking it might be drugged. It smelled OK, but to be on the safe side, I dumped it out in the sink and filled the glass from the tap. "Here, Daddy. Drink this."

While he drank, I stared at him, my mouth at half mast. "We've been looking for you since the party. We looked everywhere! The police, too."

Daddy handed me the half-empty glass, sat on the edge of the bed, and patted the space next to him, indicating I should sit down. "Not everywhere, or you would have found me!" He sounded stronger, more confident. Calm, almost cool. What on earth was going on? I'd read about the Stockholm syndrome, about people like Patty Hearst who ended up identifying with their captors. Maybe that's what had happened between Daddy and LouElla. I grabbed his hand in both of mine. "How did you get here, Daddy?"

He ran the fingers of his free hand through his short, thick hair. His eyes narrowed in thought. "The last thing I remember clearly is standing in Darlene's garden after the party." He closed his eyes as if the scene were playing out on the insides of his eyelids. "I'd had rather a lot to drink and I went out to get some fresh air." His lids flew open. "Darlene accused me of spoiling her evening. Then there was Darryl and LouElla . . ." His voice trailed off. "I was pretty low. LouElla took me in hand and talked me into Phoenix House." Daddy turned sincere brown eyes on me. "I realize now that I've had a drinking problem ever since your mother died, probably before. I should have taken that doctor's advice in Annapolis, shouldn't I?"

I nodded.

"Sometimes you have to hit rock bottom before you can start climbing back up. Well, there wasn't much lower I could go than sprawled in the dirt in Darlene's garden."

I was so stunned that it was taking a while for everything to sink in. Garden. LouElla. Phoenix House. What the hell was Phoenix House?

I looked around the room and light dawned. Smooth, off-white walls surrounded us. Cheerful drapes hung at the window. A hospital bed, a dresser, a bedside table on wheels, and a leather chair were the only furniture. A stack of magazines sat next to a CD player on a windowsill. The sink I had just used was tucked away in a corner. Through an open door in a room that might once have been a closet, I saw a toilet and shower stall. Sammy's hospital room. *This* was Phoenix House.

I was in a hurry to hustle Daddy out of there, but he was in no condition to go anywhere in his underwear. "Where are your clothes?"

He shrugged. "I don't know; I haven't really needed them."

I crossed the room to the dresser and opened the top drawer. Four undershirts and briefs lay inside, neatly folded. Fruit of the Loom, not his usual brand. In the next drawer down were my father's gray flannel slacks and blue sweater, confirming what I suspected: He'd come here the night he disappeared. In the bottom drawer lay his watch and wallet and his shoes, neatly aligned, with his socks tucked inside. "Come on, Daddy. Get dressed and let's go home."

I laid Daddy's clothes out on the bed, made sure he was steady enough on his feet to get into them, then turned my back and stared out the window while he got dressed. From his window and through the bare winter trees, Daddy would have had a clear view of the courthouse, but not much more. No wonder he was confused about where he was. I wondered if LouElla had kept him sedated.

Not wanting to alarm him, I asked, "So, LouElla's been taking care of you?"

I heard the sound of a zipper. "She introduced herself at the party as a nurse at Phoenix House. Told me all about the programs they have here." His voice was muffled by the sweater going on over his head. "When LouElla found me, she said I was practically unconscious. The next thing I know, I wake up here, in the hospital, and LouElla is telling me it's time I turned myself over to a professional." Still in his bare feet, he crossed to where I was standing at the window. "I should have done this a long time ago, Hannah. I feel *great!*"

"But, Daddy, she kidnapped you!"

Daddy threw back his head and laughed. "Kidnapped! That's the most ridiculous thing I've ever heard! I'm here because I *want* to be here." He sat down on the edge of the bed and motioned for me to sit in the chair. "And LouElla really knows her stuff. She nursed me through withdrawal, gave me something to help with the headaches—God, did I have headaches!—and sat with me until the worst of them were over." He laid both hands open across his stomach. "And this facility has a wonderful cook!" He grinned. "Who needs the Betty Ford Clinic if you have

Phoenix House?" He stared at a spot on the wall and looked wistful. "Reminded me a lot of your mother's cooking."

I started to say something in defense of Ruth, who had been chief-cook-and-bottle-washer in my father's house for the last eight months. I'm sure he appreciated the effort Ruth put into her cooking, but I knew that vegetarian chili and lentil stew didn't exactly set his taste buds racing. As if he knew what I was thinking, he said, "Last night I reached a milestone. I had a big, juicy T-bone."

I couldn't stand it. "Daddy, we've been looking everywhere for you! LouElla knew it, too, and she didn't say one word about your being here."

Daddy shrugged. "There are rules."

"We were even in the *house,* for Christ's sake, and she didn't say anything!"

"But she told *me.* From time to time I heard your voice, and today I thought I heard Emily. When I asked LouElla about it, she explained that you were allowed to check in on me, but as part of the treatment, I wouldn't be allowed visitors until I was cured. It was to give me an incentive. And it worked. The woman is a genius."

"Daddy, you are *not* in a hospital. You are not in a nursing home. You are not in a treatment center. This is her *house,* for heaven's sake."

"Does it matter?" He spread his arms wide. "I'm cured. Look at me, Hannah! I'm cured!"

Daddy did look wonderful. The sickly pallor was gone, and his cheeks had filled out, erasing the lines that had been deepening around his nose and mouth, but it was in his eyes where the real difference lay. Two

weeks ago they had been narrow, hooded slits, but today Daddy looked at me with eyes that sparkled with
life.

He bent over to tie his shoes. "I can't wait to show
Darlene."

My blood froze. So, LouElla hadn't told him about
Darlene's death. What was I going to do now? With
his "cure" so fresh, I worried that he'd not be able to
take the news without tumbling off the wagon and flat
on his face. But Darlene's house was only fifty yards
away. He'd be expecting to see her. There was no way
around it.

"Daddy, sit down. I've got really bad news for you."

"What? What?" He looked confused.

"Darlene's dead."

"She . . . she can't be dead! We're getting married."

I laid a hand on his arm. "Daddy, I'm so sorry, but
she died the night of the party."

He blinked rapidly. "She *can't* have died! She was
perfectly fine when I left her."

"When did you see her last?" I asked. I'd been spending so much time around the police I was beginning to
sound like them.

His eyes rolled around as if trying to focus on five
or six things at once. He shook his head. "It's fuzzy."
His eyebrows knit in concentration. "Everybody went
home, and we stayed up talking to Darryl." He paused
again. "Then Darlene and I had words and she went
upstairs to take her bath. Darryl stayed for a few more
drinks and . . ." He spread his hands, palm up. "That's
all I remember." Something I had said before suddenly
clicked. "Why were the police looking for me?"

"They thought you might have had something to do
with Darlene's death."

"That's ridiculous!"

"They thought maybe you'd killed her, then run away."

My father sat there, dry-eyed, stunned, as if someone had clobbered him with a blunt object and he was still trying to figure out what happened. "Killed her?"

"They found her dead in the bathtub, Daddy, and they say that somebody put enough blood pressure medicine into her schnapps to put her to sleep forever. Something called clonidine."

"My God." His eyes locked on mine. After what seemed like minutes, he looked away. "Did she suffer?"

"I don't think so. She just went to sleep."

"Blood pressure medicine?" He shook his head. "Who the hell could have done that?"

"Just about anybody at the party."

"And the police think that I . . ." His chin sank to his chest. "Where would I get blood pressure medicine? It's a prescription, isn't it? People don't just leave it lying about."

"But, Daddy, don't you see? If LouElla had access to sedatives, she may have had access to other medications, like clonidine! Did it occur to you that LouElla might be in love with you, and that she killed Darlene because she was jealous?"

"That's nonsense. She always acted properly toward me. Like a nurse. Friendly, proficient, caring, but not too personal. Very professional."

I had to admit that if LouElla had been harboring any jealous hatred of Darlene, she had hidden it well. I remembered how friendly she had been on every occasion when I had seen them together. How could this Good Samaritan, this Mother Teresa, this Florence Nightingale, this poster child for Meals on Wheels be capable of killing anyone?

"Where is she, anyway?"

"LouElla's gone to the store," I lied. "But first things first. First we get you home, then we talk to the police, then we worry about LouElla."

Daddy glanced at the bare wrist where he usually wore his watch, then looked up at me in alarm. "What day is it?"

"December twenty-seventh."

"You mean I've missed Christmas?" He looked like a little boy lost.

"If LouElla's cure worked," I said, "you'll have given us the best Christmas present we ever had. We'll have our father back."

Daddy grinned at me sheepishly. "I'm not completely helpless, sweetheart. I do have some presents wrapped up for you at home."

"Time for that later," I said, reaching for his hand. "Let's get out of here."

Daddy took two unsteady steps, then stopped dead in his tracks. "Where did you say LouElla was?" he asked again. "I need to thank her."

I knew exactly where LouElla was, but was beginning to worry that Emily would be running out of ways to keep her distracted. I hustled Daddy out of his cell, being careful to lock the bedroom door behind me. Before I helped my father down the treacherous stairs, I slipped the key back onto its hook. *Take that, LouElla Van Schuyler! A locked-room mystery of your very own. See if you can figure it out.*

I HAD REACHED A CROSSROADS, LITERALLY AND figuratively. As my car idled at the stoplight at the intersection of High and Cross, I knew what I should do. I knew I should turn left and drive straight to the Chestertown police station. I knew I should park in one of the diagonal spaces out front, walk up the steps, push through the front door, approach the counter, and ask for Captain Younger. I should tell him we'd found the fugitive. We'd found our father.

But I didn't do any of those things. I turned right and got out of Dodge as if the posse were hot on my trail.

It wasn't the posse who caught up with me, though. It was my pesky good angel. Three miles out of town on Route 213, she took control of the steering wheel and forced me to swerve into the parking lot of Dunkin' Donuts. I shifted into neutral with the engine still running. "We have to go back, Daddy."

The victim had other ideas. "Take me home."

"But you were kidnapped! We *have* to tell the police what happened."

"You can tell the police whatever you want, Hannah, but I'm not going to press charges against that woman. She gave me back my life, and I'm grateful, even if her methods were a little unorthodox." He sat in the passenger seat with his head bowed and his hands folded, as if he were praying. "I just can't believe that Darlene is dead."

I shifted into park, turned off the engine and, in the gathering silence, stared straight ahead through the windshield. I couldn't bear to look at my father, to see his pain. "That's one reason we have to see the police, Daddy. In a weird way, LouElla is your alibi."

"Not now, Hannah." He spoke so softly I could barely hear him.

"Daddy—"

"No!"

I should have known better than to try to pull rank on my father. My knuckles had been soundly rapped. After a few minutes spent staring hungrily into the window of the restaurant where doughnuts were being rearranged on large aluminum trays, I asked, "Do you have your wallet?"

"I guess so. Why?" He patted the bulge in his back pocket, reached in with two fingers, and drew out a battered tent of folded leather.

I felt my ears go red. "I left home without my purse, and I'm dying for some coffee."

He handed me a ten. "Here. I think we could both use some."

While he waited in the car, silently mourning, I went into the restaurant and bought us each a cup of strong black coffee. I doctored mine generously with milk and sugar, then with Daddy's change, I used the pay phone to call Paul at his office with the good news.

I tried to reach Emily, too, but she didn't pick up on the cell phone. She was probably still busy with Lou-Ella. Then I drove Daddy home and waited for what would happen next. *Qué será, será,* I thought. What will be, will be.

Fortunately it was Emily who first burst through our front door. "Where's Gramps? Did you find him?" She plopped Chloe and the errant Tinky Winky down on the carpet and shrugged out of her coat.

"Yes! He's upstairs. I tried to call you."

"The battery went dead on the damn phone."

I groaned. My fault. I hadn't recharged it in months.

We sat on the sofa together and traded adventures. Emily told me how LouElla had clucked over Speedo like a mother hen, but that the dog seemed unfazed by his thorough (and completely unnecessary) flea dip. Emily had dropped both dog and master off at LouElla's house, then beat it out of town, hell-bent for leather. Both of us wondered what LouElla would do once she found Daddy missing; her behavior was anything but predictable.

We kept Emily's involvement in this escapade from Daddy, who was, not surprisingly, in a blue funk. First, we installed him in front of the TV and kept him supplied with cranberry juice, soda water, and twists of lime. Then, while I began preparations for dinner, Emily called Ruth and Georgina to pass the good word. When Paul came charging through the door twenty minutes later, he found Emily sitting at the kitchen table calmly spooning strained carrots into Chloe, and me stirring the chili.

"You *are* going to call the cops, aren't you, Hannah?"

I nodded. "Soon."

"What about LouElla?"

I had to think about that. By now, LouElla would have discovered that Daddy was gone. Maybe she'd assume he'd been beamed up by aliens. I *should* let her know he'd come home, but I didn't care if her hair turned snow white with worry. How could she put us through that unnecessary suffering? Being loony tunes was no excuse.

It was very clear to me now how Daddy's car had turned up at BWI: LouElla had driven it there herself. How she'd gotten herself from the airport to Chestertown afterward, I didn't exactly know, but it had to involve a combination of trains and buses and, what with Maryland's piss-poor public transportation system, must have taken nearly all day to accomplish. Unless she sprang for a cab. I'd let the police sort that one out. I had too much on my mind right now to lose any sleep over some stupid bus schedule or cabby's trip log.

A bigger worry was that the news of Darlene's death would send Daddy crawling back down the neck of a bottle of Smirnoff, but in a way he seemed strangely calm, as if Darlene were part of a life he had chosen to leave behind, a life dulled by alcohol and grief.

That night after dinner, we settled down in the living room before a roaring fire with a Tupperware container of chocolate chip cookies and mugs of hot coffee. I put some CDs on to play, lit the candles on the mantel, and sat back to admire the tree; multicolored pin lights twinkled in synchronized waves of red, blue, white, and green, while the ornaments sparkled and twirled.

Daddy sat like a lump for a while, then suddenly spoke, as if awakening from a coma. "I see now that I wasn't really in love with Darlene. I felt sorry for her, I think, and for myself. She'd lost her husband and I'd just lost your mother . . ." His voice trailed off and he stared into the fireplace for a long moment, where the logs, still damp from the woodpile, were snapping and crackling in the flames. "Darlene had a lot of tragedy in her life."

I didn't think that was much of a reason to marry somebody. "Well, I'll never forgive her for bringing you that bottle of booze in the hospital."

With his lips pressed together, Daddy nodded. "Darlene wasn't so blind she didn't see that I had a problem; she just didn't believe I was an alcoholic."

"Why did she check you out of the hospital, then, before the tests came back?"

"She said she could teach me how to control my drinking, to cut back gradually." His head sank back into the soft cushion of the chair. He smiled sadly. "Darlene always said a little beer or wine never hurt anybody."

"Vodka isn't beer," I stated flatly.

"I know. It was LouElla who put me on the right track about that, who helped me realize that what I was doing was maintenance drinking. I'd have just enough vodka to keep from getting those monster headaches . . ." He closed his eyes and seemed to let the music wash over him. "Maybe Darlene just didn't want to drink alone," he mused.

What was it about my father, anyway? Had he stood on some street corner and shouted, *Look at me! I'm needy!* Darlene and LouElla had certainly had that in common—an attraction to men who required rehabilitation.

Using both hands, Daddy raised his mug slowly to

his lips and spoke to me over the rim. "It's like a veil has been lifted and I can see things clearly for the first time in many, many months. Even your mother's illness seems like a dream to me now, almost like it didn't happen to me, but to that person I was then. That guy whose brain was pickled in alcohol." He smiled ruefully. "I feel guilty about that."

"You have no reason to feel guilty. You were a rock to Mother. You never left her side."

"I felt numb, Hannah, like my whole body had been injected with Novocain."

"I know. I felt that way, too, when Mom died."

"We all did," Paul said.

Daddy rose and stabbed at the fire with a poker until sparks spiraled up the chimney. "We need to find out who killed her, Hannah."

At first I didn't know what he was talking about. *Mother? Killed?*

I must have looked baffled because he quickly added, "Darlene, I mean. Promise me you'll help." He stood with his back to the fire, holding the poker in both hands.

"Of course I will."

After several minutes, I picked up Paul's crossword puzzle book, turned to the back, and began making a list of possible suspects. I was operating from an advantage, after all. I knew Ruth and my father hadn't killed Darlene, so that left . . . who? I listed them in order. Darryl was my bet, or his sister, Deirdre. Darlene was hardly Mother of the Year, after all, and in spite of what Deirdre claimed, her estate must have been worth something. LouElla was a nut, but a caring, humanitarian nut. She might cheerfully cut down a terrorist with an Uzi, but poison a friend? Hardly. And

Virginia Prentice? What could have been Virginia's motive? By all accounts, she and Darlene had been only casual friends. One of the other guests at the party? I chewed on the eraser of my pencil. *Begin at the beginning*, Ms. Bromley would have advised. I started a second To Do list and wrote "Younger" at the top of it, then immediately drew a line through his name and reached for the phone.

The next day, when Captain Younger paid a house call, Daddy sat in his chair and, to put it bluntly, lied through his teeth. His interview with Chestertown's finest was a masterpiece of prevarication.

—I committed myself voluntarily, Captain, for alcohol rehabilitation.

—If I had known you were looking for me, of course I would have telephoned.

—Held against my will? Absolutely not! I needed help and Mrs. Van Schuyler was there to give it.

—So soon before the wedding? Well, that was the point, wasn't it, to be fit and sober for my wedding day?

—Of course Darlene knew about it! Encouraged me, in fact.

What an amazing collection of fibs! They belonged in *Ripley's Believe It or Not*. I just sat there, listening, my mouth flapping open and shut like a beached fish.

Younger wasn't fooled, but he could hardly make an arrest. He knew Daddy had no involvement in the hit-and-run, and there was no apparent motive for him to kill his future bride. Far better to wait until after their marriage before bumping her off, if Daddy expected to benefit from what we found out much later was Darlene's modest bank account.

Captain Younger went looking for LouElla, of course. We got this headline news from Virginia Prentice, when she telephoned to wish us a Happy New Year and say how glad she was to hear that Daddy had returned home safely. Captain Younger didn't actually talk to LouElla, Virginia informed us, because LouElla didn't answer the door. When Younger asked around the neighborhood, it turned out nobody had seen LouElla or Speedo for several days, and her car, an old Chevy station wagon, had disappeared, too.

If just the dog was missing, or LouElla, I would have worried. But the two of them together? They had to be OK. Speedo would see to that.

In my book, Darryl was a twofer. He had demonstrated a chronic need for money. He'd taken handouts from both his sister and my father. He'd had access to my father's house. He'd been among the last to leave his mother's party. Motive and opportunity. Maybe he'd decided to solve his financial problems for good by bumping off his mother before she could marry again. And you couldn't convince me that Darryl didn't have something to do with Ruth's stolen credit cards.

I decided to visit the Edgewater post office. Before leaving home, I sorted again through the photos Emily had taken at Daddy's engagement party. I found two good ones of Darryl; one staring grimly into the camera and another of his matchless profile. A little like mug shots. I tucked them into my pocket.

When I entered the spacious lobby of the new post office building, eight people were in line ahead of me. You'd think the Christmas rush would have been over. I killed some time by wandering around the lobby, studying the post office boxes, hoping to locate the one that Officer Younger told me was overstuffed. What a waste of time! None of the boxes had peepholes like in the old days, just blank, gray metal doors. With two customers still in line, I browsed through the various items for sale in the lobby shop, selecting two padded mailers, and when the last customer left, I approached the counter.

"These, please. And a book of stamps."

The clerk slapped the stamp booklet down on top of my bags.

I handed her a ten-dollar bill and waited for the change. "I'm looking for someone," I told the woman. "I wonder if you could help me."

She shrugged. "Sure."

I laid the photos of Darryl on the counter. "Have you seen this guy?"

She picked up the full-frontal shot of glamour boy and held it at eye level. "Maybe. We see so many people here it's hard to be sure."

"He might have applied for a post office box," I suggested.

"Yeah! I remember now!" She tapped Darryl's patrician nose with her finger. "He didn't have his driver's license with him the first time, and had to go back for it." She pushed the picture back to me. "He's cuter in real life."

I smiled back at her grimly. "Oh, Darryl is cute all right." I retrieved the picture. "Thanks."

"No problem."

I left the post office thinking two things. Maybe I should tape Darryl's picture up on the wall with the other FBI Most Wanted posters. And two, Captain Younger was going to get another telephone call from me.

Back home, I found Daddy sitting morosely at my kitchen table, nursing a cup of coffee, long gone cold. Ruth had dropped his mail off on her way to work and Daddy was sorting through it, his eyes looking tired and sad. Small wonder. He'd pegged the meter on his blood alcohol test and unless the judge let him off for good behavior, Daddy wouldn't be driving anywhere for a very long time. But it wasn't the suspension notice from the DMV I saw him staring at. It was a familiar blue-and-yellow folder from a local travel agent.

"What's that, Daddy?" I asked.

"Cruise tickets."

I realized at once what they must have been for: his honeymoon with Darlene. I stood behind his chair and placed my hands on his shoulders. With my cheek next to his ear I asked, "Where were you going?"

"To Cancún."

"You should be able to get a refund." I swallowed hard. "Under the circumstances."

"I don't want a refund."

"So, what are you going to do with them?" I was a silly millimeter away from tears.

"I don't know, sweetheart. I just don't know."

ON THE LAST DAY OF 1999, THE DAY THAT WAS TO have been Daddy's wedding day, we conspired to keep him busy. After a fortifying lunch of split pea soup and hunks of sourdough bread, I contrived to look so pitifully inept that he volunteered to clean the ashes out of both fireplaces. Then I walked him from our house all the way to Mother Earth with him complaining the whole way, "What? You afraid I can't take care of myself, Hannah?"

We were on Maryland Avenue at the time, just passing the entrance to Galway Bay. I thought about the cheerful bar inside and about all the other friendly Annapolis watering holes Daddy used to frequent and said simply, "Yes."

Ruth welcomed her shift as caretaker. She gave Daddy a quick lesson in cash register management—reassuring him that its computerized brain wouldn't go into Y2K-induced seizure at the stroke of midnight—then put him to work behind the counter while she busied herself restocking the shelves. I hung around for a while, chatting, until Daddy rang up a sale for Cornelia Gibbs, a widow we knew from St. Anne's Church. I eased out of the store, smiling. Daddy was attractive, charming, and sober. It wouldn't be long before he'd begin dating again, his affair with Darlene merely a chapter in a closed book. I hoped the book would end with the revelation of her killer.

Back home, Emily and Dante were preparing to leave for First Night Annapolis's gala citywide, multi-event New Year's Eve celebrations. Chloe lay placidly on the sofa and was allowing herself to be dressed in one of the outfits I'd given her for Christmas: a pink turtleneck shirt tucked into a pair of Calvin Klein minijeans that cost almost as much as the ones I buy for myself. Miniature Nike tennis shoes and pink, lace-trimmed socks completed the ensemble. As I said, the saleswoman saw me coming.

Dante picked up a Santa cap from the sofa and slipped it on his head, settling it carefully over his neatly combed ponytail. He fiddled with the snowball dangling from the end of the cap until, to my amazement, the ball began blinking. Emily giggled and kissed her husband on the nose. "A man of culture, refinement, and taste." She swatted the ball with the back of her hand, setting it swinging. "And way cool."

While Emily slipped into a coat, I pulled my granddaughter's arms through the sleeves of her pink Polartec jacket then helped Dante wrestle her into the Gerry pack. I watched with affection as the three of them hustled out the front door and down the steps.

I was waving good-bye from the porch when Emily turned. "Oh, by the way, Mom, there's a wacko message from LouElla Van Schuyler on the machine."

Dante adjusted Chloe's legs more comfortably around

his waist and added, "That woman gets stranger and stranger. She needs to be locked up."

"She's a little kooky, but I don't think she's dangerous," I said. I was actually relieved to hear that she had turned up safely.

"I don't agree, Mrs. Ives. Since your father got away from her, she's lost focus. I think she's going off the deep end."

"Yeah, Mom. Listen to the message. She was threatening Virginia Prentice." Emily pulled her gloves off and tucked them into her pocket. She took a step closer. "I don't know how you can be nice to LouElla after all the anguish she put us through with Gramps. I'll *never* forgive her for that."

I was struggling to deal with that, too, but the fact remained that Daddy was stone cold sober and hadn't had a drink in almost two weeks. But it was more than that. His *attitude* toward drinking had changed. And he'd joined Alcoholics Anonymous. I had to give LouElla full credit for that.

With long fingers circling his daughter's ankles, Dante pranced Chloe around in a tight circle. "I agree with Em, Mrs. Ives. This time LouElla's really lost it. Seems that Virginia's been putting viruses into people's mailboxes in order to take over the world for Communism."

"Or something," Emily added. "She's so wigged out that I called Mrs. Prentice to warn her. I asked her to keep an eye on Mrs. Van Schuyler. They're supposed to be friends, aren't they?"

I nodded. "I certainly thought so."

Dante sniffed. "Some friend! Keeping track of everything you do in some stupid notebook and threatening to reveal your deepest, darkest secrets to the tabloids."

I had to smile at the picture of Virginia tiptoeing around town, anointing the mailboxes in Chestertown with some exotic virus. "So, what did Virginia say to that?"

"Not much."

"She wasn't upset?"

"Hardly. She just laughed hysterically and said not to worry. Who'd believe that crazy old broad?" Emily tugged on the zipper of her jacket. "Then she wanted to know what we were doing for New Year's, so I bored her with that for a while." Emily shrugged. "That's about it."

Dante added, "LouElla said she'd try to get you on your cell phone."

Emily's face grew serious. "Why did you give your cell phone number to that nutcase, Mother?"

"When I was looking for your grandfather, I gave my telephone numbers to everyone in the world."

Emily adjusted the straps on Chloe's backpack. "Well, don't say I didn't warn you."

I promised to listen to LouElla's message and waved my little family off in the direction of their first stop, St. John's College, where they were going to see Kohl and Company, a comedy magic act that the First Night program in the newspaper guaranteed would split your sides. I stepped back into the house and closed the door firmly behind me, then leaned against it. The curious part of my brain wanted to listen to LouElla's message right away; the practical part yearned to hit the three button and send her ramblings into oblivion, then go get my sides split along with Emily and Dante. But I was expecting Paul home any minute.

Although it was only three-thirty, I opened the refrigerator, poured myself a glass of cold Chablis, pulled a chair up to the phone, and reached for the receiver. I held it to my ear for a few seconds, listening to the dial tone. Then I took a sip of wine, dialed the phone company's answering service, and punched in our code.

For someone so experienced in espionage, LouElla seemed to have very little expertise with recording devices.

"Hello? Hello?"

I heard a metal object hitting the floor.

"This is LouElla. LouElla Van Schuyler. Uh . . . uh. Hannah?"

Another clang. Maybe a pot lid.

"Virginia Prentice tells me your father came home. I'm so relieved! I spent days and days looking for him."

So that's where she's been. Serves her right! I hope she got blisters!

"Virginia says that you were very, very upset with me. That troubles me, it really does. But, please! Let me explain."

This had better be good!

"Your father entrusted himself to the Phoenix program and into my care, and I couldn't betray that trust. Doctor-patient confidentiality, as you know, extends to nurse practitioners as well . . ."

I was equally sure that it didn't.

". . . so you see my dilemma."

There was a long pause, filled with the sound of music playing softly in the background, something bouncy out of the fifties, a tune that sounded vaguely familiar.

"I must caution you, though, Hannah dear, to be more judicious in your choice of people in whom to confide. I've had my eye on Virginia for a long, long time. I find her completely unreliable. The other day I caught her on David White's porch, pawing through the items

in his mailbox. Pawing! When challenged, she showed me a package from L.L. Bean and claimed it had been misdelivered. Said she was just putting it in the proper mailbox. Hah!"

Just then I recognized the tune. Rosemary Clooney was singing "Mambo Italiano." I strained to pick up the words.

"I observed her at Ellen Swain's and Marty O'Malley's a while ago, too. There can't be that many misdelivered packages. Our postman isn't a moron! Hah! I warned Virginia over and over about this, and I've told the postmaster, too, but do they listen to me? They do not. Doesn't everyone know that interfering with the U.S. mail is a federal offense? You can never be too careful. You never know what wicked people are going to put in your mailbox."

I thought about all the junk mail I'd been receiving lately and had to agree that something wicked was indeed going on. Then I wondered about the nasty cards Darlene had been receiving. If LouElla was correct in her observations, could Virginia have been responsible for them? If so, what was her grudge against Darlene? Or had other people been receiving Nasty-Grams, too? I sipped my wine. The last time I'd heard "Mambo Italiano" it was on *Your Hit Parade,* that TV show sponsored by tap-dancing packs of Old Gold cigarettes. I was tapping my own foot and singing silently along with Miss Clooney when LouElla veered hard right and the "Oh, ho, Joe, you mixed-up Siciliano" flew right out of my head.

"I'll bet you thought that smallpox had been eradicated, didn't you?"

I was fairly certain of that. By the time Emily was

born, pediatricians were no longer recommending that children be vaccinated.

"Well, it hasn't, dear! Ronald Reagan warned us not to trust the Evil Empire, didn't he? And he was right, the man was right! With callous disregard for human life, those Russians saved some of that virus."

I remembered that the United States had saved some, too, in deep, secure vaults at Fort Dietrich in western Maryland. But LouElla was way ahead of me.

"Of course, we needed to save the virus, too, in case those scoundrels decided to use it as a biological weapon and we needed to make vaccine."

She took a deep breath, then launched in with renewed vigor, her voice spiraling upward in her excitement.

"Now one of those Russians has defected to Libya and he's taken the virus with him! Do you realize what this means? Do you, Hannah?"

If what she said were true, one could only imagine the havoc that a virus like that would wreak in the hands of a maniac like Qaddafi. Smallpox let loose in a subway tunnel? Introduced into the water supply of a major American city? Why hadn't we heard about this on *Sixty Minutes* or the eleven o'clock news?

"Everyone under the age of thirty will be dropping like flies," LouElla warned. *"We'd never be able to manufacture enough vaccine to vaccinate everybody in time. It's an evil conspiracy to get rid of all the young ones, isn't it? First the babies, then the teens, then all the brave young men who would be our best defense in time of war!"*

Then LouElla found a chink in my armor, stuck the tip of her knife in, and twisted.

"Don't you see? You'd be spared and so would I,

Hannah. We've been protected. But Emily and Chloe, precious little Chloe, they've never been vaccinated, have they?" She paused, as if waiting for me to answer her. *"No. I thought not. So, we have to be vigilant. We have to be careful. Think about it! What do we know about Virginia before she came here? Not much, do we? Virginia's husband was assassinated for a reason. Somebody wanted to stop him."*

There was more, much more, about caches of weapons in the hands of private militias right here in "Merry-Land," about the perils of our nuclear power plant at Calvert Cliffs, and about water fluoridation conspiracies that I thought had gone out of fashion with Mamie Eisenhower's bangs and fitted hats. I began to relax.

I was still sitting there, sipping wine and listening to LouElla rave on about how misunderstood Ollie North was, when Paul breezed through the kitchen door like a breath of fresh air. He approached me from behind and kissed the top of my head. "Ed Metzger was terrific!"

"Who's he?" I suspected Ed was some sort of computer guru, brought in by the Naval Academy to handle Y2K compliance.

"Plays Einstein, the practical Bohemian. I stopped by the Legislative Services building this afternoon just in time to catch his show." He pointed to the phone. "What's up?" he whispered.

I pushed 33 on the keypad, cutting LouElla off in mid-rant, then 2 to save the message in our in-box. Maybe I'd finish listening to it later . . . much, much later. "It's a message from LouElla Van Schuyler." I stood, hung up the phone, and turned to face my husband. "She wants our help saving the world from Virginia Prentice."

"And you're taking her seriously?"

"LouElla's grasp of reality is rather on-again, off-again, isn't it?" I said, more to reassure myself than my husband.

"Then let it go, Hannah. Relax." He used his thumbs to knead the tension out of the muscles over my shoulder blades.

"I'll try. Emily did call Virginia to warn her that LouElla was having one of her off days." I gestured with my glass. "Wine?"

"You read my mind."

I poured Paul a glass of Chablis and we sat down together at the kitchen table. "So, you were out gallivanting, huh? And I thought you'd be spending the afternoon making sure the math department computers wouldn't go into meltdown tonight."

"No, we didn't need to do anything special with the computers." Paul raised his glass. "Mark my words, Hannah, Y2K will go down in history as the biggest bust since Comet Kahotec." He took a sip of wine and leaned back in his chair with a sigh. "I had to write up a couple of MAPR reports is all, for some mids who have to appear before the Academic Board. But I finished early so I thought I'd catch the Einstein show." He rested his elbows on the table and rolled the wineglass between his palms. "So, what does the old dear want this time?" he asked, referring to LouElla's message.

"To warn me about smallpox virus on the loose."

"Oh." He smiled. "Is that all?"

"And to wish us a Happy New Year," I said.

Paul laughed out loud. "Are you going to return her call?"

I shook my head. "She left me her number, but I doubt I'll use it." I grinned. "That would be one sure way to spoil our evening."

Paul grinned back. "Speaking of which, what's the plan for tonight?"

"Emily and Dante already took their admission buttons and have gone with Chloe to the magic show at St. John's, then they're going to get their faces painted and after that, I think it's the *Punch and Judy Show*."

Paul glanced around the kitchen where there was absolutely no evidence of a meal being prepared, raised an eyebrow, and asked, "Dinner?"

"We're stopping by Mother Earth to pick up Daddy and Ruth, then we've reservations for dinner at McGarvey's."

Paul carefully positioned his glass in the wet ring it had made on the tabletop. "McGarvey's? I thought you'd had enough of that place."

I shrugged. "Daddy's choice. I think he's hoping to run into Darryl. He actually liked the guy."

"I thought Darryl would be arrested by now."

"Younger tells me he needs proof. Based on what the clerk at the post office said, he'll probably be able to get a search warrant. He's looking for the fake ID Darryl used to set up the post office box. And credit card receipts. There's also the possibility he's been taking advantage of his position as a waiter to steal credit card numbers from customers at McGarvey's." I remembered my recent lunch there with Deirdre and was glad I had paid cash. "There may be merchandise, too, although Younger suspects Darryl's already fenced most of it."

"And in the meantime?" Paul asked.

"In the meantime we have to live with the creep." Captain Younger had asked me not to tell anybody what I had learned about Darryl at the post office for fear it would leak back to him. I had sworn Paul to secrecy, of course, but it took every bit of willpower I possessed not to set Ruth's mind at ease. I tugged at Paul's hand. "C'mon. We need to get dressed."

Paul remained firmly seated. "If Ruth's going with us, who's minding the store?" He nibbled playfully on my fingers.

"She's arranged for some temporary help."

"Are the kids going to join us?" Paul asked, referring to Emily and her husband.

I smiled. "No. Dante didn't want to rent a tux."

"Tux? What for?"

"Dinner at McGarvey's is special tonight. Black tie." Before Paul could groan, I laid my fingers lightly on his lips and cooed, "And I'll be wearing my new electric blue number."

Paul clutched at his heart with both hands. "Short skirt? Spangles? Back bare all the way down to your ratsgazabo?"

I nodded. "The very same."

"My goose," he said, "is cooked."

"I certainly hope so." I told Paul that the kids planned to pick up a bite somewhere on Main Street and that we'd meet them at the laser light show at City Dock around eleven. Then we'd wander over to the sea wall where we'd have an unobstructed view of the count-down clock and the fireworks.

"Isn't midnight a little late for the wee one?"

I shrugged. "Lighten up, old man. It's the new millennium, a once-in-a-lifetime experience."

Paul looked around. "Does that mean nobody's home?"

"Just us chickens."

"How about a little Afternoon Delight?" He took my hand and pulled me around the table and into his lap.

Outside our kitchen window, the winter sun had set. The bare branches of the trees danced in black silhouettes against the tangerine-and-pink sky. "Five o'clock is afternoon?"

He kissed me then, soft and long, his tongue just tickling my lips in a way that drives me crazy. Later, much later, as I stood in the shower with the hot water sluicing over my head, I remembered something. First thing after the holiday, I'd call Captain Younger about it. It was about the mailboxes. Maybe Virginia wasn't putting things into mailboxes at all. Maybe she was taking things out.

NEW YEAR'S EVE IN ANNAPOLIS, MARYLAND—A symphony of lights and music and laughter. Streets in the historic district, closed to the usual traffic, thronged with people in a holiday frame of mind. Paul and I, our formal wear covered with casual coats, joined the celebration, wandering up Maryland Avenue, taking advantage of the late-night hours to window-shop and spoil our dinner with the cookies and hot, spiced cider— champagne, if we were lucky—many shops put out for their customers.

Peggy Kimble snagged us as we strolled by Galway Bay and charged us with desertion for passing up their Irish shindig in favor of the one at McGarvey's. Looking sheepish, I blamed it all on my father. The petite hostess, stunning in a white tux jacket and black slacks, good-naturedly shamed us into having a drink at the bar. When the staff began setting up for dinner, we waved a cheery good-bye and moved on.

At Aurora Gallery I oohed and aahed over a jeweled enameled pin, but Paul was being obtuse. As we left the store, Jean shot me a conspiratorial wink; she'd place the jewelry on hold. When my birthday rolled around in February and Paul turned up, clueless, she'd need to look no further than her hold drawer for a suggestion.

I dived into Nancy Hammond's studio to admire a cut-paper-and-tempera painting of a Caribbean isle that had me pining for last year's vacation in the British Virgins. I batted my eyelashes. Paul claimed he had forgotten his checkbook. Besides, he pointed out reasonably, I hadn't even found a place to hang the painting L.K. Bromley had given me.

We strolled around State Circle with hundreds of revelers, then cut through the alley next to the roped-off pit where our favorite Indian restaurant had burned to the ground two Christmases ago. Like most Annapolitans, I wanted to bury the owner of this eyesore up to the neck in his own rubble.

We wandered up to the Court House where I thought we might meet up with Emily and Dante, but they'd apparently moved on. "Let's go." I pulled on the sleeve of Paul's overcoat.

"This looks interesting." Paul planted his shiny black Corfams on a carpet of flattened cardboard which had been taped securely to the floor. From the table in front of him, he selected a red plastic disposable cup with a number taped to the side. He stared inside, as if contemplating a sip of its contents, a particularly unappealing cocktail of peacock blue paint. He looked from the cup to me to the dozens of paint-by-number portraits set up on easels around the room—Einstein, Shakespeare, Napoleon, Churchill, Kennedy, Elvis— all waiting for the next Leonardo da Vinci to step up, paintbrush in hand.

Paul smiled at me like a kid, his eyes bright with excitement. I shrugged permission. How could I resist?

I was sure he'd paint Einstein. He fooled me, though. I waited, patiently amused, until he dabbed the final splotch of silver paint on the canvas of his masterpiece. Then he made me blush by singing "Burning Love" in his ruined baritone all the way around Church Circle and down Main Street, each "hunka hunka" delivered with teenage exuberance directly into my ear.

In a window of the Annapolis Shirt Company a few doors down from Mother Earth, we watched Leigh Bo, a mime wearing a white tailcoat with a fuschia tie and cummerbund, perform magic maneuvers with her top hat. By the time we barged through the door at Mother Earth, extracted the owner and her father, said hello to the temp, and listened to Ruth tell us three times how she should have gone the temporary route a long time ago, Leigh Bo was being replaced by the Beauty Shop Quartet wearing pink satin shirts and black bow ties.

Darryl, oozing so much charm that I wondered if it hurt, met us at the door of McGarvey's. I could hardly bear to look at him. Exuding bonhomie, he escorted us to a round table in the back. Before sitting down, Daddy extended his hand to shake Darryl's while simultaneously gripping the younger man's bulging biceps. "I'm sorry I wasn't around to help after your mother died."

"I heard you came unglued," Darryl said bluntly.

Daddy mustered up a smile from somewhere. "It's as good an explanation as any."

Darryl laid beer label coasters about on the table. "What can I get you to drink?"

I wanted a beer in the worst way, could practically taste it, could feel the hops and the malt exploding on my taste buds. I ordered an iced tea. With a quick questioning glance in my direction, Ruth ordered a coffee. When Paul followed suit by requesting a Diet Coke, Daddy shaped his hands into a T. "Wait a minute! Time out!"

All heads, including Darryl's, swiveled in his direction. "Don't coddle me, please! I've got to learn to live in the real world, a world where other people drink alcoholic beverages. Otherwise, what's the point?" He pointed a finger at Darryl. "Sam Adams all around, Darryl. And bring *me* a cup of coffee, black."

When Darryl returned with our drinks order, Daddy said, "Can you join us for a moment?"

I held my breath, dreading a yes.

Darryl laughed. "Not if I want to keep this job. I'm not even your server." He waved a slim blond woman over to the table. "Take good care of these folks, Mary Ellen," he told her. "They're relatives of mine." He tipped an imaginary hat. "Later, dudes!"

Mentally, I shot arrows into his retreating back while Mary Ellen took our orders. When my quiver was empty, I sat back and watched Daddy as he sipped his coffee, trying to decide if he was comfortable with it or fighting with every molecule not to reach out, grab Ruth's beer, and down it in a single gulp.

My father must have read my mind. "LouElla was a gift from God," he said.

"How can you say that, Daddy?" Ruth fumed. "She held you prisoner, like that poor guy in the Stephen King story." She looked to me for support. "You know, the movie with Kathy Bates and James Caan?"

"*Misery?*"

"Yeah, that one."

Daddy smiled. "LouElla wasn't offering to break my legs with a baseball bat if I didn't shape up."

"Still, you were being held against your will."

"For the last time, Ruth, I was there because I wanted to be there."

I decided to jump in before Ruth ended up spoiling the evening. "You know, Ruth, I was thinking back to the party, and what happened may have been partly my fault. I was going into the living room to check on Chloe and I remember pointing to Daddy and asking LouElla to keep an eye on him. I didn't realize she'd take me quite so literally."

"She lied to us, Hannah."

"I'm certain that in her own mind, she wasn't lying, just giving us her own cockeyed interpretation of the truth." I nibbled on a bit of the smoked bluefish that had just appeared on the table in front of us. "For example, she told me, 'I'm sure he'll turn up hale and hearty'—"

Daddy interrupted. "And abracadabra! Here I hale and heartily sit!"

I stared at him suspiciously, wondering if he weren't trying too hard to be jovial. "And when she said . . ."

"George?"

I paused in mid-sentence, unaccountably annoyed at the interruption, and turned in the direction of the speaker. Deirdre wore knee-high black boots and a slim, shimmery strapless gown in an odd shade of green that did little to detract from her pale, washed-out face. Her too-black hair stuck up in overmoussed spikes. She looked like a "before" photo in a magazine makeover.

Daddy sprang to his feet, nearly knocking over his

chair. "Deirdre! Do join us!" He grabbed a chair from
the adjoining table and dragged it over to ours, squeezing it into the space between his chair and Ruth's.
Deirdre heaved herself into it with a grateful sigh.
"Thank God! A friendly face."

"Here for First Night celebrations?" Ruth asked.

"What a zoo! I had to park way down on South
Street." Deirdre turned to Ruth. "I'm only here to
switch cars with Darryl. He's going skiing again and
doesn't trust his jalopy to make it all the way to
Vermont."

I wondered what had happened to Darryl's fancy
motorcycle. I hoped it had been repossessed. It would
have been a sight, though, to see him riding up I-95
with skis and poles tied to the side of his Harley.
I wondered how he'd attach them to his mother's
Porsche.

Paul passed me a plate of crab balls and I picked
one up with my fingers. Just as I popped it into my
mouth, my beaded bag began to squawk. I plucked out
the cell phone and stared at the illuminated window
where the incoming number was displayed. "LouElla,"
I groaned. I made an executive decision. LouElla had
interfered with one too many family dinners, so I decided to punish her by stuffing the phone back into the
depths of my bag. I chewed on the crab ball and tried
to ignore the ringing tone that Emily had changed
from Mozart's 40th Symphony to laser gun warfare
from *Star Wars*.

"Why don't you want to talk to LouElla?" Deirdre
inquired.

Ruth beat me to the draw. "She's got some crazy
theory about Virginia Prentice. What was it, Hannah?"

She stared at me from across the table. "Smallpox virus in the drinking water?"

"Who's Virginia Prentice?" Deirdre wanted to know.

Paul pushed the empty crab ball plate across the green-and-white checked tablecloth toward the center of the table. "You probably remember her from the engagement party. Stark white hair, red plaid suit?"

"Boston accent," I added.

"Not really Boston," Daddy corrected. "She's from Row Die Lan."

"Rhode Island?" I poked him in the ribs with my index finger. It was wonderful to have my old Daddy back, along with his sense of humor.

Deirdre leaned back to allow Mary Ellen to set a steaming bowl of Maryland crab soup in front of her. "I remember her now." She picked up her spoon. "You know, that name Prentice rings a bell." Squinting thoughtfully, she tapped the spoon against her chin. "I think Carson McPhee was married to a woman named Prentice before he married Mother."

Now it was Ruth's turn to ask, "Who's Carson McPhee?"

"Lucky husband number two." She grinned wickedly over her soup spoon. "He augered his Piper Cub into a cornfield in New Jersey rather than stay married to Mother. My theory, anyway."

Something LouElla had said was nibbling at the edges of my brain. Wasn't Carson McPhee from Fall River, Massachusetts? Or was it the Tinsley guy? The Lizzie Borden house was in Fall River, too. I had visited the Borden house once, and remembered Fall River being just across the state line from Tiverton, so close to Rhode Island it was practically in it. And didn't

Virginia tell me she came from Tiverton? With growing curiosity I asked, "Who was the first Mrs. McPhee?"

Deirdre wrinkled her brow. "I don't remember. Maybe Darryl does."

When Mary Ellen returned with our entrees I asked her to find Darryl and send him over to our table.

Eventually Darryl swaggered over, tucking a plastic bill server into the back of his pants. "Whatcha want, Didi?"

"Didi" rolled her eyes. "Do you remember the name of the woman Carson divorced so he could marry Mother?"

Darryl squinted and wagged his head back and forth like a metronome, thinking hard. "Can you give me a hint?"

"She was youngish. Had a name like an actress, you know, the one with the fat lips?"

Darryl's face brightened. "Kim Basinger?" he tried.

Deirdre shook her head. "Not that one. She was with Hugh Grant . . ." She turned to me in triumph. "Julia Roberts! That's it. Her name was Julia. Julia Prentice."

I tried to remember if Virginia had mentioned her daughter's name, but couldn't.

Deirdre favored her brother with a plastic smile. "Thank you, Darryl. You've been *such* a help!"

"Don't mention it, dudette." He thrummed his fingers on the top of his sister's head, disturbing her over-laquered do, then moved quickly out of the range of the flat of her palm.

"Does that help?" Deirdre asked as she fluffed up her hair with nimble pinches.

"Yes, thank you." I nibbled thoughtfully on a cracker.

"Virginia told me she'd had a daughter once, but she died. I wonder what her name was."

"You could always ask her," Paul suggested.

"That would be insensitive."

"I'll bet LouElla knows," offered Deirdre. "She knows everything."

I remembered LouElla's dining room lookout post and was sure she knew a lot about a lot of things. The problem was sifting the truth out of the fantasy. I sat there in a haze listening to the banter going on around me—the subject had shifted to Super Bowl XXXIV—but I couldn't have cared less about the Rams or the Titans. In my right ear, Ruth's voice was insisting that the Rams were from Los Angeles and on my left Paul was saying St. Louis, St. Louis, while a voice in my head kept repeating Prentice, Prentice, Prentice, Julia Prentice. What if Virginia Prentice's daughter had been married to Carson McPhee and Darlene had broken up the marriage? That would give Virginia a powerful motive to bump off Darlene. Revenge.

Then there was the funny business with the mailboxes. Something I'd overheard at Darlene's party was gonging loudly in my head. Hadn't Marty O'Malley, the charming retiree, mentioned something about getting his prescriptions by mail?

Ruth was conceding that the Titans were from Tennessee when I excused myself and took the stairs to the second floor. I parked myself in the hallway next to the cigarette machine, reached into my bag, and pulled out the cell phone. I dialed four-one-one and asked directory assistance for Marty O'Malley's number in Chestertown. For an extra thirty-five cents I let the operator connect me, then waited impatiently through the rings, praying that Marty was spending the waning hours of 1999 at home in front of his television set.

On the sixth ring, someone picked up. "O'Malley."

"Marty, this is Hannah Ives. Remember me? From Darlene's party?"

He remembered me, down to the sweater I was wearing.

"Sorry to bother you tonight of all nights but I was just wondering something. You get your prescriptions by mail, right?"

"Saves me money."

"Has any medicine ever gone missing?"

"Once or twice a shipment got lost, but they always replaced it."

"What medicine did you lose?"

"Vitamins once. And my stress medicine."

"What do you take for stress?"

"I can't remember. Just a minute." Marty clunked the receiver down. While I waited, listening to his TV playing softly in the background, I paced the hallway outside the rest rooms. It seemed like forever before he returned, rattling the pill bottle in my ear.

"Something called Compres."

I swore softly and sagged against the wall. Must be a brand name. "What do they look like?" I asked.

Marty rattled the bottle again. "Little orange buggers with a seven on 'em."

My heart did a *rat-a-tat-tat* on my ribs. Clonodine hydrochloride! I thanked Marty and wished him a happy New Year. I leaned against the wall, still holding the phone, trying to catch my breath and wondering what to do next. Circumstantial evidence, I told myself. Nothing that would hold up in a court of law. But Captain

Younger needed to know about this. I rummaged in my bag, looking for the card he had given me. You'd think I'd have the blasted number memorized by now. I couldn't find it in any of the pockets or nooks and crannies so I called 911, asked to be connected to the Chestertown Police, and left a message for Younger to call me. I was putting the cell phone back in my bag when Darryl appeared at the top of the stairs.

He swaggered in my direction, his lips twisted into a half smile, half sneer. "Hannah! We can't go on meeting this way."

I looked for an escape route, but I was standing in an alcove next to the cigarette machine. Now Darryl hovered between me and the emergency exit on the landing. He was so close I could tell he'd had garlic for dinner. I lifted my bag and clutched it to my chest, like a shield, fighting the urge to clobber him with it. "I had to make a phone call."

He loomed closer. "Calling the boyfriend, huh?"

I hugged my bag even closer. "Do you mind if I tell you something?"

He folded his arms and leaned toward me. "What?"

"You are disgusting."

"That's no way to talk. Didn't your mother teach you manners?"

That wounded, as he knew it would. I yearned to slap that triumphant look off his face. "Get out of my way, Darryl."

He touched a finger to my cheek. "I could have been your brother."

My head was so far back against the wall that I had to duck to one side to escape. "But now, happily," I shot back at him, "that doesn't seem very likely."

"I'm just trying to be friendly."

I prayed somebody would show up to use the rest room soon. Usually there was a line a mile long. If nobody came, I might have to get physical with this irritating creep. "If you don't get out of my way, I'm going to start screaming."

He ignored me. "Didi is such a stuck-up bitch. Thinks she knows everything."

I put my hand against his chest and pushed him away. "Move!"

Darryl raised his hands, palms out, and took a step backward. "OK, OK. Don't get all bent out of shape."

I scurried around him and bolted for the stairs.

"Don't you want to know about Julia Prentice?"

As much as I wanted to put twenty-five miles, maybe even an ocean, between me and the Dearly Departed's son, his question pulled me up short. Halfway down the stairs I turned and looked up at him.

"I thought so." He leered.

"What about her?" I asked, hoping that he wouldn't ask me to do him any favors in exchange for this information.

"Come here."

"If you can't say what you have to say from up there, forget it."

He shrugged. "OK. Just thought you'd be interested to know that Julia Prentice killed herself."

I swallowed my revulsion long enough to ask "How?"

"Jumped off the Mount Hope Bridge."

I shuddered. "Does anybody know why?"

"Couldn't deal with the divorce, I suppose, and the prospect of raising her baby alone."

"She had a child?"

"Sort of. She was seven months pregnant when she took the plunge."

I staggered back, catching myself against the wall. Poor Virginia. If she held Darlene responsible for her daughter's death and that of her grandchild . . .

"Mother considered it a lucky break," he continued, peering down the staircase and studying my face as if to gauge my reaction. "Carson not having to go through the trauma of divorce and all."

Maybe my father had a lucky break, too, then. The words hovered on the tip of my tongue, but I remembered I was supposed to be a grown-up. I clamped my lips tight and forced myself to look at Darlene's poor excuse for a son. "My father is devastated by your mother's death."

Darryl leered. "Yeah, well, I'm sorry about that." He started down the steps. "I can think of a lot worse things than being your stepbrother, sis."

I'd have a better chance of being struck by an asteroid than ever being related to a troglodyte like you. With admirable self-control, I managed a grim smile. "As I said, Darryl. I don't think that's very likely."

"Don't count on it, Hannah. I've seen how your father's been looking at Deirdre lately." His teeth gleamed white in the shadows at the head of the stairs. "How does Uncle Darryl grab you?"

The duck I had eaten for dinner rose to the back of my throat, and I thought I might do a Linda Blair all over the loathsome toad. Rather than give him the satisfaction of seeing me rattled, I turned and fled down the stairs, into the lights and comforting din of the crowded restaurant.

And ran smack dab into Ruth, who had been

appointed head of the search party sent to find out what was keeping me. "Hannah! You're red as a beet. Are you OK?"

"That Darryl is a creep."

"You won't get any argument from me." She peered into the depths of my eyes as if more information were hidden there. "What happened?"

"I'll tell you later. C'mon, let's get back to the others."

Paul, looking relieved, stood up when we appeared and held my chair out until I'd settled down into it. He kissed my cheek. "Thank God. I thought maybe you'd fallen in."

I patted his cheek and managed a smile. "It took longer than I thought." I'd fill him in later. Paul, who took care of business in men's rooms as if they had revolving doors, always claimed to be completely baffled by why women took so long to accomplish the same thing, so he accepted my explanation without question.

Deirdre was staring at me curiously. I wondered if my cowlick was misbehaving again, or if I had spinach on my teeth. How old was she, anyway? Twenty-eight? Twenty-nine? How would I feel having a stepmother fifteen years younger than I was? I shook away the thought. The hell with Darryl; he was just rattling my cage. I sprinkled some salt and pepper on my duck and took a bite, surprised to find it hadn't grown cold, and consoled myself by picturing *him* behind bars.

Deirdre pushed her soup bowl toward the center of the table and stood. "Well, sports fans. Gotta go."

Daddy and Paul rose politely. Daddy extended his hand; when Deirdre took it, he covered both their hands with his left. "Are you sure you wouldn't like to stay and see in the New Year with us?" I held my breath, hoping she had other plans. Like having to alphabetize her spice rack. Or neuter her houseplants.

"No, sorry. I've got to get back to Bowie. My roommates are having a party and I'm expected to make the pizza." She turned to us. "Bye. Happy New Year."

We watched her go, Daddy looking wistful, whether from melancholy over what might have been with Darlene or for some hope of a new relationship with her daughter it was impossible to tell.

I worried about this through the rest of my roast duck, but by the time Mary Ellen cleared the dishes and began hovering tableside for our dessert order, Daddy had remained so cheerful that I knew Darryl was full of baloney.

When my cell phone rang again, catching me in mid–Key lime pie, I hurried to answer it, thinking it had to be Captain Younger.

But I was wrong.

"Hannah, thank goodness I got you!"

I closed my eyes. "Hi, LouElla."

"No time to chat! Hurry! You've got to find Emily and warn her!"

"What the hell are you talking about?" All eyes at our table and several pairs from the adjoining tables glommed on to me.

"Virginia's gone crazy! She just came over here and demanded my log book."

That was the silliest thing I ever heard, but there was no use telling LouElla that. "Why would she do that?"

"She hit me in the face. Knocked me over," LouElla whimpered. "I'm going to have a black eye."

"I'm sorry, LouElla, but what can I do to help?"

"She's going to destroy it, obliterate it, wipe it off the face of the earth! Oh, my poor log book!"

An alarm clanged in my head. "What does all this have to do with Emily, LouElla?"

"Emily?" LouElla paused, as if she'd lost her train of thought.

"Yes, Emily. What were you saying about Emily?"

"Oh! It was Emily who told Virginia about my log book. I'm sure Emily didn't mean any harm by it, and I certainly don't hold anything against the dear girl, but Virginia says that now Emily's seen what's written in it, she'll have to be stopped."

I sighed. Another one of LouElla's loopy conspiracy theories. "That doesn't make any sense, LouElla. You *wrote* the log book and she didn't stop you."

"That's what I told her, but Virginia said that *no-body'd* believe a crazy old witch like me." She snuffled noisily. "Except she used the B-word."

"I'm sure you're overreacting."

"No, I'm not. You should have seen her face! All red and purple and the veins in her neck popping out."

I needed to drag LouElla back on track before she wandered down a divergent path. "You said she went looking for Emily?"

"She blames you, Hannah, for messing up her plans. She said there was only one way to make you understand why she had to do it. You were going to find out, firsthand, how it feels."

How it feels? Adrenaline suddenly shot through my veins, cold as ice water, but I had to ask. I had to be sure. "How what feels, LouElla?"

"How it feels to lose a child."

I leapt up from my chair, clutching the cell phone to

my ear with both hands. "LouElla! Look out your window. Is Virginia's car still parked in the lane?"

"Just a minute."

I filled the time with silent prayer: *please, oh, please, oh, please, oh . . .*

"She's just leaving!" LouElla seemed suddenly focused. "But don't you worry! I'll follow her. I'm good at it."

"Don't hang up!" I shouted. "Wait a minute!"

"It'll be OK," LouElla soothed. "I've trained with the best."

"What makes Virginia think she can find Emily, LouElla? It's New Year's Eve. The city is packed with people."

"Emily told her where she was going."

"Oh, my God!"

"And, Hannah?"

"What?"

"I know for a fact that Virginia owns a gun."

The phone went dead in my ear.

EVERYONE STARED—RUTH'S MOUTH AJAR, PAUL'S brow deeply furrowed, Daddy's eyes like slits—as if trying to determine if I'd lost my mind. "We need to find Emily and Dante," I blurted at last. "Virginia's come unglued. LouElla thinks she's on her way here to kill Emily!"

"That's crazy!" Paul said.

"Maybe so, but there's usually an element of truth in what LouElla says." I smiled grimly, thinking about my father. My eyes locked with Paul's. "Can we afford to take that chance?"

Ruth grabbed my hand and jerked me back into my chair. "But where do we look?"

Paul's chair screeched against the floor as he scooted closer to me. "Hannah, can you remember where the kids were going?"

"I didn't ask! Oh, God, I didn't ask." Panic seized me. *Where did they go? Oh, Lord, where did they go?* I shook my head violently, trying to drive the random bits of memory that were ricocheting around inside my skull into their proper slots. "The magic show finished at four-thirty, so that's out. After the face-painting, there was the *Punch and Judy Show* . . ."

"Wait a minute!" Daddy nearly knocked over his coffee cup as his hand shot across the table in front of him. "How will Virginia find Emily in all these crowds?"

"Emily *told* Virginia where she'd be going, Daddy! When she called Virginia to warn her about LouElla." I buried my face in my hands. "Oh, how did things get so bass-ackwards?"

I peeped out through my fingers. "We need a plan." I pulled the First Night Annapolis program out of my bag and spread it on the table. I scanned the program, looking for events marked with a balloon indicating their suitability for children. "There's a comedy juggler at St. Mary's. Ruth, you take that. And there's some sort of sand craft workshop at Annapolis Elementary. You can check that out, too—"

Paul shook his head. "No, forget that, Ruth. Chloe's too young for sand crafts."

I threw up my hands in frustration. "What, then?"

Paul stabbed his finger at a green section of the program: Zone 5, the U.S. Naval Academy. "There. The Harlem Wizards."

"A basketball game? With Chloe?" I thought Paul had lost it. "What makes you think so?"

"Dante's a nut for basketball, Hannah. Trust me. After watching puppets duke it out and having his face painted, he'll be ready for something like this." He tapped the program where a balloon was drawn next to the event. "Besides, this *is* an event for kids. And it's practically at the Visitors' Center where we agreed to meet and watch the fireworks."

A wave swept over me, half of sadness, half of shame, that I had distanced myself so much from my son-in-law that I didn't even know he enjoyed basketball.

I checked my watch. "If LouElla is right, it will take Virginia an hour to get here, another twenty minutes or so to park . . ." I turned to Paul for reassurance. "The game doesn't start until nine-thirty, so that gives us plenty of time to find them. Doesn't it?"

He nodded. "I certainly hope so."

My cell phone burbled to life. With frantic fingers, I fumbled for the talk button. It was Captain Younger, returning my call. I blurted out my suspicions about Virginia Prentice and about Marty O'Malley's missing Compres tablets, then babbled on about LouElla.

"Whoa! One thing at a time, Mrs. Ives."

"That's just it!" I was practically shouting. "If Lou-Ella's right, we don't have much time!"

Captain Younger's voice took on such a soothing tone that I wondered if I'd reached Dial-a-Shrink. "I hear what you're saying, Mrs. Ives, and we'll check into it, of course. Your immediate concern is for your family, I know, but I'm certain there's virtually nothing to worry about. Just in case, however, the minute I finish talking with you, I'll notify the Annapolis police to be on the lookout for Mrs. Prentice."

I heaved a sigh of relief. "Oh, thank you."

"I'll have to warn you, though, that LouElla Van Schuyler isn't going to be a very credible witness."

"I know she's a little kooky, but—"

"Not just a little, Mrs. Ives. Last year we charged Mrs. Van Schuyler with assault when she got into a brawl with a clerk at the grocery store over the sale price of a canned ham. Both women ended up in the emergency room at Kent Queen Anne's Hospital. I the hospital, Mrs. Van Schuyler became irrational and kept threatening to kill herself, so we got a court order to commit her."

I let that soak in. "Commit her where?"

"To the Upper Shore Mental Health Center."

Just great! I was about to send my family running all over Annapolis chasing the paranoid schizophrenic fantasies of a character right out of *One Flew Over the Cuckoo's Nest.* But for some reason, I believed LouElla, and to my great surprise, I found myself defending her. "But they released her, didn't they?"

"They did, but who's checking to make sure she's taking her medication?"

IT WAS STILL THIRTY MINUTES UNTIL GAME TIME, so while Daddy and Ruth checked the events going on at St. John's College and the area around the county buildings and the Court House, Paul and I retraced our steps from Maryland Avenue, around State Circle to Church Circle and down Main Street.

Opposite Chick & Ruth's deli, I thought I spotted Chloe riding on Dante's shoulders about half a block down Main Street, near Hats in the Belfry. "There they are!" I grabbed Paul's hand and dragged him down the middle of the street, playing dodge 'em with boisterous clots of teenagers and little families traveling in pods. "Emily! Dante!" But they didn't hear me. I could see Chloe's head above the crowds, bobbing farther and farther away.

Suddenly my path was blocked by a giant pink blob with green eyes and a yellow spine. I gasped, then recognized it as an inflatable fish; its fat purple lips swam menacingly in front of my face. I turned and bolted for the sidewalk, yelling for Paul to follow me.

In front of Brown's Furniture, I collided with a character swathed in red silk, wearing long gloves and a stark white Venetian mask. The sinister figure raised its lantern and peered at me closely in the dim light, scaring the bejesus out of me. Behind it, other faceless figures floated threateningly in robes of green, yellow, purple, and white. I froze in my tracks. "Out of my way!" I shrieked. I needed to keep my eyes glued to Chloe. I could just see the top of her golden head as she crossed the street with her father, heading for the giant Christmas tree at Market Square.

A gap opened, and Paul and I charged through. At last we were gaining on them. "Emily! Dante!" Heads turned, but not the ones we were pursuing. It wasn't until I had grabbed the back of his blue jean jacket that I remembered Dante had been wearing a black windbreaker and that Chloe would have been sitting in a Gerry pack. The surprised face that turned to me was that of a stranger. "Sorry," I stammered. "I thought you were somebody else."

As the couple walked away, I bent over double, my hands resting on my knees as I tried to keep my lungs from exploding. Paul rubbed my back. "OK?"

Still panting, I looked up at him sideways and nodded.

"Where next?"

"Let's try the juggler."

Paul and I cut right, dodged the Pillsbury Doughboy and his entourage at the crosswalk, and hurried up Green Street and across Duke of Gloucester to the auditorium at St. Mary's Catholic School.

"Sorry, it's full." The usher offered us second-chance tickets for the ten-thirty show.

I turned to Paul in desperation. "But that'll be too

late!" To the usher I said, "It's an emergency. Have you seen a tall guy with a ponytail carrying a baby? He's with a woman. Kinda short with reddish hair and an earring in her eyebrow?"

The usher smiled. "There could be a dozen of 'em in there just like that."

"He might be wearing a blinking Santa hat."

The guy shook his head.

"Please let me in, just for a minute. I need to find them."

Paul pinched the fabric of the usher's sleeve. "Let my wife look. It's important. I'll stay here as collateral."

Before there could be further argument, I pushed through the doorway and into the auditorium. I threaded my way through the aisles, squinting down each row, practically swimming through the waves of laughter that erupted from the crowd as Michael Rosman fooled around up on the stage with a life-size dummy. I kept a low profile, not wanting anyone to confuse me with a volunteer from the audience and clap a fake animal nose on my face. But in spite of what the usher had said, there was no one in the audience even remotely resembling Emily, Dante, or little Chloe.

We hurried back the way we had come, across Market Space and down Randall Street to the Academy, following a string of revelers through Gate One, several wearing hats made of recycled computer parts. A woman dressed as a parlor maid raced by with ice skates slung over her shoulder. "She's going to the ice rink," I panted. "Let's try there."

At Dahlgren Hall the public session was still in progress, and DKGB and the Kremlin Crew had settled down into a reggae groove. We took the steps to the second level of the Victorian-era building two at a time and made a quick circuit of the balcony, scanning the faces in the crowd as well as those skating down below. As I leaned over the railing, I half expected to see Dante and Chloe watching from the sidelines while Emily performed mohawks, crossovers, spirals, and simple jumps on the ice—as a faculty kid she'd taken lessons at Dahlgren and had gotten pretty darn good before giving it all up during her Dungeons and Dragons phase. We waved halfheartedly to a few friendly faces, but no one we were related to.

"C'mon, Hannah." Paul grasped my upper arm and tugged on it gently. "Let's get over to Halsey in case they make the game."

I tagged along behind him, still scanning the faces in the crowd. At the field house, we stood outside for a while letting the fans flow around us as they arrived for the basketball game, but there was no sign of Dante and Emily.

Inside, the field house was packed. I wrinkled my nose at the odor of commingled sweat and old tennis shoes.

"Ma'am?"

The door attendant seemed to be addressing me. "Yes?"

"Your shoes."

I stared down at my feet uncomprehendingly. The peacock blue T-straps seemed perfectly fine to me. "What about my shoes?"

"You can't wear heels on the floor in there."

"Oh?" I was too exhausted to argue. I slipped off my shoes and stuffed them toe first into the pockets of my coat, one on each side. "OK, now?"

"Sir?"

Paul sighed, slipped out of his Corfams, tied the

laces together, and slung the shoes over his shoulder. Satisfied, the attendant waved us through into . . .

Cacophony!

The *ja-bung, ja-bung, ja-bung* of the ball being dribbled down the court. The *thrump* of it hitting the backboard. The *whoosh* as it streaked through the net. The *sqweep* of athletic shoes on the polished floor. Add the shriek of the whistles and the cries of the crowd ricocheting off the hard walls and high, rounded ceiling, and I wanted to cram my fingers in my ears.

Paul scanned one side of the field house and I took the other. I tried to take in every face, but with so many people in the audience, it was impossible. I looked at Paul and shook my head. Maybe he'd been wrong about Dante attending the game, and I'd been right, but this was hardly the time to say *I told you so,* not with my family in possible danger.

I located a uniformed security guard and explained that someone might be showing up to make trouble. I begged him to be on the lookout for a woman matching Virginia's description. White hair like Barbara Bush, I said. She's distraught, I said, and unbalanced. The guard nodded. I could practically hear him thinking: *If there's any nut here, I must be looking at her.* "I'll keep my eyes open." One thumb hitched in his pants pocket, he was watching the game, not my face. "Anybody looks like that comes through, I'll let you know."

I didn't know how it was possible, but the noise in the arena intensified. Wearing bright purple uniforms emblazoned with red *W*'s and gold stars, the Harlem Wizards streamed onto the court and began their antics to the delighted shrieks of the crowd. While buzzers and whistles assaulted my ears, Paul slipped his arm around me and pulled me close. "I'm sure it's a false alarm, Hannah, aren't you?"

"But LouElla seemed so sure!"

"Like the smallpox?"

"I see your point." We must have appeared to the outside world like a comfortably married, middle-aged couple, standing around looking for front-row seats.

Suddenly Paul's arm tightened around me. "Look! There she is!"

"Who? Virginia? LouElla?" My eyes vibrated in their sockets as I struggled to look everywhere at once.

"Virginia! Over by the doors!" I followed the long line of Paul's arm as he pointed across the court. So many people were to-ing and fro-ing near the entrances in a vibrant, colorful patchwork of winter outerwear that I missed her at first. And then it was as if a spotlight had been turned on: Virginia stood there, arms plastered to her sides, solid as a tree, her familiar white head shimmering in the blaze of lights.

I took a step forward and watched, petrified, as Virginia's arm rose like a turnstile until it extended from her body at a ninety-degree angle. In her hand was a gun. She pointed the weapon toward a spot in the bleachers, straight at Emily, who was sitting next to her husband, bouncing little Chloe on her lap. In that split second, I realized I had been looking for Dante's Santa cap, but he wasn't wearing it. It lay across his knees and was no longer blinking. Dante was cheering for the players as they thundered down the court toward the basket.

I shouted "Look out!" but my cry was drowned by the screech of a referee's whistle.

What's wrong with these idiots? Can't they see what's going on?

Without hesitation, Paul and I dashed onto the floor and raced down the middle of the court toward a herd of basketball players stampeding in our direction. Emily turned toward me, her eyes wide. Dante stood, his hands aloft, frozen in mid-cheer. The crowd around him stood, too, roaring with approval, thinking we were part of the show—Mr. and Mrs. America vs. the Harlem Wizards. Someone started to chant "Go, go, go, go . . ." and then the rhythmic clapping began.

"Look out!" I screamed again as the Wizards streamed by us on both sides. "She's got a gun!"

The crowd went wild—*"Go, go, go, go!"*

I raced toward Virginia, my lungs exploding, waving my arms wildly over my head. "A gun! A gun!"

Suddenly the mood of the crowd changed. The clapping became sporadic as first one section of the audience and then another realized something other than basketball must be going on. Heads turned this way and that in puzzlement and confusion. On the court, the Wizards froze. First a player, poised with the ball in one hand, about to wrist-flip an effortless basket. Then his teammates. Then a referee, arms extended, whistle dangling from his lips, who, thank God, called a time out. *Screeeeeeeeeeee!*

I focused on Virginia. Someone had turned down the volume on the crowd, and in the muffled chaos she turned her head lazily toward me. But the arm holding the gun remained steady. I imagined her finger bearing down slowly, slowly, on the trigger and willed every molecule of adrenaline I possessed into the muscles propelling my legs.

All at once, an object hurtled out of the shadow of the bleachers and launched itself at Virginia in a streak of purple fury. A broad shoulder caught Virginia just below the knees in an NFL-style tackle that sent her sprawling. Virginia's right arm shot skyward; the gun, gray-black and ugly, spun away, sliding across the polished floor and coming to rest against the athletic shoe of an astonished Wizard. "Gotcha!" exclaimed LouElla. In a single, practiced move, she twisted Virginia's arm behind her back and rolled her over so that the other woman's cheek lay squashed against the floor. By the time I reached her side, LouElla was sitting on the small of Virginia's back, pinning her down.

"Thank you, thank you!" I drew in a ragged breath.

"Are you all right?" Paul extended his hand to LouElla, offering to help her to her feet, but she shook her head.

She wiped her brow with the sleeve of her sweater. "Phew! I'm a little out of practice." Still balancing on Virginia's back, she used the fingers of both hands to tuck long strands of hair into the elaborate French twist at the back of her head. All around us the crowd had grown strangely quiet, and I was aware of Dante standing next to me with Emily and Chloe peeking out from behind his back.

Eyes bright and round as coins, LouElla surveyed the faces surrounding her. "Well? Isn't anybody going to call the police?"

The security guard employed by Halsey Field House happily took over for the exuberant LouElla, who couldn't help but preen in the spotlight like the Comeback Kid. For the photographers who materialized out of nowhere she posed prettily, but when the Department of Defense police arrived to make a formal arrest, she positively glowed.

In short order, Virginia would find herself locked in a holding cell on Hospital Point, while DOD and the Navy Criminal Investigative Service sorted out jurisdictional issues. We'd be interviewed by NCIS in the morning, we were told. What a way to spend the first day of a new millennium!

In the meantime, the Wizards had resumed their zany tricks, and Ruth had called my cell phone to report in. We'd given Ruth and Daddy the startling news about Virginia and, although badly shaken, we agreed to stay at Halsey Field House until they appeared.

I settled down on the bleachers sandwiched comfortably between Emily and LouElla. Paul, with Chloe on his lap, sat next to Dante in the row above us and behind. Adrenaline still coursed through my veins; I knew I wouldn't have any trouble staying awake until midnight.

"Lady?"

I turned and stared into the freckled face of a gap-toothed kid around eight years old. He held a needle-point purse in both hands, its tortoiseshell handles hanging limply to each side. "Yes?"

"My mom told me to give this to you. That other lady dropped it." He straightened his elbows and thrust the purse in my direction.

I squinted at the kid in confusion. "What lady?"

"The one the cops took."

Holy moley! I laced my fingers and squeezed my hands together while staring into his innocent, pale blue eyes. My good angel advised me to pat the kid on the head and tell him to give Virginia's purse to the security guard, but there was a bad angel whispering in my other ear so I smiled, said, "Thank you," and relieved him of his burden.

And burden it was. Even without the gun, the bag weighed a ton. I settled it on my knees and stared at it, trying to decide what to do.

Emily elbowed my arm. "I don't remember that purse."

I positioned my mouth a few inches from her ear and said, "That's because it's not mine."

"Then who . . . ?" she began. Her jaw dropped in a pantomime of surprise until she snapped it shut with a quick tap on her chin with the back of her hand. "Mother!"

"I probably should look through it," I said.

"To find out who it belongs to?" Emily grinned.

"Naturally." I grabbed the handles and pulled until the purse yawned open on my lap. A black wallet lay on top. I plucked it out and handed it to Emily.

Emily unfolded the wallet, smiled, and turned it in my direction. A younger, darker-haired Virginia Prentice scowled out at me from the corner of her driver's license. "It's evidence now, huh?"

Emily returned the wallet and I flipped through its plastic sleeves checking the names embossed on each credit card before I remembered that Darryl would have to account to the police for that particular crime. I reached the last sleeve and flipped it over, not to a credit card, but to a picture of a young bride. My stomach clenched. Julia. Her dark brown hair swirled high on her head in an elegant crown interwoven with seed pearls and orange blossoms. Soft spit curls nestled against each cheek. She was smiling. "Oh . . ."

Emily leaned close. "That's Virginia's daughter, isn't it?"

"Must be."

"So sad." I tucked the wallet into the purse and leaned back against Paul's knees. "We'll take it to the police in the morning."

I was able to keep my hands off the purse for the space of two free throws before being compelled to peer into the bag again—a lipstick, hairbrush, ballpoint pens, some loose coins. I thought I knew why the damn thing weighed so much. I felt along the dark silk lining and discovered a zipper compartment large enough to accommodate several paperback books. I drew the zipper across and pulled out what I knew had to be there, LouElla's log book, plus a DayTimer, a packet of business cards, and a flat paper bag. I handed the miscellaneous items to Emily and turned to LouElla with the log book.

"Look what I found, LouElla." I handed the log back to its owner.

"Oh, thank you!" LouElla clasped the log to her chest for one joyful moment, then lowered it and addressed her remarks to its black and red covers. "*You* are going right home with me, you little rascal."

I laid a gentle hand on her arm. "I think you'll need to give it to Captain Younger, LouElla. It may help prove that Virginia poisoned Darlene."

"It will?" LouElla's eyes widened in genuine surprise. "How?"

I retrieved the log, opened it at random, checked the date heading, then leafed forward several months to early December. "Look." I tipped the log toward her. "This is the day you first saw Virginia fooling around with Marty O'Malley's mailbox. Darlene died of an overdose of clonidine. The police will check with the AARP Pharmacy Service to see when they sent out Mr.

O'Malley's Compres pills. If that date corresponds with the shipment that disappeared, it may help to convict her."

LouElla nodded her head. "Good. Shouldn't be tolerated. Tampering with the mail is a federal crime, you know." She stabbed the air with an index finger. "Not a good idea to mess with the feds," she continued knowledgeably. "Because they mean business."

While I still had the log in my hands, I thumbed back to early summer, remembering the curious notations I had seen there previously. I pointed at one now: *jb23.*

"LouElla? What does jb23 mean?"

LouElla's eyes remained glued to the court where a red-white-and-blue basketball whizzed from one Wizard to another, over heads and under legs, upside down and backward, at a feverish pace. "June bugs," she explained. "Pulled twenty-three of 'em off the roses that day."

Of course. Why didn't I think of that? "Silly me," I said.

"Mom?" Emily was elbowing me frantically. "Look at this!" She passed me a newspaper article about a fatal plane crash. Stuck to it was a lime-green Post-it note: *Too bad you weren't aboard.* "It was in the bag. There's a card in there, too," she said. She handed the card to me. "It looks like it came off a computer." Written across the face of a bucolic landscape were the words *You can make the world a better place.* I opened the card. *Leave it!*

Emily stared at me with troubled eyes. "I guess Virginia got tired of waiting for Darlene to go voluntarily."

* * *

As much as I wanted to hear the bagpipers, we were too exhausted and drained to make it back downtown for the annual Parade to Midnight, or to the laser light show in the tent at City Dock. As the magic hour approached, we wandered from Halsey Field House to the terrace outside the Naval Academy Visitors' Center which overlooks Annapolis Harbor and Spa Creek. Across the harbor, a large neon crab pot steamed on the roof of the parking garage of the Marriott Hotel. As midnight approached, the countdown began and the blue crab began its inexorable descent.

Fifteen, fourteen, thirteen . . .

My cancer behind me, my family safe around me. A new millennium, I thought, and a new beginning for everyone.

Twelve, eleven, ten . . .

Daddy standing side by side with Cornelia Gibbs. However "accidentally" Cornelia had run into him at the fast-food concession in Halsey that night, he would negotiate a postponement of his cruise until March so that he and Cornelia could sit in adjoining deck chairs on the *Wind Star* off Belize.

Nine, eight, seven . . .

Emily nestled in the shelter of Dante's arm with Chloe napping, open mouthed, on his shoulder. Years later Chloe's parents would tease that she slept through the new millennium on the very night her baby brother was conceived.

Six, five, four . . .

Ruth sat alone on the seawall, feet dangling over the water. Before the week was out, her financial problems would be over, when Darryl Donovan was arrested and charged with ten counts of grand theft, theft over five hundred, theft under five hundred, and credit card theft. Now the lawyer handling her case seems to be taking more than just a professional interest in his client. Ruth calls him "Hutch."

Three, two, one . . .

Paul kissed me once, curling my toes. And later? Well, you can imagine.

Happy New Year!

The millennium crab plunged the final few inches into the pot, flashing from blue to red. Cheers erupted from points all over the harbor as a salvo of fireworks was launched into the night. In the first flash, I caught sight of LouElla, her cheeks glistening with tears. I was filled with shame. In my happiness, I had nearly forgotten about her. In the past year this woman had lost her only son, had pulled my father from the depths of alcoholism, had thrown herself between my daughter and the bullet that was meant for her. With Darryl going to jail, I planned to put in a good word with Deirdre so that LouElla could keep Speedo, at least. I reached for LouElla's hand, gathered it up into mine, and squeezed.

"Do you know something, LouElla?"

"What?" she said dreamily.

"J. Edgar Hoover would have been very proud of you today."

She beamed as red-white-and-blue pinwheels exploded over our heads. "He would, wouldn't he?"

"He'd pin a medal on your chest."

She bowed her head and concentrated on finding something in her bag while I watched the double hoops in her ears revolve like iridescent Catherine wheels. "You know, everyone thinks I'm crazy."

I swallowed my denial. Even LouElla wouldn't have believed it.

She pulled an envelope from her purse and handed it to me. I slid my finger under the flap, withdrew a piece of paper, unfolded it, and squinted at it in the dark. Some sort of form. In the next second, brightly illuminated by a burst of white chrysanthemums, I saw that I held a discharge certificate in the name of LouElla Van Schuyler from the Upper Shore Mental Health Center.

"I carry it with me everywhere." LouElla lifted her face to the night sky. Sparks rained down on us like spangled confetti. "Virginia's the crazy one, not me. And I have a paper to prove it."

About the Author

Marcia Talley's first Hannah Ives novel, *Sing It to Her Bones*, won the Malice Domestic Grant in 1998 and was nominated for an Agatha Award as Best First Novel of 1999. *Unbreathed Memories*, the second in the series, appeared in 2000. Both were Featured Alternates of the Mystery Guild. She is also the editor of a collaborative serial novel, *Naked Came the Phoenix*, where she joins twelve bestselling women authors to pen a tongue-in-cheek mystery about murder in an exclusive health spa. Her short stories have appeared in magazines and collections.

Marcia lives in Annapolis, Maryland, with her husband Barry, a professor at the U.S. Naval Academy. When she isn't writing, she spends her time traveling or sailing. Marcia and her husband recently returned from the Bahamas, where they lived for six months on *Troubadour*, their thirty-seven-foot sailboat.

SARA PARETSKY

"Paretsky's name always makes the top of the list when people talk about the new female operatives." —*The New York Times Book Review*

___ Bitter Medicine	23476-X	$6.99/9.99
___ Blood Shot	20420-8	$6.99/8.99
___ Burn Marks	20845-9	$6.99/8.99
___ Indemnity Only	21069-0	$6.99/8.99
___ Guardian Angel	21399-1	$6.99/8.99
___ Killing Orders	21528-5	$6.99/8.99
___ Deadlock	21332-0	$6.99/8.99
___ Tunnel Vision	21752-0	$6.99/8.99
___ Windy City Blues	21873-X	$6.99/8.99
___ A Woman's Eye	21335-5	$6.99/8.99
___ Women on the Case	22325-3	$6.99/8.99
___ Hard Time	22470-5	$6.99/9.99
___ Total Recall (os 9/01)	31366-7	$25.95/39.95

HARLAN COBEN

Winner of the Edgar, the Anthony, and the Shamus Awards

___ One False Move	22544-2	$6.50/9.99
___ Deal Breaker	22044-0	$6.50/9.99
___ Dropshot	22049-5	$6.50/9.99
___ Fade Away	22268-0	$6.50/9.99
___ Back Spin	22270-2	$6.50/9.99
___ The Final Detail	22545-0	$6.50/9.99
___ Darkest Fear	23539-1	$6.50/9.99
___ Tell No One	33555-5	$22.95/32.95

RUTH RENDELL

Winner of the Grand Master Edgar Award from the *Mystery Writers of America*

___ Road Rage	22602-3	$6.50/8.99
___ The Crocodile Bird	21865-9	$6.50/8.99
___ Simisola	22202-8	$6.50/NCR
___ Keys to the Street	22392-X	$6.50/8.99
___ A Sight for Sore Eyes	23544-8	$6.50/9.99